Acclaim for
The Boys in the Brownstone

"*The Boys in the Brownstone* is a laugh-out-loud comedy of manners. Kevin Scott tells the story from the perspectives of multiple characters, capturing the poignant contrast between how we see ourselves and how others see us. He has a remarkable, uncanny range, orchestrating the work from a vast array of viewpoints.

This novel is a great read, full of deadpan wisdom, madcap plot twists, and basic human truths. It locates the little internal contradictions that make people so exasperating and tackles the big questions head on. The author sheds light on parental expectations, addiction, and self-delusion; he explores such topics as why we marry people with our parents' most annoying traits; and he makes gentle fun of postmodernism along the way. Best of all, he mines the comic gold of the dysfunctional American family."

—Jenny Lyn Bader
Co-author, *He Meant, She Meant:*
The Definitive Male-Female Dictionary;
Playwright, *None of the Above*

"Kevin Scott joins distinguished company—James and Wharton, Auchincloss and Hijuelos—in his keen ability to chronicle life and manners in New York City. This brownstone differs only in that it has possibly more closets, and their doors are thrown wide open. These 'boys,' whose lives overlap and intersect here, form a family as comforting and dysfunctional as any in literature or real life."

—Marion Abbott Bundy
Co-author, *Talking Pictures;*
Co-owner, Mrs. Dalloway's
(independent bookstore, Berkeley, California)

The Boys
in the Brownstone

HARRINGTON PARK PRESS
Southern Tier Editions
Gay Men's Fiction
Jay Quinn, Executive Editor
Greg Herren, Associate Editor

Through It Came Bright Colors by Trebor Healey

Elf Child by David M. Pierce

Huddle by Dan Boyle

The Man Pilot by James W. Ridout IV

Shadows of the Night: Queer Tales of the Uncanny and Unusual edited by Greg Herren

Van Allen's Ecstasy by Jim Tushinski

Beyond the Wind by Rob N. Hood

The Handsomest Man in the World by David Leddick

The Song of a Manchild by Durrell Owens

The Ice Sculptures: A Novel of Hollywood by Michael D. Craig

Between the Palms: A Collection of Gay Travel Erotica edited by Michael T. Luongo

Aura by Gary Glickman

Love Under Foot: An Erotic Celebration of Feet edited by Greg Wharton and M. Christian

The Tenth Man by E. William Podojil

Upon a Midnight Clear: Queer Christmas Tales edited by Greg Herren

Dryland's End by Felice Picano

Whose Eye Is on Which Sparrow? by Robert Taylor

Deep Water: A Sailor's Passage by E. M. Kahn

The Boys in the Brownstone by Kevin Scott

The Best of Both Worlds: Bisexual Erotica edited by Sage Vivant and M. Christian

Some Dance to Remember: A Memoir-Novel of San Francisco, 1970-1982 by Jack Fritscher

Confessions of a Male Nurse by Richard S. Ferri

The Millionaire of Love by David Leddick

Transgender Erotica: Trans Figures edited by M. Christian

Skip Macalester by J. E. Robinson

Chemistry by Lewis DeSimone

Friends, Lovers, and Roses by Vernon Clay

Beyond Machu by William Maltese

Virgina Bedfellows by Gavin Morris

The Boys in the Brownstone

Kevin Scott

Southern Tier Editions
Harrington Park Press®
An Imprint of The Haworth Press, Inc.
New York • London • Oxford

Published by

Southern Tier Editions, Harrington Park Press®, an imprint of The Haworth Press, Inc., 10 Alice Street, Binghamton, NY 13904-1580.

PUBLISHER'S NOTE
This is a work of fiction. Names, characters, places, and incidents either are the products of the author's imagination or are used fictitiously, and any resemblance to actual persons, living or dead, business establishments, events, or locales is entirely coincidental.

Cover painting, "Outing at Flamborough," by Bruce Sargeant. Reprinted by permission of the artist.
Cover design by Kerry E. Mack.
Author's photo by James Manfredi.

Library of Congress Cataloging-in-Publication Data

Scott, Kevin, 1952-
    The boys in the brownstone / Kevin Scott.
      p. cm.
    ISBN 13: 978-1-56023-295-7 (soft : alk. paper)
    ISBN 10: 1-56023-295-1 (soft : alk. paper)
    1. Men—New York (State)—New York—Fiction. 2. Upper East Side (New York, N.Y.)—Fiction.
3. Bars (Drinking establishments)—Fiction. I. Title.

PS3619.C674B695 2005
813'.6—dc22

                                                                                    2004024573

For Richard York

Think well of me, in years to come,
When you sing my little songs.
Though I wrote them all,
Not all the credit belongs
To me but to the guys
Who told me about the guys
And boys they were mad about.
I've told no lies.
I've told the honest truth
About each lover's heart.
After all, that's why the gods
Gave men like me this gift of art.

Strato (circa 120 C.E.)

Every man is guilty of all the good he didn't do.

Voltaire

CONTENTS

The Quarry

It was the night before the night before Christmas, it was snowing, and the Brownstone would be just a block away when Roberto got off the tram from Roosevelt Island. The staid-looking Brownstone reminded him of the '21' Club, or at least the picture of it he'd seen in a book he'd just finished reading, the biography of a Brazilian industrialist who had dined at '21' with his northern counterpart, Henry Ford. Granted, neither of them would have been caught dead in the Brownstone for all of its armchairs and hunting prints. But times were changing. That very morning, in a daze of grief—his wife had fled home to São Paolo with the kids just days before—Roberto had come upon a photo spread in *The Times* of a house on the Amalfi Coast owned by two men, lovers and business partners, who were not only celebrated for their taste and hospitality, they were neighbors of his favorite American writer, Gore Vidal. That *The New York Times* could be so matter of fact about, so approving of, gays was exhilarating. He was right to have finally told Olga the truth. She was spiteful to have been so stupid. What was Brazil? A swamp, the Amazon. New York was a snowglobe, magical and real, as the tram slipped through the air into Manhattan.

> *The sun is shining, the grass is green*
> *The orange and palm trees sway*

"White Christmas": Roberto beamed knowingly at the introduction.

> *I've never seen such a day*
> *In Beverly Hills, L.A.*

Roberto loved all the old songs being sung round the piano. The best English teachers he'd had in high school were Frank Sinatra, Ella Fitzgerald, and the other singers favored by the Kowalciks, his "host parents" as an exchange student in Pasadena. Fun-loving and unpretentious, the Kowalciks were everything his real parents were not. Their generosity lent the old songs a warmth and a casualness the newer songs could never match. The newer songs—by Andrew Lloyd Webber and the others he didn't know the names of—had come to represent for him all that was sapless and insincere about the English-speaking world. During his other stints away from home, a year at Georgetown and two years at the London School of Economics, where the only gay bar he could slip away to was a pub in the West End, he had added "Stephen Sondheim: What's His Problem? Can't He Get Laid?" to the small repertoire of topics he could rely on to impress cute guys with his rambunctious masculinity. (Other provocative topics: "Philanthropy: What a Scam" and "Princess Di: Ninny or Psychopath?")

For once, Roberto wasn't nervous at all as he joined the crowd bellying up to the bar at the Brownstone. He'd lost a little weight, trimmed his mustache; he felt almost attractive. Short and just a bit chubby-cheeked, with wavy black hair and a swimmer's shoulders, Roberto, if hardly a knockout, was decidedly pleasant-looking, even cute. Well-employed by Colcutt and Company, an investment bank that guaranteed him a green card and, any day now, an end-of-the-year bonus, at thirty-four, for the first time in his life, Roberto was self-supporting and soon-to-be single: in short, he was free to take somebody home. All afternoon he'd been tossing toys into plastic baskets and shifting Olga's toiletries from the rim of the tub to the back of the medicine cabinet. The snowstorm, of course, had made it less likely anyone would be willing to accompany him to Roosevelt Island. But as good-looking men continued to squeeze into the room, shoving all but the most steadfast showqueens downstairs to the darker room where they played disco, Roberto was in such a good mood, he found himself translating Sondheim just for the hell of it: *Nao e delicioso? Nao e esquisito?*

Two years before, on his first visit to New York, Roberto had found his way to the Brownstone but he hadn't stayed very long: he had a job interview at Credit Suisse in the morning. The only patrons he passed in the wood-paneled expanse that night were middle-aged queens, barefoot in tasseled loafers. He couldn't understand: what was the point of liking men if the men looked just like women? It was no wonder he'd made so little impression; he could barely hide his contempt. All those jowls and chrysanthemums: it was a funeral parlor. Finishing his drink in a couple gulps, he took off for Chelsea.

The place was different tonight. The storm had cast a spell, keeping the few hundred gays who had not yet migrated downtown uptown. As the snow fell inch by inch, stupefying commuters, unnerving cabbies, scattering the homeless to underpasses and subway stations, the last of the Uptown queers found themselves far from the dance music of Chelsea, trapped in the Brownstone, listening to *Les Miz,* safely suspended in a warm solution of liquor and lust.

Roberto couldn't help smiling. The hearty Christmas trees with little red apples, the swags of evergreen drooping over seascapes of Maine: it was A New England Parlor, circa 18-something. Crowding into the room, however, was a troupe of revelers Currier and Ives could have never imagined. (Unless, of course, Currier and Ives were more than partners; you never know.) There were tenors in yuletide bow ties holding hands with hairy-armed baritones. There were Chinese toothpicks in turtlenecks and stockbrokers in camouflage pants. Too broke for the coatroom, sales boys in plump down jackets were tethered to the bar like balloons before the Macy's parade. Bags under their eyes, drug dealers and hospital interns counted their beers, dreading their beepers. Hypnotized by hustlers with improbable bulges, frail CEOs of nonprofit organizations moved through the throng like sleepwalkers.

Flushed with freedom, Roberto beamed. He wriggled through a thicket of bodies, smiling at each man he passed as if one by one, they had trudged to the Brownstone just to reassure him: You've got nothing to worry about. She knows. You told her. You survived. Merry Christmas.

An older man in houndstooth trousers was bopping to *Guys and Dolls* like a chorus boy. "Still snowing?"

"Uh-huh." Roberto tried to get the attention of the bartender: "Rum and coke."

Downtown, amid the personal trainers and Ecstasy-heads, Roberto felt out of place. Not here. One part Carnival, two parts Bloomingdales: who could feel out of place in a place like this?

"You want lemon or lime in that rum and coke?" the hardpressed bartender shot out.

"Uh, uh, lemon. Thanks."

Sitting on a shelf, interspersed with the cocktail glasses, were decoy ducks, a thin blue condom package stuck in each bill.

Hey there, you with the stars in your eyes

Roberto drifted awhile, dreamy as a schoolboy taking in the Christmas lights on neighbors' houses. There was no reason to hurry home. Olga would not be waiting up to weigh his story with anxious eyes. He could take his time, canvassing the crowd for the physiognomy of his dreams. A Thai here, a teddy-bear there, guys returned his gaze occasionally, casually, in passing, but only one showed serious interest, a kind of Protestant social worker type—cute, blond, eager to please, a middle-aged boy with a jaw rectangular as his wire-rimmed glasses.

"You know who else went to LSE?" The social worker pointed to the crest on the pocket of Roberto's sports coat.

"You?"

"No. Oh, hardly."

"Mick Jagger."

"You're kidding."

"He did. You don't believe me?"

The social worker looked skeptical. But before Roberto could explain about Mick Jagger or find out who the other unlikely alumnus was, he was borne away on a wave of newcomers bound for the bathroom.

If I never had a cent
I'd be rich as Rockefeller

Roberto's second lap around the bar yielded one arresting sight: two black men in gray suits arguing in sign language—and an intriguing shard of conversation—"Incest was the *least* of her problems"—but nobody who resembled the man of his dreams. Just as well, Roberto consoled himself. For some reason, every guy he met who fit the bill of his fantasy (short, fair-skinned, dark-haired, handsome and straight-looking) turned out to be a real handful. Only one, the little mechanic at Barracuda who disappeared with his wallet, had actually done him any harm. But why fuck with fate? What he needed, and in fact, almost wanted, was a guy like the social worker, easy to talk to, easy to look at, an instant boyfriend for a screw and a cuddle. They could kiss on the tram; they could fuck on the rug. In the morning, with Ella and Louie singing sympathetically in the background, he might even admit how many years he'd been waiting to watch the sunrise with a man in his arms without wishing he were dead.

Rooting through the crowd for the social worker, Roberto was getting a little woozy from the smell of wet wool when he was stopped in his tracks by a wiry young guy in a ski cap with the hard handsome face and coy stubble of a young artist or musician or mathematician or Web designer, maybe. Roberto knew him from somewhere. Where? At least a couple years younger than Roberto, he seemed intelligent, troubled, humorless. Squinting down at his snow boots, his jaw would clench and his fist would tighten around the neck of his beer as if he were wrestling some inner urge to do what? Burst into tears? Pull out a gun? Play the lead in an Elia Kazan movie? With glances and business cards flying all around him, the guy never once looked up; he just stood in the eye of the storm, head bowed, clenching his fists in anger—or anguish?

Take it easy, Roberto was dying to tell him. Things are never as bad they seem. A few days ago, he was ready to kill *himself*. And he would've done it—jumped from the tram into the East River—if it hadn't been for the kids. His wife had informed him she was taking the kids to Brazil and no matter what he did he was never going to see them again. Heart pounding in panic, he began to wheeze. Then he realized, bullshit: she's bluffing. What the hell is she gonna live on?

You can't keep yourself in Laura Ashley teaching ESL in São Paolo. Fine, go!, Take the kids, *tchau!,* he told her. Live with your parents! Wear your mother's old clothes! Olga ran downstairs: Ivan! Maria! Wake up! *Teu pai e um bicha!* Roberto raised his fist. Olga froze. Dr. Weiss had assured him if she ever did tell Ivan and Maria he was *homossexuais,* they wouldn't be shocked; they'd just be baffled. They were too young to understand.

When the guy in the ski cap looked up and, head unmoving, began to let his eyes wander the crowd, well, Roberto could hardly have been more excited if Jesus himself had sat up from the Pieta, flexed his muscles, and started checking out the Swiss Guards. He *did* know the guy: what a god. He had met him last summer. But what was his name? Luther. Calvin. *Wesley.*

Who knows? Maybe we're all just chicks imprinted with the silhouette of someone—Mom, Dad, or the paperboy—who happened to walk by just as the mold of our deepest desire was setting. For attractive as he was to the other men in the Brownstone, Wesley struck a deeper chord in Roberto. Give or take thirty pounds and twenty years, he was the spitting image of a boy who had kissed Roberto and jerked him off under a waterfall, at the very moment the neuroplaster of his deepest desire was fixing.

The youngest son of a man who worked for Roberto's grandfather in Uchoa, Pedro-Paulo was lighter skinned than the other kids whose fathers drove trucks and showered behind the barn. A sullen boy, he kept a distance from Roberto, returning soccer balls without enthusiasm. With his cigarettes and buddies, he was the last kid on the plantation Roberto could have expected to tug him into the spray, to hang onto his shoulders as they struggled to stay upright on the slippery moss. They were hugging when it happened, the fateful hard-on that, like an eon of evolution, would specialize Roberto's libido from that day forward. Twenty years and many thousands of hard-ons later, he was still looking for Pedro-Paulo, still dreaming of that downpour of abandon and belonging.

Heart pounding, Roberto waited, the head of his cock budging up his shorts.

Sad as an icon, Wesley's eyes followed the eyes of other guys around the room.

Roberto tightened his paunch, perfected his profile, and said a little prayer as the moment approached.

For several seconds, he could even imagine that his gaze was being returned. But Wesley was looking at two Hasids behind him, causing a stir as they swept into Sodom in their overcoats and side curls. Skimming over Roberto without focusing, Wesley's eyes returned to the floor.

We three queens of Orient are
Bearing gifts we traverse afar

He wasn't ugly; he wasn't worthless; he was doing something wrong, Dr. Weiss insisted. Like what? Gay people didn't talk. They just made small talk as they looked over your shoulder for a cuter guy. It was a beauty contest.

The next time Wesley raised his head, Roberto could see what a fraud he was—with his James Dean bullshit—and his agonized brow!—as if only a grueling act of will could've wrested him from introspection for the mere prospect of a blow job. To hell with Ella: a kiss, a wrestling hold, and he'd prong the little punk till he howled out loud that he'd never been fucked before. Not like this. Never. He'd flop like a fish in a wave of sweat. His eyes would yearn for more. What was beauty? It was nothing compared to a man who could slam it in hard and tight as a doorstop.

Oh-oh, star of wonder, star of night

Looking up again, Wesley skimmed the faces facing him. Like the exhausted steel ball of a roulette wheel, his gaze finally fell on Roberto. Then with a little shy grin of acknowledgment, he looked away.

Roberto inched forward, camouflaging his progress toward Wesley with little pit stops to pick up a napkin, to check the time, to admire a creche.

"You want anything?"

"What? Sorry?" Roberto turned.

A cute young waiter was balancing a tray with one hand; with the other he held something high in the air.

"What's that?"

"Oh, this? It's mistletoe."

"Right, right. For Christmas."

"Want another?"

"Yeah, thanks. Rum and coke."

"You want lime in that?"

"Yeah, sure."

"That's all you want?" He looked away coyly, the little satyr, dangling mistletoe like grapes.

Wesley was watching.

"Merry Christmas." Roberto kissed the waiter, then turned to Wesley. "You want anything?"

"What?"

"You want a drink?"

"Me? Oh, no. Thanks."

"You're sure?"

"Really?"

"Why not? What are you having?"

"Oh, this? It's just a Guinness."

"Have a real drink."

"No, Guinness is fine."

"You don't remember me."

"Yes, I do."

"From where?"

"That's what I can't remember."

"We met on Stonehaven."

It was to amuse his wife—whose disdain for bankers could be softened by a good command of a romance language—that, five months earlier, Roberto's boss, Gordon Farr, had invited Roberto to bring his family to Maine for a week of summer vacation.

Roberto had mixed feelings about the invitation. He liked his boss. Bald and affable Gordy, Colcutt's chief analyst for South America, was the doting father of two pre-school boys and the deferential husband of a handsome, wry redhead who taught Comp Lit at NYU. It wasn't Gordy, it was his wife, Virginia, who had Roberto a little worried. He quite enjoyed talking to her; she could be very funny; but he was afraid that she had more than conversation in mind. Moreover, he doubted that there would be opportunity, under his boss's nose, to slip into the dunes for a hand job with another restless dad, as he might have on Long Island. As it happened, he decided to go: there was nothing to pay for, really, except airfare; he could brownnose the boss; the kids would have kids to play with; and Olga would have the very thing she liked best, the audience of another couple. It bugged him: the cooler their marriage became, the more Olga enjoyed illustrating their Wedded Love with little tokens of togetherness on other people's sofas. All it took was a few drinks, an unfamiliar coffee table, and she began flaunting their illusory intimacy like a tango contestant. Their first night on the island, she pursued him to the far edge of a couch and, wrapping herself around him, confided to Virginia how, just like a man, Roberto showed no regard at all for the little things a woman cares about. Roberto was tempted to counter that, her clitoris aside, there were few aspects of domestic life to which he wasn't far more attentive than she. But for some reason—maybe it was the thought that he would leave her some day, or the poignancy of her laughter as she told Virginia how he had pursued her over the objections of his snobbish family—he suddenly felt sorry—sorrow—for her, and headed off to the kitchen, talking rubber futures with Gordy.

In fact, he *had* pursued her. He quite liked her. And she was crazy about *him*. In just the week before he proposed, he took her to *Noises Off* in Portuguese, a French restaurant and a sort-of ballet. He wrote her a poem that she still kept in her jewelry box with the ticket stubs of their courtship. And having achieved penetration in the pantry before his grandmother's funeral, he was so encouraged by the experiment and so worried that changing a major variable might jeopardize the success of any repetition, he had asked her to marry him before he'd even swept up the dried beans and broken glass, trusting that marriage would cure him of the doubts about his masculinity that made his penis so equivocal in the first place. Over time, though his daydreams about men occasionally brought him to the brink of panic, he had become an effective husband, translating his anger at Olga— for her ignorance of how much work was involved in making love to her—into a wrenching brutality she had come to mistake for ardor.

"Daddy, look!" Every day on the beach in Maine, Ivan searched for rocks with something squiggly-looking embedded in their speckled surfaces.

"*Otimo!*" Roberto studied each improbable fossil, imagining a career for his little boy as one of those scientists whose prose wins praise in the *Sunday Times*.

"Daddy, look," Maria competed, grabbing anything—a rake, a dandelion—and holding it up for a blessing.

"*Que lindo,*" Roberto cooed.

Gordy's preschoolers, Todd and Junior, were big, blond dynamos who would rather watch *Fear Factor* and wrestling on television than explore their father's countryseat. Expelled from the house to play with their guests, their good-natured roughhousing often went too far. More than once, roused from his book (Gore Vidal, *Palimpsest*), Roberto was called on to referee. Prying Ivan from a half nelson, he wiped his tears: "Ask Todd to race. You're fast. You can beat him." Hiding his relief when the little geologist declined, Roberto headed back to his book, stiff-limbed as Frankenstein, Maria clinging to one leg, Ivan to the other. Each night, he lay beside Olga, confounded by her beauty and afraid to share her happiness. When it got chilly, he looked in on the kids. It scared him to see them splayed out on the bottom bunk bed, mouths open, like victims of an airborne catastrophe. Pulling the blanket from the top bunk, he covered them, kissed them, and sat awhile. Pacing his breath to the tempo of the waves, he tried to picture Dr. Weiss, his sturdy furniture, his kindly spectacles on a chain.

Each morning, Stonehaven proved to be a much grander place than Virginia, scourge of the immodest, had allowed herself or her husband to let on to their guests the day before. Twelve miles out in Penobscot Bay, forty-five minutes on the ferry, the bumpy little island was all grass and fir trees and hiking trails, with a trim of white-shingled houses round the harbor. Here and there, on the blue, a white sail billowed or a motorboat idled at a rickety dock. The docks belonged to the summer residents who, like Virginia, had left behind mothers and tennis skirts in Camden and Rockland for the bohemian Eden of Stonehaven. Only two thousand people lived on the island, year-round. A few hundred more visited in the summer. Most of the men who lived on the island were lobstermen. Those who were not, and often their wives, worked for the summer people as gardeners, nannies, and handymen. It reminded Roberto of his childhood: you were either a landholder or a serf. But in Brazil the have-nots, as a rule, were darker and leaner than the haves. On Stonehaven, a couple centuries of inbreeding and perhaps a lingering excitement over the convenience of prepared foods (the general store was a time capsule of cake mixes and blue boxes of macaroni and cheese) had given the permanent residents pale round faces and lower bodies the size of tree-stumps. Holding hands as big as mittens, their children stood in the dirt, watching lovely old houses float by on flatbed trucks en route to the hilltop estates of the slender rich.

Until the last two days Roberto spent with the Farrs, things went smoothly on the busy estate. Little posses of workmen banged away at outbuildings, installed phone lines, and motored up to the dock to drop lobsters in a cage Roberto's kids couldn't stop opening the trap door of. When they weren't pitying the lobsters or being rough-housed by Todd and Junior, Ivan and Maria played amicably, trampling the vegetable garden, cutting their feet on the pebbly beach. Gordy and Olga did chores, carrying the lighter furniture from a house about to be winterized to a barn the Farrs had turned into their living quarters.

The day he first saw Wesley, Roberto spent the morning down at the harbor, meeting Virginia's friends among the handful of artists who had decamped to the island from careers that had stalled in New York. He was flattered by the way she introduced him to a bearded old artist, hinting, as she brushed grass from the seat of his pants, that they were enjoying a summer fling. Later he would wonder if it was an omen, meeting that artist, that day, Robert Indiana, the guy who made the LOVE sculpture, its lopsided O reproduced a million times on postage stamps.

Roberto never would have seen Wesley at all that afternoon, let alone seen him naked, if Virginia hadn't insisted on taking him to "the nude quarry."

"I thought Brazilians were totally shameless about their bodies."

"Maybe in Rio. I'm from São Paolo."

"Oh, come on. I look like an old stick and I'm not ashamed."

"You look fine. You look good."

"For my age."

He was a guest. "For any age."

As Virginia explained it, until the turn of the century Stonehaven had been a source of top-quality granite for big projects like the base of the Brooklyn Bridge and the columns of the New York Customs House. But when the advent of structural steel and concrete put the island out of business, someone had the idea to fill the quarries with water and turn them into swimming holes. An inverted diamond, the "nude quarry" was a jagged pool of water surrounded by shelves of granite on which a few naked families frolicked like seals.

"How 'bout a swim?"

Roberto was tempted. He loved to swim. And in this crowd he felt like Adonis. That is, until he saw Wesley stepping out onto a ledge, his muscles as honest, his face as sharp as any stonecutter's in Walt Whitman. Sticking out his arms, flexing his calves on tiptoe, he froze like a physique model in a frame of film. Diving into the quarry, his furry privates breezed backward, jaunty as the tail of a raccoon cap.

"That's Wesley Wilson."

"Who?"

"Him. The diver."

"Oh."

"He's the most sought-after man on Stonehaven."

"He knows how to dive."

"And fix a toilet."

"What?"

"He's a plumber—the only half-decent plumber on the whole island. How 'bout it?"

"What?"

"A swim."

Roberto would have agreed if he hadn't seen Wesley grabbing his Levi's as he emerged from the water, pulling on a T-shirt, rushing to leave.

"Maybe tomorrow."

All the way home, he thought of Wesley, his sinewy calves tensed on the ledge, as Virginia cataloged the pretensions of the dot com *nouveau riche* who had rearranged the lobby of her apartment building, Feng Shui-style, to enhance their chances on the stock market; required the doormen to wear gold braid on their uniforms; gilded the acorns on the wainscoting to the sheen of a boudoir in Versailles; only to cut and run from the building the minute the market crashed.

"Sorry, what?"

"Am I boring you?"

"Oh, no, no. I went to Versailles—when I lived in London."

Without agreeing to do so, neither of them mentioned the nude quarry to their spouses that day. Nor did Roberto mention his second visit, alone, the next day, either. Despite his tummy, Roberto felt quite comfortable naked among the islanders, big as Botero sculptures. But Wesley never showed. Almost finished with *Palimpsest,* Roberto got back on his bike, reproaching himself for obsessing about someone who could be a serial killer or a sissy, for all he knew. He was leaving tomorrow. There was nothing he could do about it. Face it. He would never see Wesley again.

That evening at sunset, as the kids played tag in their pajamas and Olga made a third caipirinha just for him, Roberto looked out on the flower garden and the cutting garden and the vegetable garden and the picket fences illustrating perspective as they intersected in a distant blur. Civilization, if he understood Freud, was mainly a process of renunciation. You've got to make choices. You can't have everything. Any man would be lucky to have the life he had.

"I thought you were going to change," Virginia scolded Gordy as he sat down in the lime-green shorts she had sent him inside to change out of. "At least take off that silly necklace."

"Not till I get the profit reports for the second quarter." Lifting a little silver cross from his freckled chest, Gordy showed it to Roberto. "Franco in Buenos Aires gave it to me for good luck." There was a little silver scroll over the head of Christ with something in Latin written on it.

"It wasn't a very lucky day for Jesus." Virginia sipped at her martini.

"Yeah, but three days later, he was on top of the world."

"You must've been raised a Catholic."

"Not really," Roberto said. "My parents don't believe in much, except plastic surgery."

"You're kidding. Your father too?"

"He's had his chin and his eyes done twice and he's not even sixty. That's Brazil for you."

"The dishwasher's still iffy." Gordy handed his wife a fresh bowl of crab dip.

"You said you'd call."

"I'll call him tomorrow."

"I'll do the dishes," Roberto offered, hoping to shame his hosts into summoning Wesley.

Neither was in the mood to protest.

"What's your wife making in there?" Gordy asked. "Some kind of witch's brew?"

"We saw Wesley in town." Virginia winked at Roberto.

"Who?"

"Wesley, the plumber."

"Oh, right."

"Now, *there's* a character."

"You don't say."

Smiling to himself, Gordy savored his drink, shuffling the facts in his mind before dealing his story.

"He's half and half." Virginia took over impatiently. "Half islander, half summer people. His father was a fisherman; his mother Sally was a Wescott."

"A vest?"

"That wasn't funny the first time, Gordy." Virginia nibbled at an olive. "She was one of the Philadelphia Wescotts: lots of land but not much money. When her grandfather died, she sold her share of the farm in Newport and moved out here to live off the rest. She took up with a fisherman, a total stud—"

"How would you know?"

"If only. They married; they—"

"No, they didn't."

"Gordy."

"They didn't."

"They did. Veronica was there, at First Methodist. They raised Wesley together."

"He was a terrible drunk."

"Wesley Senior . . . they took the boat out in a storm . . . drunk, as usual. They never came back. End of story."

"He's very well-read," Gordy said.

"Wesley? Bullshit. He doesn't know the difference between Dickens and that stuff you read."

Gordy smiled. "What's wrong with John Grisham?"

"Please. People say he takes things."

"Virginia."

"They do. The Boltons, the Pomeroys. He's never taken anything from us. Maybe I should be insulted."

"He's an incredible gardener. You should see his greenhouse."

"All right," Virginia snapped.

"What?"

"He's a genius. He's a sweetheart."

"I didn't say *that*."

"Besides, he charges a pittance and he'll come out at any hour."

"Shit," Roberto let out, loudly.

"What's the matter?"

"Do you have some allergy spray or something?" Roberto took off his wedding ring. With the fingernails of one hand, he started itching the knuckles of the other.

"Honey, what's wrong?" Returning with the caipirinha, Olga knelt down at his side.

"Let me see."

"It's nothing. It itches."

"There's Lidocaine in our bathroom." Virginia put down her drink.

"No. Stay. I'll get it."

"*Eu vou pegar,* honey."

"No. Sit. You've been on your feet all night. I'll be right back."

Inside the house, transfixed with guilt, he looked back at Olga settling on a chaise lounge as the kids rushed up to nestle in her arms. She put a hand to Ivan's forehead, as she had put a hand to his, those Sunday mornings when he lay in bed, hungover from a night in Chelsea.

Locking the door, Roberto flipped up the toilet seat. He held the gold ring between two fingers. The water was blue. What was he thinking? Was he crazy? What about the sink? He studied the pipes. Convoluted like a snake, the pipes of the sink were a better bet; surely the ring would plop onto a plateau and stay there without sailing farther down the drain.

With his left hand, he pushed aside a glass door of the medicine cabinet and took out the Lidocaine. In the other pane of glass, he saw himself, empty of expression as a passport photo. How could he do it? Was he having a breakdown? You'd think that Wesley was the last man on earth. There was no chance of sex. Just a few words and a muscular arm as he wielded a rusty wrench.

With the tip of his index finger, Roberto flicked the ring down the drain of the sink.

"Honey, what is it?"

"I can't believe it."

"What?"

"I think I dropped my wedding ring down the sink."

"I'll call Wesley." Virginia put a hand on Olga's shoulder.

Wesley was there in half an hour. His grease-stained T-shirt, which he stubbornly continued to wear even as Roberto complained of the heat, had a motto on the back—WORK HARD, PLAY HARD, DIE BROKE—which enchanted Roberto with its rudeness.

"We should let you get on with it," Gordy said to Wesley, encouraging Roberto to return to dinner.

"You go on ahead. I'll be right down."

"You want a beer, Wes?"

"No thanks. I've got the Obsornes after this." On his knees, toolbox beside him, he wrenched away at the pipes.

"What's the matter there?"

"At the Osbornes? Their fuckin' kid got pissed at the sitter and flushed her car keys down the toilet."

"Incredible."

Left alone with Wesley, Roberto felt happy for the first time all week. Hovering in the doorway, he admired Wesley's musculature even as he struggled, without much success, to get another glimpse of his face. "I hear you read a lot."

"I guess. What's a lot?"

"What are you reading these days?"

"Lincoln."

"A biography?"

"Sort of. It was a best seller."

"By Gore Vidal?"

"Yeah, right."

No way. "I love Vidal."

"I don't know about this one. He's pretty hard on Lincoln. I liked the other one better."

"Burr?"

"Yeah, you read it?"

"Years ago. I'm reading his memoirs, *Palimpsest.*"

"Never heard of it. Good?"

"What?"

"Is it good? Are you enjoying it?" He wiped the sweat from his forehead on his forearm.

"Yeah, I like it, so far. I mean, the guy's led quite a life."

"So I've heard." Craning his neck, he looked up at Roberto.

"What?"

"So, you're from New York." He returned to his plumbing.

"I'm from Brazil. But I live in New York."

"Brazil. Uh-huh. What's that like?"

"It's beautiful. Poor. But beautiful."

"I get down to New York—a couple times a year."

"Business or pleasure?" Roberto asked.

"You know, a little of both."

"Right."

"So, what do you do for fun in New York?"

Jesus Christ. "There are plenty of places."

"Uh-huh. Like what?" Wesley asked.

"You mean restaurants? What kind of food do you like?"

"I don't know. I'm not much of a gourmet."

From below, Roberto recognized Maria's wail revving up like the siren of a squad car.

"Know any good bars?" Wesley asked.

Pulling the door with him, Roberto took a half step into the room. "There are plenty of bars."

"If you gotta pee or something, just go ahead."

"I can wait," Roberto said.

"This is gonna take awhile."

"Roberto!"

Shit. "Olga, what?"

"Roberto! *Venha logo, e a Maria!*"

Maria had fallen off the deck. Rushing downstairs, Roberto took her in his lap and examined her forehead. There was barely a bump, but she was terrified. Holding her tight, he told her of Pedro Pan who could fly off decks, children in tow.

Virginia reassured Olga there was nothing to worry about. Finally, she calmed down, resumed speaking English, and finished off a bottle of wine as the sun set on the bay.

Roberto took Maria to bed in his arms. Exhausted from fear, she fell asleep beside her brother. Later that night, Olga took Roberto's hand, slipped the wedding ring back on his finger, and hugged him close.

Wesley was long gone. Apologizing for his stupidity, Roberto insisted on paying for the plumber. The Farrs refused him. Not only had Wesley found the wedding ring, he'd taken a look at the dishwasher and found the espresso spoon that had been throwing it out of whack.

Stepping out on the empty deck, Roberto found his caipirinha still waiting for him. He sat in the moonlight, thanking God that his daughter was safe and begging him for forgiveness. When the chill drove him inside, he poured his drink down the garbage disposal. He eviscerated the lime and the stick of sugar cane with a twist of self-disgust.

"They gave you the ring."

"Oh, right, yeah," Roberto said. "Thanks. So, how ya been?"

"Where is it?" Wesley touched the side of Roberto's glass to still his hand. "You take it off when you come in here?"

"No. Not anymore. I mean, my wife and I, we're . . . not together."

"Oh."

"Since Friday."

"Oh."

"No, for good. She went back to Brazil with the kids."

"Oh, shit. I'm sorry." Wesley's eyes narrowed as if approaching a highway disaster.

"Yeah, well."

"You must be wrecked. I mean, emotionally."

"Oh, yeah. Kind of. I miss the kids."

"I bet."

"I mean, it's rough, but . . ." Roberto stopped.

"What?"

"You're not married?"

"Are you kidding?" Wesley said.

"It's like pretending all the time. It drives you crazy."

"You mean, you told her?"

"Uh-huh."

"Good for you."

"She was sort of hinting about having another baby. I just blurted it out."

"Congratulations." He knocked his bottle against Roberto's glass.

I used to be married. I have two kids. This is who I am now, Roberto marveled. "So, how are *you?*"

"Good."

"You look good."

"Thanks," Wesley said. "You too."

"Isn't this weird?"

"What?"

"Meeting here."

"I know," Wesley said. "I never come here."

"Me neither."

"Gordy told me about it."

"Gordy?"

"Yeah."

"You're kidding. Gordy."

Wesley looked worried. "Wait."

"Gordy comes here."

"You didn't know?"

"No way." Roberto was delighted.

"I thought you knew."

The world was full of gays. It was one big Brownstone. "I can't believe it."

"I thought the two of you . . ." Wesley stopped.

"What?"

"You know."

"What?"

"Got it on."

Roberto stiffened. "Jesus Christ."

"What's that supposed to mean?"

"Me and Gordy?"

"He's a very nice guy."

"Yeah, right."

"He is."

Roberto shuddered. Is *that* what he thinks? I'm only fit to fuck an old fart like Gordy?

"Don't tell him I told you."

"What? Oh, no."

"Promise."

"I promise. I can't. He's my boss. I can't just walk in and tell him, 'I hear you're a regular at the Brownstone.'"

"Don't tell him you saw *me* here either."

"No, no. I won't mention it at all. Does Virginia know?"

Wesley shrugged. "He doesn't *think* so."

A shameless old showqueen was doing the samba with the piano player's bowl of tips balanced deftly on his head—just one of the dozens of dowdy men in the room Wesley counted him among. "He doesn't *sing,* does he?"

"Who?"

"Gordy. When he comes here."

"No, only in the shower."

Roberto turned. "You mean, when you're plumbing?"

Wesley looked away, abashed.

"You don't mean . . ."

"What have you got against Gordy?"

"No, no, nothing."

"He's a great guy, really."

"I know, I know," Roberto said. "I just didn't picture—"

"What is it with everyone in New York? You've got to be Brad Pitt with like perfect muscles or you might as well roll over and die."

"I didn't mean—He's a wonderful guy," Roberto said. "I just didn't . . . y'know, *know.*"

"Well, now you know."

"Cool. Take it easy. I just didn't know."

Wesley shrugged.

Looks didn't matter to him. Amazing. Roberto was astonished by his decency.

"He's got a great big dick," Wesley added.

Roberto hesitated a second. "And it's a tiny island."

For a moment, Roberto regretted the stupid remark that had cost him the poke of his life and, who knows?, some kind of relationship, long-distance, the phone ringing eagerly for him in his empty apartment. But then Wesley laughed. Shadow boxing giddily, Roberto gave him a playful right to the gut. "So what brings you to New York?"

"Oh, lots of things. I had to pick up some books." Wesley kicked a paper bag at his feet.

Roberto reached for an old hardcover. "*Latin Grammar?*"

"I just need the prefixes and suffixes."

"You're studying Latin?"

Wesley looked pissed. "Believe it or not."

"I don't mean—I mean, I'm impressed, but who studies Latin anymore?"

"I'm not like planning to read *The Aeneid*. I just need to figure out the names of plants. They're all in Latin."

"Oh, right."

"It was like one of my best subjects in school."

"Really? Cool. They teach Latin on Stonehaven?"

"At boarding school."

"Oh. Where'd you go to boarding school?" The words were barely out of his mouth before Roberto saw he had revealed too much class-consciousness.

"Connecticut. My grandmother paid for it." Wesley looked away irritably.

Looks didn't matter. Class didn't matter. And he was cuter than Tom Sawyer.

"*Manual of Cultivated Trees and Shrubs. Winter Ornamentals.*" Roberto read the titles. "You're a serious gardener."

"I'm starting this business. *Trying* to start it—a nursery and a mail-order catalog."

"Wow."

"Gordy's gonna be a partner. But, first, I gotta find plants I can raise on Stonehaven and then ship by mail to other places with the same kind of climate."

"What a great idea."

"You know, everybody on Stonehaven complains about how like there's not much choice about what they can grow. We've got maybe five warm months and these terrible winters. And it's worse in Canada."

"So, where do you find them—the plants—to sell?"

"I haven't found them yet," Wesley said. "I'm going to Scotland and Scandinavia."

"Cool. When?"

"Tomorrow."

Roberto tried to hide his disappointment. "Oh."

"Yeah. I'm really psyched."

"Tomorrow morning?"

"Tomorrow afternoon."

"No way."

"If the airport's open."

Roberto took heart in the blizzard. "I wouldn't count on *that*. You want another beer?"

"Nah. Not right now." Wesley's eyes wandered the crowd.

"Can I ask you something?"

"What?"

"What's that about?"

"What?"

"Your hands. You keep going, left, right, left." Roberto squeezed one fist and then the other.

"Oh, my wrists are for shit. I'm tryin' to work 'em. The doctor says it's carpal tunnel syndrome."

"Right, right."

"It probably is. I'm like ten hours day with a wrench in my hand and then ten hours at home on the computer. I'm designing this Web site, for the nursery."

"Not to mention the chat rooms."

Wesley smiled. "You got *my* number."

"Is that how you meet people?"

"It's not like we've got a lot of bars on Stonehaven. We haven't got *one*. Is it hot in here?"

"Take off your sweatshirt," Roberto suggested.

Crisscrossing his hands to tug off his sweatshirt, Wesley grimaced, "My neck is killing me too. I pulled a muscle or something." His T-shirt rode up over his stomach. A trail of hair disappeared in his pants.

"You go into the chat rooms?"

"Now and then," Wesley said.

"Ever meet anybody?"

"You mean, make a date, to meet in real life?"

"Yeah. Is that how it works?"

"I'm meeting somebody here."

Roberto blinked. "No way. You're kidding."

Wesley scanned the crowd.

"You must be nuts," Roberto said.

"What?"

"He could be a murderer."

Wesley laughed. "Not this guy."

"Who? Why?"

He checked his watch. "Trust me. He isn't a murderer."

"You'll land up in the morgue."

"He's probably stuck in the snow."

"You know what he looks like?" Roberto said.

"This isn't the first time we've hooked up."

"Oh, you know him already."

"Uh-huh."

"What's he look like?" Roberto scanned the room.

"Glasses. Brown hair. Says he's thirty-nine."

"That's half the men here."

"I wonder what's keeping him."

It was now or never. "It's getting late. If you need some place to stay."

"Really?"

"I mean, I've already seen you naked."

Wesley frowned.

"I *have*."

"How much have you had to drink?"

"At the quarry. The naked quarry."

"Oh. You're kidding." Wesley looked shy and proud at once. "So, you mean I'll do."

"Oh yeah, you'll do." Roberto cupped a hand on Wesley's butt. "You'll do what I say." He hammed it up like that wrestler, The Rock.

Wesley scowled in amusement. "We'll see about that."

"Wesley?" A voice interrupted.

It was the social worker. Shit.

"Mike." Wesley turned to embrace him. "This is my friend . . ."

"Robert."

"You get stuck in the snow?" Wesley shifted his stance to face both his admirers.

"It's a long story. How long have you been here?"

"I don't know." Wesley shrugged. "Maybe an hour." He pulled off his ski cap and mussed the curl back in his hair.

He looked like a handsome Roman youth in one of those heartbreaking coffin portraits. With Mike's arrival, Roberto despaired of ever having the chance to tell Wesley things like this. "So you met on the net?"

Mike smiled. "Why not?"

"We hooked up last summer—in Provincetown."

He was a fool to have thought he could spend the night with a guy so beautiful. "Where'd you get *that?*" Roberto recognized something—the chain around Wesley's neck.

"Gordy gave it to me." Wesley proudly held out the little silver crucifix. "There's something in Latin."

Mike examined the scroll above the crown of thorns. *"Christus Vincit."*

"You speak Latin too?"

"Uh-huh."

"What are you, a priest?" Roberto said.

Wesley shook his head in warning. Mike froze.

Fuckin' asshole, he *was.* "What? It's nothing to be ashamed of. I'm *married.*"

Wesley's eyes shot venom at Roberto.

"What?" Roberto relished their embarrassment.

"It's just two words: *Christus Vincit,*" Mike went on. "You can translate *that.*"

Wesley hesitated. " 'Christ is risen'?"

"Right," Mike allowed, equivocally. "Christ is triumphant. But as you say, it's usually translated 'Christ is risen.' "

Priest, pedant, pedophile. "I'm getting a drink." Roberto turned on his heel.

"Robert. Hang on."

Life is nasty, brutish and short. And so am I, Roberto reminded himself as he pushed through the noisy crowd to the bar.

"See you around," Father Mike called after him with a note of re-proach that made Roberto want to kick him in the balls. He could hear the little closet case saying *See you around* to his bored parishioners as they slipped out a side aisle before the Consecration.

Beauty's a commodity, Roberto acknowledged, like tin and lumber and the other commodities he had to analyze for Colcutt and Com-pany. In the current market at the Brownstone—face it—he was not much in demand.

Insinuating himself into the throng at the bar, Roberto renewed the vow he made the day after he and Pedro-Paulo had jerked off to-gether. He would never let himself get quite so stupidly happy and hopeful again. Waiting by the waterfall, day after day, he had come to realize that Pedro-Paulo would never return. When he finally saw him on the road to school with his soccer buddies, Pedro-Paulo kicked the ball right past him, dashing by without even a nod.

At the bar, too timid to stick out his arm with the other storm troupers, was a half-decent-looking kid with a buzz cut—nothing to write home about—a law student or an accountant or a lab techni-cian. Roberto sized him up in a second: he was the kind of kid who'd be so grateful for any attention, he'd gladly blow you on the tram.

Wiping his eyes, slipping in beside Buzzcut, Roberto brushed a hand up the back of his head. "So, what are you having?"

The Assistant Pastor

Of all the busy establishments on the north side of New Brunswick, from Danube Travel to the Gentle Panda Laundry, from Roger's Trophy Engraving to The Main Squeeze (For All Your Accordion Needs), none was busier at Christmastime than St. Paul's Church, where Father Michael Dougherty had been serving for more than a decade. Nearing forty but very much younger-looking, with the gentle features and wire-rimmed glasses of a soft-rocker from the seventies, Father Mike seemed, even in his hour of desperation, the kind of genial, savvy, ballplaying priest that altar boys imagined themselves as they nodded off during the Consecration. On the night before Christmas Eve, as the snow waltzed down on Danube Travel and the wind tore the umbrellas from the Chinese girls slipping into the laundry, Father Mike stood at his window overlooking the churchyard, smoking a joint and checking the train schedule.

There was no way he could drive to New York. The snow was halfway up the hydrant.

He had to go. There was no getting out of it. His boyfriend was waiting at the Brownstone. He had promised Wesley some spending money for his trip to Scandinavia. It had been six weeks since he'd seen Wesley. He would've walked to New York to see him.

There was a train leaving in an hour. It would take half an hour just to give out the presents: songbooks for the choir, tie-clips for the ushers, St. Christopher medals for the acolytes rehearsing for midnight mass. Before that, he had to drop in on the monsignor, see how he was doing, and slip a check out of his checkbook. Then write out the check, run to the liquor store, and get the manager to cash it.

The five o'clock chimes. A tight last toke. His little church had never seemed so poignant. Stuck between two tenements, St. Paul's had gone uncherished for decades until Father Dougherty became assistant pastor. The first thing he'd done, after settling in for a decent interval, was persuade Monsignor Szathmary to sandblast the facade. The veil of years lifted from its neo-Gothic face, the church began to sparkle with friezes again: Christ cast out devils, called Lazarus forth, and calmed the waters capsizing His apostles.

His second achievement was convincing the parish council (who were afraid that twelve-step meetings would bring blacks into the building) to rent rooms in the basement, weekday nights, to Alcoholics Anonymous, Al-Anon, and the group he'd considered attending himself, Debtors Anonymous. This accomplished, Father Mike, as everyone now called him, set about reviving organizations that put the beatitudes into practice: the old ladies of the Emmaus Society brought covered dishes to the sick; the old marrieds of the Pre-Cana Society disillusioned the engaged; the Youth Ministry visited homeless shelters and Three Flags, Great Adventure.

There wasn't much he could do to make the church more hospitable to homosexuals. He decried violence against gays, women, blacks, and immigrants in his sermon on the Sermon on the Mount. On a Day Without Art, the day AIDS organizations set aside for commemorating those who have died of AIDS, he let Emil, the choirmaster, drape the statues in the church with the purple cloths ordinarily reserved for Lent and Advent. When individual gays—teenagers, husbands, nuns—turned up in the confessional, their voices shaking with sobs, he chided them: "Stop. Who were Christ's friends? Women, Samaritans, adulterers—the outcasts of His day. So stop beating up on yourself. And call this number," he insisted, slipping them through the grille the card of a gay psychotherapist he'd met at an Almodovar movie at Rutgers. Clicking down the marble aisle through the colored shadows into the sunlight, the footsteps of the forgiven sped up giddily.

There were days he felt dizzy, looking down from the pulpit on so many faces that would shrivel in disgust if they only knew what Web site he'd been whacking off to, just a few minutes before Mass. But most of the time, it just seemed inevitable: what could he do? He hadn't chosen to become a priest: he had been chosen; he was a priest forever. He wasn't a pedophile; he didn't diddle parishioners. Maybe some day in the future, a half century from now, there'd be a John XXIV (but younger and cuter and unobtrusively gay) who would sit under the undulating pillars of St. Peter's and issue an encyclical, *Amoris Natura,* on the drawbacks of celibacy and the dignity of all varieties of love. Until then, whenever he got panicky—bumping into a parishioner in South Beach, daydreaming of Wesley in love with a layman—he could do what he'd just finished doing: smoke a joint and reread a bit of *Brideshead* (or Graham Greene or Chesterton) and marvel at the crooked path that led even the most libertine protagonist to God. No matter how hard he struggled, no matter how far out he swam, God would hold onto the line and tug him in.

Neither weed nor Waugh, however, could alter the fact that Father Mike had been swimming pretty far out financially in the eighteen months since he'd met Wesley in Provincetown and driven back with him to Maine. He had always been spendthrift—with beggars and boyfriends especially—but never quite this reckless. In less than a year, he had maxed out his credit cards and cashed in his CDs. By the end of the summer, he was borrowing hundreds, thousands, at a time from Monsignor Szathmary who, suffering from Parkinson's, had no idea that the checks on which he eked out his signature were paying for airline tickets, computer games, Irish sweaters, and cocaine. The lion's share of the money, however, was not being squandered on coke and computer hockey. It was being invested in Wesley's business, the nursery he was planning to stock with plants from Scandinavia and other cold climes to sell to the gardeners of Maine. Once the business got going, Father Mike would pay back the pastor (or the parish, his beneficiary) every penny he'd borrowed—with interest. But how could he *not* spoil Wesley a little? Both parents gone, he had no one else to spoil him. Surely, the God who had modeled his beautiful hands had not meant him to be a plumber. What kind of God would have brought two people to a tiny island, to a futon under the stars, just to begrudge one of them a few thousand dollars to fix up a proper greenhouse?

"I'm going now, Father Michael."

"Oh. Hang on, Agnes." He opened the door. (The room reeked of weed but the old housekeeper could hardly smell or hear a thing.) "Agnes, wait!" he shouted.

"Jesus, Mary, and Joseph."

"Want me to see you home?"

"You don't have to yell."

"It's bad out there."

"What?"

"It's really bad out there," he said. "Bad weather."

"Can't I see it myself? It's Alaska."

"You want me to see you home?"

"What?"

"You want me to see you home?"

"Don't be daft. I'm right down the street." She arranged a scarf over her nimbus of teased white hair. It was even whiter than usual.

"Look at you. You've had your hair done."

"What?"

"You've had your hair done. Your hair looks nice. You've had your hair done."

"Get away with you." She knotted the scarf under chin. "I just gave it a little whoosh with Adorn."

"How's the monsignor?"

"The monsignor?" She frowned. "You know I don't go in there."

"Oh, right, right."

She was at odds with the Indian fellow from the hospice who was looking after the monsignor.

"I'll be back tomorrow by noon."

She scowled. "I'll be here at nine, come rain, come shine."

"I know *you* will. I'm just saying, *I* should be back by noon. I'm going to New York to see a sick friend."

"New York? In this weather?"

"I know. I have to. Amrit will be here."

"What?"

"Amrit will be here," he said. "Amrit."

"He's with the monsignor."

"He's staying the night. He's sleeping over—on the daybed."

"You want me to make it up for him?"

"No, no. You go home. I'm just saying, he promised to stay all night with the monsignor—till you get back in the morning."

She thought for a second, shrugged, and headed downstairs. "What harm can he do now?"

" 'Night, Agnes."

"Tell him to call me if anything happens."

"I will."

If the monsignor dies, is what she meant.

For years, despite the shivering grip with which he offered parishioners a sip from the chalice, Monsignor Szathmary had not let his Parkinson's get the better of him. He still had the Scouts to tea—four at a time, two boys and two girls—and managed the teapot himself. He still taught his interfaith pottery class at Temple Bethel: his shaky hands gave rise to some arresting vases. He still lowered the needle on his scratchy old Rubinstein records by hand, finding the groove of his favorite Chopin. If he was more absentminded than usual, he didn't let it get him down. When a package of chicken breasts turned up under the tax forms on his desk, he just sniffed them and insisted that the parish council president stay for dinner: "It won't take a second. I'll make paprikash."

Then, ten months ago, in March, he had genuflected during the Offertory and disappeared behind the altar for several minutes. It was not until a Filipino nurse in the congregation came up and tapped him on the shoulder that he got up and resumed the Mass, as if nothing had happened. "This is My body," he held the bread in his trembling fingers. And froze again. The nurse tapped him again. Halting a few more times, he finished the Mass, unperturbed by his dying battery.

From that day on, Father Mike had made sure the pastor was attended at all times by someone ready to rouse him from his nap in the jaws of death. He took turns with Agnes rationing the monsignor's drugs in little envelopes—Morning, Noon, Bedtime—and making sure that he took them on schedule. By the end of summer, however, the monsignor's wonder drugs were failing to work their wonders.

His tank all but empty of dopamine, the affable pastor was losing his temper, hurling missals at lectors, groaning at the campfire kitsch of the Contemporary Choir, spitting out the "dog food" served up by the Rosary Society. Convinced that the conservative Catholic League was bugging his phone, he startled callers with rude claims about more orthodox clergy designed to unnerve the eavesdroppers: "Bishop Rorty? He told *me* there was too much of a fuss made about Mary. She gave birth. She took Him to the temple. She watched Him die. End of story." His views on contraception, Fatima, and the varying Gospel accounts of the Resurrection progressed from the liberal to the peculiar. On Easter he argued that the young man in the white robe who surprised the women at the empty tomb was Mahatma Gandhi. On Earth Day his portrait of the crowded household on Noah's Ark upset the younger children. In short order, word came from the archdiocese that the monsignor was not—under any circumstances—to be allowed in the pulpit again. This final blow only confirmed his conviction that the bishop was in league with Opus Dei.

Though his lungs soldiered on, in recent days the monsignor's other systems had all but failed him: he couldn't swallow; he couldn't defecate without a nurse working his buttocks like a bellows. The hospice people agreed he could die at home: what he needed was morphine and an antipsychotic. Sure enough, a morphine patch, a few milligrams of Klonopin, and he took to bed calmly, slipping into childhood reveries of Hungary. Cheeks sunken, seldom blinking, he whispered to friends from the past (*Szia, Bela!*) and toasted their health (*Egeszsegedre!*). Most of the time, he seemed to be listening to something difficult and beautiful—Liszt? "Everybody's asking for you," Father Mike reassured him as he wiped the drool from the old man's mouth. "I can't get out the door without people grabbing me. 'How is he?' 'Tell him we're praying for him.' 'Give him my best.' 'Give him my love.'"

The Sunday before the snowstorm, Father Mike himself got out, "I love you, Monsignor," but he felt like a fraud. For his grief was mixed with relief: the monsignor's right hand was hard as a claw—too stiff, finally, to sign another check. Never again would Father Mike be tempted to manipulate the dying man like a dummy. Even forgery—

though riskier—seemed less awful than guiding that bluish hand to the bottom line of the check and, when it stopped in mid-signature, prodding it back to business. The indulgent monsignor, he scolded himself for thinking, would be the first to forgive him his sins. But he had no right to let himself off the hook so easily. Not until he paid back everything he'd borrowed and confessed everything he'd done.

The bed was empty. The room was dotted with odd, ambitious vases full of flowers sent over by pottery students.

"Excuse me, Amrit?"

On his cell phone, as usual, the brawny Sikh was sitting at the desk where the Monsignor kept his checkbook.

"And I'm like, 'What the fuck did you say?' And he's like, 'Dude. You said some mean shit to me last night, and there comes a point when I gotta evaluate a friendship.'"

"Amrit, where's the monsignor?"

"And I'm like, 'Yo, dude: evaluate *this*. Everybody knows you're a whiny little bitch who just sits on his ass all day, eating Fig Newtons.'"

"Amrit."

"He's like mad jealous I get all the booty and he's so stuck in his room, watchin' Comedy Central."

"Amrit!"

"Call ya back, dude." With a show of forbearance, Amrit clicked off the phone and hooked his hair behind his ears. "What's up?"

"Where's the monsignor?"

"He's at the Meadowlands."

"What?"

"*Duh.* He's in the bathroom."

"By himself?"

"It was his idea."

"Can you do me a favor?"

"What?" Amrit looked suspicious.

"Run down to the kitchen and get me a cup of tea."

"Are you kidding? She hates me."

"Who?"

"Agnes."

"She's gone. She left already."

"She leaves at six."

"No. She left early. 'Cause of the storm."

Amrit yawned. "I'm not going nowhere till the monsignor takes a shit."

"Amrit."

"You think I'm wack? Look. He had a couple sips of Ensure," Amrit pointed.

A can of Ensure sat on the bedtable, a flexi-straw sticking out like a pinky.

"Then he's all, 'Amrit, I've gotta go the bathroom.' I stick the jug on his dick. He says, 'No, I want to go to the toilet.'"

"Is that you, Mike?"

Little more than a whisper, still it was audible.

"He's talking?"

"You believe this shit?" Amrit beamed.

"I'll be right out."

"I come in; he's asleep. Then, pow!, his eyes are open and he's all, 'Amrit, what time is it? Get me the phone. I gotta call the rabbi.'"

"The rabbi?"

"I'm ready, Amrit."

"Chill, dude, I'm coming!" Amrit got up wearily. "It's gotta be the new pill."

"The Klonopin? It was putting him to sleep."

"Not anymore."

"Amrit?"

Amrit went into the bathroom. "Buddy, how'd we do? Take it easy. Lemme help you."

The checkbook was in the desk under a pile of mass cards. Ripping out the topmost check, reaching for a pen, Father Mike hesitated: he wouldn't have to fake the monsignor's signature if the old man could still sign for himself.

A bag of bones in Amrit's arms, the monsignor groaned as Amrit carried him out of the bathroom and lowered him into the nest of pillows on his bed.

"How ya feelin', Monsignor?"

"Mike?"

"Uh-huh."

"What day is it?"

"Thursday." Father Mike took his hands.

"Is it Christmas yet?"

The fingers were stiff as wood: no go. "It's the day before Christmas Eve."

"Can I have the phone?"

"The phone?"

"I've got a cell." Amrit reached into his carpenter pants.

"You want Sister Phil?"

"Rabbi Singer."

"Is he in the book?" Amrit grabbed the address book.

"I want to get him a present. For Hanukkah."

"You're too late. It was like a week ago." Father Mike reached for a tissue to wipe the monsignor's mouth.

"Where's the checkbook?"

"Let *me* worry about that."

Amrit opened the desk. "Here it is."

"You can't call him tonight. It's Thursday night. He's with his family."

"Heads up." Amrit tossed the checkbook onto the bed.

Father Mike grabbed it. "He reads his Torah portion on Thursdays."

"How much do I have?"

"Don't you worry about that."

"I got the number." Amrit started dialing.

"Amrit. Go down to the kitchen and get us some tea."

"The home number?"

"Amrit. Stop. *Now.*"

"What?"

"Get the tea."

"It's ringing." Amrit held out the phone.

Father Mike grabbed it.

"What?"

"Get the tea."

"Fuckin A. I'm not your fuckin' servant."

"Amrit. I know that."

"Right away, sahib." He grabbed his phone back.

"Amrit. I didn't mean to sound—"

"Fuck you, faggot," Amrit let out, not quite under his breath, as he slammed the door behind him.

The monsignor was smiling. "He's quite a handful."

"No kidding. So, how ya' feeling? Want some Ensure?"

The monsignor shrank away from the straw bent toward his lips. "I need your help."

"Sure. Anything. What is it?"

Mouth open, he froze. Mike touched his jaw with a finger.

"I had a friend."

"Uh-huh."

"Bela Katzner."

"Uh-huh."

"We were seventeen."

"Oh, way back then."

He looked away.

"In Hungary, you mean. Before you came to America."

The monsignor spoke very slowly. "I was leaving for the seminary. His father . . . Dr. Katzner. They passed a law. Only twenty percent of the . . . doctors and lawyers . . . Jews could only be twenty percent."

"The Nazis."

He shook his head. "Not yet. It was our prime minister. Daranyi. Or . . . Imrédy." He looked lost.

"They passed a law?"

"Dr. Katzner was fired. From the hospital."

"That's terrible."

"He got a job . . . far away . . . in Sopron . . . at a factory . . . making plates." The monsignor grimaced. "Kitsch . . . for tourists in Vienna. Emperor Josef. The Lipizzaner stallions."

"Uh-huh."

"Dr. Katzner. They had a little house . . . with a pottery wheel. He put my hands in the clay. He showed me how to hold them." He tried to open his hands.

"Uh-huh."

"I was good at it."

"You are good."

"Better than Bela," he whispered.

"I bet you were."

"His father told me."

"You're still good."

His brow tightened. He looked out the window. "I came home from seminary . . . for Christmas. I went to Sopron. Their little house . . . it was full of Jews."

"Uh-huh."

"Bela and his father . . . the whole family . . . there were seven . . . living in one room."

"Ah, Monsignor."

His tears sparkled. "Such beautiful plates . . . and vases. Every sister was an artist."

"Incredible."

"Six years, they lived in that . . . room." He stopped.

Mike touched his forehead.

"Forty-four . . . the Germans came," he resumed. "I went in May . . . to show off my vestments."

"You'd been ordained."

"Bela was gone. They were all gone." His shoulders heaved.

"Ssssh." Shifting about, Father Mike pressed his head against the monsignor's shoulder.

"The plates, the vases . . . they were all just . . . broken pieces."

"You really loved him."

The monsignor looked up.

"Bela. You really loved him."

His eyes filled with gratitude as the sobs were wrested from his bony chest.

"He loved you too."

Father Mike held him like a lifeguard floating a swimmer back to shore. He didn't deserve this chance, he knew full well, to comfort the monsignor, but wasn't it just like God to use him, utterly unworthy as he was? That was the mystery of the priesthood: God offering His love, His sacraments, through sinners.

"Here, blow." Mike wiped his nose.

There was no need for Extreme Unction now: this was it: tears and a Kleenex.

"I want to buy him a kiln."

"A what?"

"I want to buy Rabbi Singer a kiln." The monsignor pronounced the word carefully.

"Of course, we will."

"Can I afford it?"

"Absolutely."

"You're sure?"

"Why not? What is it, exactly?"

"A kiln? You know, it's an oven."

The wind rattled the windows. In the courtyard below, the snow stuck like a yarmulke to the statue of St. Paul. They were quiet awhile, Father Mike and the monsignor, sitting shiva for Bela, Dr. Katzner, Mrs. Katzner, and the four talented Katzner girls.

"They don't have a kiln . . . at Temple Bethel. We put our stuff . . . in a station wagon . . . and take it to campus . . . to Asia House."

"Uh-huh."

"You're sure I can afford it?"

"Absolutely."

"It's big as a room."

"Don't you worry about that."

"The parish council—you can't tell them."

"No way."

"They're expecting every penny."

"I know."

The monsignor smiled. They were close as lovers.

"You're a good boy, Mike."

Before he knew it he was crying, at once relieved and saved. In the choirloft across the yard, the handbell choir began "Away in a Manger." A bad boy too long, he'd be good from now on.

"Okay, ladies, who wants milk? Who wants lemon?" Amrit minced into the room, three handmade mugs and a box of teabags on a tray.

Having met online in a chat room, Father Mike was just Mike to Wesley. A week before they met in the flesh, he finally 'fessed up to being a priest. Wesley was skeptical, at first:

HANDYMAN
lol

MIKE
honestly don't laugh

HANDYMAN
you're shittin me

MIKE
no honestly

HANDYMAN
cool brb gotta turn off the sprinkler

Mike was a day late getting to Provincetown for their first non-virtual meeting. He'd left a message for Wesley at the guesthouse but he thought it best not to give the silly queen at the desk the reason he was delayed. He'd been summoned to give out First Communion: the shaky monsignor could not be trusted with so many hosts and so many shy little tongues.

When his bus finally made it to Provincetown, Wesley was waiting beside the car in sandals and cut-offs. He looked just as good as his jpeg pictures and even browner for a weekend at the beach.

"Wesley?"

He didn't even take off his sunglasses.

"I'm so sorry. Did you get my message? There was nothing I could do."

"Uh-huh."

"I was all set to leave last night—"

"Shit happens."

"But something came up. I tried to reach you."

Rubbing his wrist with his other hand, Wesley looked away to the beach.

"I know you're not gonna believe this, but this is so unlike me. I'm almost never even five minutes late."

"I'm gonna take a last swim." Wesley slipped out of his sandals.

"You know, the guy I work with . . . the guy—"

"Are you comin' to Stonehaven?" Wesley interrupted.

"What? Yeah. Sure. I'd like to. I mean, wasn't that the plan? If you're still in the mood."

He cast a cold eye on Mike. "I'm gonna take a quick swim." He handed Mike the keys. "Put your bag in the trunk. There's a gas station on the corner."

"You need some gas?"

"Yeah. Fill 'er up." He handed Mike his sunglasses and slipped out of his shorts.

"I'm really sorry."

"Point taken." In his snug little Speedo, he ran down to the beach. Mike picked up the shorts and the sandals and, half-hard with excitement, started on his errand.

Almost an hour off the coast of Maine, the little island of Stonehaven was miles away from anything Mike had to worry about. Watching Wesley at work in his little "greenhouse"—slapped together from storm windows and doors—gave him a rush of contentment he hadn't felt since his altar boy days. He lay on the hammock under the trees, watching for hours as Wesley snapped off dead branches with his clippers, or put stakes in the flowerpots to support the tuberoses. More than once, when Wesley summoned him inside the little greenhouse, he reached out to bless himself from a holy water font that wasn't there. Lifting a leaf to reveal a new bud, Wesley's rapt, unshaven face was proud as a dad's showing off his son's first tooth: "Look at that little bugger. It's gonna bloom already."

Everything in Wesley's life had a purpose. Beside the sink in the kitchen, he kept a dozen little dishes, receptacles for used teabags, squeezed-out lemons, chicken bones, nutshells: the nutrient-rich garbage he used as fertilizer for particular plants each morning. Mike helped with the chores: there was soup stock to boil down, deckchairs to fix, portable heaters to order for the new greenhouse from gardening sites on the Web.

Over eighteen months, the new greenhouse had progressed from a Web site dream (Professional Solarhut Greenhouse, Model 8514) to a permit to build; from a pile of boxes beside the old greenhouse to a rectangle of red bricks on a concrete floor; from an aluminum frame the size of a small chapel to its present state, fiberglass walls in place, just the glass on the rafters yet to be hung. Nervous at first, climbing a ladder to attach a gutter or weather-strip the frame, Mike now looked forward to working side by side with Wesley, quiet as Cistercians praising God with their activity.

Without cocaine, Wesley didn't talk much; about his family, he hardly talked at all. As far as Mike could gather, Wesley's mother had come from a wealthy family that had summered on the island. Defying her parents, she had married Wesley's father, a football hero at Stonehaven High. Scraping by on his wages and her mother's largesse, they drank, fought, and eventually drowned in a sailing accident when Wesley was just sixteen. Since then, he'd gotten by on his wits, his wrenches, and his dreams of a gardening business.

"If you had one of those round driveways like Gordy's, and you wanted—"

"Who's Gordy?"

"That guy I introduced you to—when I stopped the truck?"

"Who?" Mike said.

"Last time you were here. His wife just kept talking and talking, remember?"

"Oh, right."

"He's got this big round driveway and he wants bushes to go all around it. Which looks better to you: this one?" Wesley clicked a photo up on the computer screen. "Or this one?"

"Let me see the first one again." It was a sturdy evergreen with clusters of white flowers. "Look at the name: *cotoneaster Rothschildianus*."

"I gotta learn Latin."

"It's easy. I'll teach you. Look at the one at the bottom."

"This?"

"Yeah. *Hebe recurva*. What do you think that means?"

"I don't know."

"Try."

"What does it mean?"

"Think."

Wesley took a second. "Jew?"

"Jew? Where'd you get that?"

"*Hebe*. Jew."

"That isn't funny."

"I wasn't trying to be funny."

"What about '*recurva*'?"

Wesley laughed. "Jew with a big curved nose."

"Shut up."

"What?"

"You're a terrible person."

"That's why you like me."

"No, it isn't."

He grabbed Mike's ass. "Bullshit. That's why you like me in bed."

It was hard to argue with that. Strokable as a puppy afterward, Wesley was cool, at best, in the heat of sex. The first time they got down to it, bags from Provincetown still on the bed, he grabbed Mike's head like a basketball he was ready to shoot from the foul line. Mike's eardrums roared as Wesley shoved his dick into his mouth.

"Got any rubbers?"

"In my shaving kit," Mike managed to say.

Unzipping Mike's knapsack, he grabbed a black leather bag. "What's this?"

Distracted by Wesley's balls, downy as peaches, Mike didn't look up until Wesley had taken out the little chalice and the long white scarf embroidered with loaves and fishes.

"Stop. No." Mike bolted backward. "Don't touch that."

"What is this shit?"

"Put it back. Please. Now."

Wesley examined the gold plate. "Take it easy. What's this?"

The gold plate was the paten Mike used to say Mass away from St. Paul's.

"Oh, shit. I'm sorry."

"Just put it away." Mike sat back on his heels.

Wesley cupped a hand under his chin. "You want to take a break?"

There were plenty of people, Mike knew, who would consider what had just happened a sacrilege. But if God had been squeamish about genitalia, you have to ask yourself, would He have sent His Son to earth equipped with a dick? Would He have made Wesley's dick so poignant, soft, so noble and sumptuous, hard? "No, I'm okay."

Finding the rubbers, Wesley wriggled Mike's asshole down on his dick. The practicality of Wesley's approach was made to order for Mike. Nothing more or less than a body, he felt unashamed: he felt like a porn star. There was no need to feel guilty: he was beneath reproach. Some of the greatest saints had been masochists, martyrs; St. Lawrence was worse than he was.

"Do you ever think you'd like to live with somebody?" Mike ventured one evening as he lay in bed beside Wesley, after sex, watching *Law and Order*.

"Ssssh."

"Sorry."

"You want to live with me?" Wesley asked during the commercial.

"I've thought about it. Is that something you'd like?"

"To be honest, I like my privacy."

"Uh-huh."

"I like the way we are—online all the time, then we get together."

"I know. But sometimes I miss you."

"I miss you too." Wesley patted his head.

"I wonder what you're up to when I'm not here."

"Nothing much. The usual shit."

"Do you see other guys?"

"On Stonehaven? Christ."

"You can't be the only gay guy on the island."

Wesley tilted Mike's head up to look at him. "You wanna know the truth?"

"Uh-huh."

"Once in a blue moon, like I get my rocks off."

"Uh-huh."

"But that's just sex."

"Uh-huh. What's this?"

"Sex Plus."

"Sex Plus what?"

"Sex plus I really like you."

"I like you too." Mike pressed his head against Wesley's chest.

"We're partners."

"You mean in the business."

"There wouldn't *be* a greenhouse without you. The fuckin' bank won't give you five hundred dollars if you haven't gone to Harvard Business School."

"You're gonna be a big success."

"*We* are."

Mike grazed his hand down Wesley's thigh.

"Nobody ever really believed in me," Wesley said quietly. "Except my grandmother. And what could she do? She had to listen to her old man."

"What was she like?"

The show was back on. "I've seen this one before." Wesley reached for the *Law and Order* fanzine he'd downloaded from the Web. "The coed's a hooker, right?"

"I think."

The last day they spent together on Stonehaven, Wesley got a call to fix the boiler of the guy, Trevor, whose big estate was right above them on the hill.

Alone in the house, Mike wandered in a daze of affection. Wesley's Raiders cap, his lead soldiers in kilts, his bar of soap speckled with grease: Taking each relic in hand, Mike said a little prayer, thanking God for putting so much of Himself in ordinary people and ordinary things.

Having emptied the dishwasher, washed the salad stuff for dinner, he picked out a novel from Wesley's bookcase, *A Separate Peace*. In the hammock by the greenhouse, he read only a few pages before putting the book down on the grass and falling asleep.

The car was back when the raindrops woke him up.

"How'd it go?"

Wesley was sitting on the couch, flipping through the *TV Guide*. "It was a pain in the ass."

"Why? What happened?"

"Can you get me a beer?"

"Sure," Mike said. "What happened?"

"Nothing."

"You look pissed."

"Fuckin' Trevor's an asshole."

"Why? What'd he do?"

"Nothing. He's just an asshole. He was an asshole in school."

"You went to school with him?"

Mike raced through the TV channels. "Yeah. Big man on campus."

"I thought he was a summer person."

"He is. He's here in August."

"But you went to school with him?"

"In Connecticut. He was like the captain of everything," Wesley said. "He still is. Asshole."

"When did you live in Connecticut?"

"At boarding school."

"Oh. You went to boarding school? How was that?"

"It was bullshit."

"Oh."

"Shit. Is that rain?"

"You're right."

Wesley went out to shut the car windows. Mike was patting lettuce dry with a paper towel when he came back with *A Separate Peace*.

"What the fuck did you do?"

"What?"

"Look at this."

"Oh, sorry," Mike said.

"It's fuckin' ruined."

"It'll dry. Just leave it out in the sun."

He had the book opened to the title page. "There was writing. It's all . . . fucked."

"Oh, shit. Sorry. What did it say?"

"None of your fuckin' business."

"Calm down," Mike said. "Come on. I forgot. I'm sorry. It's not that big a deal."

"Is this your book?"

"What?"

"Is this your book?"

"No. Of course not."

"It's my book. You fucked it up." Wesley tossed the book on the couch and grabbed his rain slicker.

"Where you goin'?"

"You are fuckin' useless."

"Wes, wait. I'm starting dinner." He grabbed Wesley's sleeve.

Wesley struck him in the stomach with the side of his fist. Mike doubled over.

The door banged.

When he caught his breath, he picked up the book. He could just make out: . . . *good boy . . . Love, Gran.*

By the time Mike got to the Brownstone, there was a line of guys waiting to get in. A big white sheepdog was snoozing in the snow, just at the foot of the steps. A little lady in a raincoat was trying to get the dog to move as the pissed-off manager of the Brownstone assured the guys in line, "It won't be long now." Shrinking into their overcoats, the patrons stomped the sidewalk to stay warm. Snowflakes broke on their neat goatees and relaxed the spiky frontiers of their buzz cuts.

On a beautiful night like this, Mike reckoned, not even an atheist could believe in oblivion. Christ was everywhere: He offered Mike earmuffs through the kindness of an older man who'd found an extra pair in his pocket. How could anyone doubt that a world as wondrous as this was a world without end? Across the street, it was Bela, the monsignor's buddy, pulling down the gates of a Pottery Barn. And there were his grandparents, whose deaths within a year of each other had inspired him to become a priest, struggling home from Tuscan Pizza, their half-eaten slices in a paper bag.

There would always be a place in his heart for Wesley but his soul belonged to Christ. On the train from New Brunswick, he had vowed to tell Wesley there was just no way he could give him the money he'd promised. Moreover—and it would hurt him to say this—it was time to stop seeing each other. As the New York skyline backlit the cease-less shower of snow, he slipped the monsignor's check from his wallet and ripped it in half. The moment he did, he was flooded with for-giveness: he glowed like the snow-covered chemical drums rushing by the window of the train.

It was funny how close you could come to the brink before Christ snapped you back to your senses. "New Brunswick Priest Embezzles from Dying Pastor: Money Intended for Temple"—no, "Holocaust Memorial." A Jewish judge would throw away the key. "No Charges Against Priest's Boyfriend." Wesley *was* innocent. He had no idea where the money was coming from. "Local Priest Raped"—no, "Mur-dered in Prison Rape." God would be waiting with open arms.

Brightly shone the moon that night,
Tho' the frost was cruel

None of the boys singing around the piano were saints but they were good people, blinded by pleasure. So they boasted of blow jobs. It wasn't easy to be gay. No wonder they got shit-faced and shut out the world. At the wedding feast of Cana, wasn't Christ a party animal Himself?

"We buried the placenta and planted a tree on top of it."

"Eeeek. Why?"

"Don't ask me. That's what she wanted."

"Whose sperm did you use?"

"We mixed it together."

"You're kidding. Like with a spoon?"

"No, no. It was a surgical instrument."

"Yuck."

"Bill and I didn't want to know like who's the real father. So we're both the real father."

"How old is he now?"

"Ten months. He's adorable. You gotta see him. He looks just like Eminem."

It's love that we need, Mike understood: sex is just what we do to get it. The thing about Christ is, His love is *always* there—for the good, the bad, and the flabby.

On his way downstairs, Mike passed a short dark guy who looked lonely. "You know who else went to LSE?" He pointed to the crest of the London School of Economics on the guy's blazer.

"You?"

"No. Oh, hardly," Mike said.

"Mick Jagger."

"You're kidding."

"He did. You don't believe me?"

But before he could find out if the guy was pulling his leg, or show off his own nugget of knowledge about George Bernard Shaw, Mike was shoved aside by a party of theatergoers pressing into the room, *Hairspray* playbills in hand.

The downstairs room was darker and much less demure. The picture frames that held seascapes and landscapes upstairs, downstairs held photos of fifties physique models in little loincloths and muscleboys in spandex, their abdomens mapped in chiaroscuro.

Desire is nothing to be ashamed of, Mike knew, unless you let it run away with you. He said a little prayer for the horny and the hopeless, standing against the wall like suspects in a police lineup. He asked God to look after the hustlers and the goateed stud in a leather jacket absorbing the lust of lawyers.

It's rainin' men, Hallelujah
It's rainin' men, Amen

"Can I get you another?"
The waiter looked like the cute Jewish guy on *Friends.*
"Yeah, thanks. Vodka and tonic."
Had Bela and the monsignor ever kissed or even just leaned against each other on a train?
Mike stopped: it was wrong to think of Bela in a place like this. Poor Bela on the back of a truck, headed for a train, headed for Auschwitz.

God bless Mother Nature
She's a single woman too

Wesley was gonna kill him; Mike had to prepare himself. Or cause a scene. Or say he'd never even liked him at all, he'd just been fucking him for the money.
He was tempted to leave and just send Wesley an e-mail from home: "Where were you? I looked everywhere."
But there was no need to panic. His future was in God's hands. And Wesley had only been violent once—under stress—and even then he had apologized.
"That's six."
"Oh, thanks."
The waiter made change for a twenty. "Still snowing out there?"
"Uh-huh. It's unbelievable."
"Merry Christmas."
He checked his watch. Back at St. Paul's, Emil was waiting with the choir kids for their parents to pick them up. The handbells were back in their red felt cases. The monsignor was asleep or lying awake or passing from this life to the next.
"Hello."
It was the bald guy in the leather jacket.
"Hello."
"What's your name?"

"Mike."

"Aaron."

He had an accent. "Is it still coming down?"

"Yeah. It's unbelievable."

"And this is the coat I have. I'll have to buy one."

He was built like a bull. "Are you from Russia?"

"I was born in Bucharest. We moved to Israel when I was ten."

Why had *he* survived—his parents; his *grand*parents—and not Bela?

"Ever been there?"

"Israel? No, but I'd love to see it some day."

"Wait a year," Aaron said, "till the settlers calm down."

"I was supposed to go in the spring."

"That's a great time. We've got a big Pride Day in Tel Aviv." His grey goatee was like the scrub brush Agnes cleaned glasses with at the rectory. "Watch yourself." He put a beefy arm around Mike to draw him out of the way of people squeezing through to the bathroom.

"Is this your first time in New York?"

"No, no. I did a year at Columbia. I come all the time."

"On business?"

Aaron nodded. "I pick up programs for ITV."

"Uh-huh."

"I got in this morning, before they closed the airport. Lucky me."

Lucky you: you might never have been born.

"I got myself settled; had a nap; worked out. They've got a great little gym at the Four Seasons."

"Oh, that's where you're staying?"

"Yeah. It's just round the block and down Fifty-Seventh."

"I know. I mean, I know it from the outside."

"You should see it from the inside. Do you party?" He rubbed his thumb against his nose.

Mike froze. "I'm meeting somebody."

"You like getting fucked?"

"Uh. Well, I . . ."

"Is your friend cute too?"

"I better go find him."

"I'm not your type."

"No, I mean, you're . . . attractive . . ."

"Here take the room number." Aaron reached into his jacket for a pen. "I'd really like to get naked with you."

"I can't tonight."

"Bring your friend. Here. Eleven-o-two. Aaron Toma. You know any of these hustlers?" He cast his eyes around the room unenthusiastically.

"No."

"Talk to your friend. I'm not leaving yet."

I loves ya Swanee
How I loves ya, how I loves ya

Upstairs, the boozy show tunes were rippling from the piano round the room. People pushed to the bar like passengers making light of a lifeboat drill.

Maybe the snow had delayed Wesley's flight. Better yet, he was stuck in the Portland airport.

When Mike finally spotted him under the ski cap he'd bought him at the drugstore on Stonehaven, Wesley was talking to some short guy in a blazer. He was playing with his wrist, the way he did when he was nervous about something. For a moment, Mike wavered. How could he hurt this boy? He had been hurt too much already.

He finished his drink. It was no wonder he was having second thoughts. You can't just love somebody for eighteen months and then turn it off like a spigot. What the hell was God thinking, making the spirit so willing and the flesh so weak?

The die was cast. He had ripped up the check on the train. "Wesley."

"Mike." Wesley turned and gave him a hug. "This is my friend . . ."

"Robert."

It was the guy from LSE.

"You get stuck in the snow?"

"No, I've been here," Mike said. "How long have you been here?"

"I don't know," Wesley said. "Maybe an hour." He pulled off his ski cap and ran his fingers through his curls.

"So you met on the Net?"

It was the way Robert said it. "Why not?" Mike stood his ground.

"We hooked up last summer in Provincetown," Wesley said.

Suddenly, Robert reached out for something—a silver chain around Wesley's neck. "Where'd you get *that?*"

"Gordy gave it to me." Wesley showed them both a little silver crucifix. "There's something in Latin." He turned the cross toward Mike so he could read the tiny inscription.

"*Christus Vincit.*"

"You speak Latin too?" Robert said.

"Uh-huh."

"What are you, a priest?"

He made it sound like an insult.

"What? It's nothing to be ashamed of," Robert said. "I'm *married.*"

Wesley glared at him.

"What?"

"It's just two words," Mike stepped in. "*Christus Vincit.* You can translate *that.*"

Wesley narrowed his eyes and took a second. "'Christ is risen'?"

"Right. Christ is triumphant. But, as you say, it's usually translated, 'Christ is risen.'"

Robert turned on his heel. "I'm getting a drink."

"Robert. Hang on."

"See you around," Mike said without thinking, as Robert took off.

"He's pretty drunk," Wesley said.

"You know him?"

"Not really," Wesley said. "We met for two minutes this summer at Gordy's."

"Are you all right?"

Wesley looked nervous. "You want a drink?"

"What's wrong?"

"I gotta pee."

"Wes. What is it?" Mike held on to his T-shirt as he headed for the line to the bathroom.

"I thought you weren't coming."

"Tell me what's wrong."

"I'm a fuckin' asshole."

"You're not sick?"

"No."

"What?"

Wesley closed his eyes. "Trevor complained."

"Trevor? About what?"

"About the greenhouse. It's too big."

"Too big for what? You got permission. Didn't you?"

"For up to ten feet."

"Uh-huh."

"It's a foot too high."

"That's the way it came," Mike said.

"I know."

"You ordered it too big?"

Wesley hit himself on the head. "A fuckin' foot."

"Oh God."

"The smaller size was a shoebox."

The whole greenhouse would have to come down. "Oh God."

"I know. I'm an asshole."

"Wes."

"I'm a fuckin' asshole."

"What's he want you to do?"

A black guy tapped Mike on the shoulder. "Are you in line?"

Wesley said, "No. We're waiting for this one." He pointed to the private bathroom for people in wheelchairs.

"Can you take it down a foot?"

"It's *glass,*" Wesley said.

"I know; I know."

"Maybe he'll calm down."

Wesley closed his eyes. "I don't think so."

"What? *What?*"

"I'm an asshole."

"What did you do?"

"I hit him."

"No. Bad? How bad?"

Wesley turned away, "I don't know."

"You don't know?"

"I ran. I took the ferry. I was late."

"What did he say?"

Wesley laughed. "He didn't say anything."

"Stop. He was . . . breathing?"

"I'm not *that* strong."

Mike said a quick *"Jesus, please help us."* "You checked?"

"Yes. I checked. He was breathing."

"But he was . . . unconscious."

"Yeah. Shit, he was out cold."

"Did you call a doctor?"

"I tried from the ferry," Wesley said. "But no one had a cell."

"Jesus Christ."

"I really fucked myself this time."

"You gotta go back."

"I know."

"To hell with the trip."

"I *know.*"

"What the hell were you thinking of?"

"He called me a faggot. He said we didn't need any more faggotty flowershops on Stonehaven."

"You're gonna need a lawyer."

"I know."

"Can you mortgage the house?"

Wesley laughed. "It's already mortgaged."

"Get a second mortgage."

"I've already got one."

"Oh Christ."

"How much did you bring?"

Oh shit. "Let's get out of here."

"I gotta pee." Wesley stayed put. "How much did you bring?"

"We gotta talk."

"You don't have it?"

"No. Sorry. I don't have anything. Maybe fifty. I'm broke."

Wesley laughed. "Well, that's it, then."

"What do you mean?"

"I mean I'm fucked."

"They give you a lawyer if you don't have the money."

"Yeah. Some retard who doesn't know his ass from his elbow. What's he doin' in there?" Wesley banged on the bathroom door.

"Take it easy."

The door opened. The Israeli TV guy was putting on his leather jacket. "Hey, fella." His eyes moved from Mike to Wesley. "This your friend?"

"Uh-huh."

"Does he party?" He touched a thumb to his nose.

"Not tonight."

"Speak for yourself." Wesley stepped into the bathroom. "What's your name?"

"Aaron."

"Wes, you can't."

"Stay there," Wesley said.

"Wes, wait. I'll get the money."

Aaron misunderstood. "Oh. You a workin' man?"

Wesley looked flattered. "You got a problem with that?"

"No. As long as I get a bargain."

"I'm no bargain."

"Wes, wait," Mike said.

Wesley pulled the door closed.

Mike prayed: Dear Christ, tell me what to do.

The colossal lobby of the Four Seasons Hotel was sullen as an Aztec temple. Up its marble stairs, businessmen on cell phones led their lanky dates to dinner.

"If you're coming up, Mike," Aaron said, "you gotta get high."

"I just wanna talk to Wesley a minute."

"Will you drop it already. I'm a big boy. I can take care of myself."

Aaron grabbed Wesley's crotch. "How big?"

The tone sounded. As they rode up the elevator, Mike tried to figure out how much he could get at a pawnshop for his silver chalice and paten.

"How's it goin'?" A handsome guy in jeans and a parka slipped into the elevator as they got out on Aaron's floor.

"Keep up the good work," Wesley said.

"You know that guy?" Aaron headed down the hall.

"Shit, no. *You* know who he is," Wesley said. "He's on *Entourage,* isn't he?"

The suite was unbelievable. On a high school visit to the White House, Mike had seen fancier rooms but he had never actually sat down in one.

"Nice place." Wesley strolled around.

"Wes, how are you gettin' home?" Mike looked out the window at the snow coming down. "Is there a train to Portland?"

"What's the hurry?" Aaron said. "How 'bout a drink?"

"You got scotch?"

"I got everything." Aaron handed Wesley a vial of coke with a tiny spoon attached. "There's a joint there in the ash tray. I gotta take a pee."

Wesley picked up the joint.

"Wes, just listen," Mike said. "Then I gotta go."

"Here, take a hit of this."

"No, thanks."

"No, take a hit. You take a hit; I'll listen."

What could he do? Mike took a hit.

"What kind of music you like?" Aaron called from the bathroom. "The TV's on the music channel."

Mike pleaded with him. "Wes, all I'm sayin' is you should call a lawyer and say you're on your way back to turn yourself in."

"I'm gonna. In the morning." Wesley called to Aaron, "Where the fuck is the TV?"

"In that cabinet thing."

Mike tried to make him focus. "Wes, you promise?"

"Here. One more hit. This is incredible shit."

"No, thanks."

"Take it."

"You got money for the plane?"

"Yeah." Wesley laughed. "I'm gonna hock my iPod."

"Here's forty." Mike reached for his wallet as he took a toke from the joint Wesley pressed to his lips.

"Keep it."

"No. Let me help."

"No," Wesley said. "You've helped enough."

"I gotta keep ten to get home."

"Keep it." Wesley pushed his hand away. "Aaron's gonna give me a thousand if I stay the weekend."

"Wes. You gotta go home."

In his underpants, stepping out of the bathroom, Aaron looked liked a bodybuilder gone to seed. He picked up the remote and clicked on the music. "That was scotch all around?"

"Not for me, thanks." Mike tried to get up but he was wobbly already. "I gotta go."

"What's the hurry?" Wes pulled his T-shirt over his head and tossed it to Mike.

The T-shirt was warm. His head was spinning.

"Aaron thinks you're hot."

He would never again see Wesley kick off his shoes, drop his pants, his underpants, and stand before him, his legs taut with muscle, his dick sticking out.

"Suck it."

"Wes."

"Come on. Suck it once. For old times sake."

What difference would it make? On MTV, a hundred college boys in bathing suits were dancing on a beach as if their bodies were God's gift to the world.

"Suck it."

Which, of course, they are, in a way, if you don't get distracted entirely from doing some good for people.

"*Suck* it."

Like those people in Africa who get their hands cut off and have to be dressed and spoon-fed like children.

"That's good."
What good did it do *them* to forgo a dick?
"That's nice."
What good did it do Bela?
"Me next." Aaron stood nearby.
Aaron was *alive.*

The Curator

Every parent has a favorite child. Most parents have the cunning to conceal their preference. Mine didn't. Try as they may, my parents could not disguise their pride in the blessings the Creator had bestowed on my older brother, Perry.

Perry was a beautiful boy with corkscrewy hair and improbable dimples. His portrait—in cowboy hat and holster—occupied the cubbyhole just above the TV in our family's teak "entertainment unit." It was also displayed on an easel in the window of the Marblehead Photography Studio run by my mom. Cute as Perry was, it was his startling intelligence that gave him the glow of a wonderchild. No sooner had he learned his ABC's than he had dashed through all of *Dr. Seuss* and lay curled in a corner with *Treasure Island.* The potholders he wove on a little loom showed an uncanny appreciation of the chromatic spectrum and mathematics. My father's guitar, he just picked up and played as readily as he dribbled a basketball. And yet his accomplishments—which would have swelled the head of any other prodigy—did little to make Perry boastful or bored or contemptuous of his fellows. He waited his turn. He did his best to fit in. Like the boy Jesus we learned about in Sunday school, he made every effort to defer to his parents and to conceal his miraculous abilities. It was only in the clutch—what choice did he have?—that he flexed his faculties in public, helping Dad with the fractions confounding the completion of his income tax returns, sparing his school the ignominy of a second place finish in the state science fair. Even in victory, laying down his last five tiles for a triple word score in Scrabble, his smile was modest, his eyes as pityingly affectionate as Gandhi's, Einstein's, Garbo's.

In high school, he shot up in height, put on muscle, and began to date the better-looking girls on the honor roll. When he left home for Harvard, my mother could barely bring herself to cook for the poor mortals remaining. The following winter, when my father died suddenly—of pancreatic cancer, only five months after diagnosis—my mother turned to Perry more than ever for direction. She got an extra phone for the bedroom and Call Waiting, so as never to miss his call. She sat on the steps, waiting for the mailman to reboot her will to live.

Success at Harvard led Perry to further success—and tenure—at the University of Chicago Law School. He was barely thirty years old when he was tapped to be a regular commentator on constitutional law for *ABC News*. Wry but judicious in analysis, he held onto his column inches in *The New York Review of Books* even as he sparred with the wacky right-wing lightweights ABC paired him off with on *Nightline*. Throughout the month-long battle between Bush and Gore for the electoral votes of Florida, he was on the air almost constantly. Offered his own program on CNN, he turned it down, to the dismay of his agent and mother, lest putting on record his views on too many contentious legal issues jeopardize his chance of some day sitting on the nation's highest bench.

Fourteen months younger than Perry, I was no slouch at school myself. But as far as my parents were concerned, I had none of the same star quality. I was slight, asthmatic, nearsighted; I wore glasses from fourth grade on. I plunked out tunes on the piano with hesitant hands. My potholders were cautiously colored. Playing soccer, dizzy with dread, I often ran in the wrong direction. Homework took hours; I double-checked every sum, every synonym. After dinner, as my father graded papers from BU, and Perry read his latest article from "The Headlight" (the high school page of *The Marblehead Reporter*) to my mother in the kitchen, I lay on the couch in the "family room" eating Fritos and watching TV. *Murder, She Wrote* led me to Agatha Christie and Sherlock Holmes; I dreamed of becoming a mystery writer. My earliest effort, however, *Murder by the Yearbook*, discouraged me; the bodies piled up; I had no idea who done it. When my father became ill and almost before we knew it, died, I tried my hand at poetry, without much inspiration: I hardly managed a haiku.

Not an obvious nerd, I had friends to hang out with: wisecracking Randy who watched old movies, metalhead Brett who blasted Aerosmith. We hung out in the mall. We smoked dope under the bleachers. I told none of them my secrets: I was a total loser; I was relieved my father died before he found out I was gay; I wanted to kill myself.

At Columbia, I was pleased to discover, it was taken for granted that life is unfair. Blacks were bitter, whites sardonic: even the boys who played ball did it as a hoot. On Saturday night, I went out to bars and went home with any guy who seemed to like me. I worked harder than ever even as I surrendered all hope of ever competing with my brother. Cultural Studies let me write essays on *Mary Tyler Moore* and the other TV shows I knew by heart. I learned to patronize even the most ambitious of shows; to scrutinize them for any hint of racism, sexism, heterosexism, ageism, imperialism; and to write about their every signifier in a vocabulary so abstract, only fellow postmodernists would ever know what the hell I was predicating. At the suggestion of my advisor, one of the few professors who had resisted initiation into any of the prevailing intellectual cults, I wrote my thesis—a straightforward history—on the earliest years of television news. For my PhD, I expanded the book, interviewing Fred Friendly, Robert Trout, and the other surviving pioneers of TV journalism. With a little help from my brother, the book was published by Chicago, reviewed respectfully, and discussed on Public Radio. When a job turned up at the Museum of Television Arts and Sciences, I had just begun teaching at NYU.

I owed the museum job—I hated to admit it—to the reflected glory of my brother's celebrity. The portly president of the museum, Harlan Bigelow, spent much of the job interview pumping me for stories about Perry and the other demigods of ABC News.

"I hear Koppell is pissed at Perry for taking meetings with CBS."

He knew more than I did. "Really."

"Hewitt wanted him for *Sixty Minutes.*"

"Uh-huh."

"Mike Wallace told me. Hewitt denies it. But I think that's just 'cause nobody's ever turned him down before."

Learning the ropes, my first year as curator, I managed to enjoy myself now and then. I got to honor *Maude*, meet Mary Tyler Moore, and with my new paycheck, place a down payment on a sharp apartment on Sixty-Second between Third and Lex. Granted, I had to hold my nose occasionally to host *An Evening with Aaron Spelling* or celebrate *Thirty Years of The Hollywood Squares*. But I trusted that when I took the reins of programming in my own hands, there would be no more screenings of second-rate sitcoms, no more tributes to advertising gurus who bought expensive tables at the museum's gala.

"Who do you think pays your salary?"

"Excuse me?"

Bigelow tossed me the Annual Report. "We'd be up shit's creek without CBS."

"There are other CBS shows we could honor."

He fumed, "What's wrong with *Touched by an Angel*?"

"It's crap. Sentimental crap."

"It's won awards."

"From the Christian Coalition. From the Catholic League."

"People say it was charming," he said.

"You've seen it?"

"I've heard about it."

"It was total kitsch. There's a white angel and a black angel and they go about rescuing crack babies and high school kids with machine guns planning to mow down their class."

He was losing steam. "What about *Party of Five*?"

"It was nothing special either."

He closed his eyes. "It was on Fox, right?"

"Uh-huh."

"Is it better than *Touched by an Angel*?"

I shrugged.

"We should honor them both."

"The same evening? We can't," I said.

"Sure we can. We can do *Touched by a Party of Five*."

I had to smile. "I wish."

He looked at his watch. "I gotta run."

"Just watch 'em." I put the cassettes on his desk. I hoped that seeing the shows would change his mind.

"I already promised CBS."

"Oh Christ."

"Lighten up." He grabbed his briefcase. "This is a TV museum. It's not the fucking Louvre."

Many nights I came home so sick of it all, I turned on the gas, opened the door of the oven, removed the shelves, and knelt there, weighing the pros and cons of sticking my head in: fuck this shit. The smell of gas, the woozy promise of oblivion, relaxed me. I'd turn off the gas, take a couple of Benadryl, turn on the TV, and pop in an old movie—something screwball—say, *Bringing Up Baby* or *The Awful Truth*.

The one compensation that came along for my demoralizing job at the museum—and my other demoralizing job teaching the history of television to NYU students who only wanted to "break into" TV—was my boyfriend, Emmett. I met him at a cocktail party at the museum. The party celebrated the opening of one of the museum's even more than usually lackluster exhibitions. On the walls of a narrow hallway (the Rod Serling Gallery) were hung the yellowed sheets of staff paper on which composers had jotted down the melodies that would become TV's most famous theme songs. Throughout the party, Emmett played the piano, improvising a nonstop medley of show openers: the peppy intros to *I Love Lucy* and *Bonanza,* the rinky-dink song from *All in the Family*.

"Don't you get a break?" I asked him.

"I guess. But I'm enjoying myself."

"Can I get you a glass of wine?"

"No, thanks. Have they got Perrier or something?"

"Yeah. Sure."

"That would be great," he said.

"You don't have any music."

"No. I play by ear."

"You're kidding."

"I can't really read music."

"But wow, you're really good."

When I returned with the glass of water, Emmett was hemmed in by a stooped old man on a walker for whom he was playing the theme song from *Dr. Kildare*.

"Thank you." He smiled.

What a smile. He had little square white teeth, slitty eyes and fuzzy hair like a koala bear. In his navy blazer and navy tie with little grey anchors on it, he looked like a big soft toy from FAO Schwarz.

I lingered in the lobby as the party broke up. "You were great."

"Thanks for the drink."

Before I could introduce myself, he was grabbed by the elbow and spun around to meet other admirers.

Luckily, it was raining. I took my time, putting up my umbrella, till he emerged.

"Which way you walking?"

"North," he said. "I've got a gig at this place, the Brownstone."

"Oh. I live near there. You been playing there long?"

He got under my umbrella. "Six months. You know it?"

"The Brownstone? Yeah."

"I *thought* you were gay."

"You did? Why?"

"I don't know."

"Why?"

"You paid attention to me."

"Where are you from?"

"Annapolis, Maryland," he said. "What do you do?"

"I work at the museum. I'm the curator."

"Cool."

"It's not *that* cool."

"You've got like every show ever made."

"Not really."

"There's a show I always wanted to see—"

"What?"

"*Our Town.*"

"The musical." I loved it. "With Frank Sinatra."

"Right."

"And Eva Marie Saint."

"She's in it too?" he said.

"You should come and see it. I'll get you a pass."

"Cool. Great."

At the steps to the Brownstone, the rain trickled down the wrought-iron railing.

"Come in for a drink." He took my arm.

"I can't."

"You've got a boyfriend."

"No. A deadline," I said. "Come by tomorrow. You can watch *Our Town.* And I'll take you to lunch."

"Okay. Thanks. I will."

The next day, I found him in a carrel, earphones on, listening to Sinatra sing "Love and Marriage."

"No. Finish it. I'll come back later."

"No. I watched it already. I rewound this part."

We had lunch at a little bistro. He was nervous, at first. He let me do most of the talking. I confessed that what little I knew about Irving Berlin, Cole Porter, and the other songwriters he admired, I had learned putting together a series of screenings: *Sinatra on Television; The Fred Astaire Specials;* and *Ed Sullivan and the Great Songwriters.*

He wasn't eating.

"Are you all right?"

"I should tell you something."

"Uh-huh."

"I'm an alcoholic," he said.

"Oh."

"And a drug addict."

"Uh-huh. But you're getting . . . treatment."

"I'm in a twelve-step program."

"AA."

"And NA. Uh-huh."

"NA?"

"Narcotics Anonymous."

"Oh, right. How long?"

"Eleven months."

"Good for you." I patted his hand.

"Have you ever heard the expression, 'You're as sick as your secrets'?"

"No. I don't think so."

He squeezed his eyes together tight.

"What's wrong?"

"I should call Trey." He got up.

"Who?"

"My sponsor."

"No, sit," I said. "Let's have dessert."

"I'm not ready for this."

"For what?"

"Dating. Relationships."

"Fine. We're just having lunch. Come on. Sit. They've got great
desserts here."

He sat down. "My last two boyfriends committed suicide."

"Oh, shit."

"I'm bad news."

"No, you're not," I said, though it had already occurred to me that
he was.

"I should go."

"Tell me about it."

"I can't."

"Yes, you can. You're as sick as your secrets."

He smiled, and then for the next twenty minutes, told me more
disturbing stuff about himself than I'd ever expected to hear from
anyone with whom I was sharing a bowl of sherbet. In fourth grade, it
seems, while I was mapping out Magellan's voyage with magic mark-
ers on posterboard, he was sucking off his father, a Navy captain, his
older brother, and his older brother's playmates. In high school, he
had countered his sissyish image as the star of every spring musical
with a more acceptable reputation for chugging six-packs of beer and
half-pints of bourbon in record time. On a junior year abroad in
France, he fell in love with an older married man, Luc, an executive at
Fiat. Luc set him up in an apartment and convinced him to switch
from the University of Maryland to the American University of Paris.
Together they discovered cocaine, crystal, K, and cavorted through

the clubs and bathhouses of Paris. When Luc showed up unshaven, hallucinating, at an annual meeting of Fiat brass in Milan, he was fired and, soon thereafter, sued for divorce by his wife of nineteen years. With his assets tied up in court, and nowhere to go, Luc moved into the little flat he'd been renting for Emmett. Together they lived for a year on Emmett's meager earnings as a teacher of English. When Luc's money was cleared, he announced he was leaving Emmett for a disc jockey from Belgrade. High on coke, Emmett tried to strangle him but succeeded only in dislocating his own collarbone. Returning from the hospital, his neck in a foam-rubber collar, he found Luc swinging from a rope tied to the skylight.

"My God. That must've been . . . awful."

The second boyfriend to commit suicide was Jean-Michel, a young man from Gabon who worked as a proofreader for a French company that printed labels and inserts for pharmaceutical products. No less fond of drugs than Emmett, his job performance was not all it should have been. Overlooking a misplaced decimal point, he approved a label for an anti-anxiety drug which, when distributed, resulted in the hospitalization of over a hundred people and the death of a much-loved puppeteer. As the investigation closed in on the culprit, he leapt to his death from the roof of a parking garage.

"You can't blame yourself," I said.

"No. Not entirely. But I have to take some responsibility."

"For what?"

"The drugs we did. The way we lived."

"When did you come back to the States?"

"Last year," he said. "I got a room in the Ninety-Second Street Y. I started looking for work. Well, I should have been looking. I was mostly dealing. I don't remember what happened exactly. All I know for sure is, they had to break down the door of my room and bang on my chest to bring me back to life."

"Oh God."

"They put me in Roosevelt for a month, the addiction clinic. When they let me out, I started going to AA meetings at Gracie Square."

"And the rest is sobriety."

"So far."

"God," I said, "you've been through a lot."

"Yeah. It sure feels like it."

"But you're okay now."

"Let us pray. I'm getting better. One day at a time."

"Good."

"What about you?"

"What?"

"What are *your* secrets?"

I was hard-pressed to compete. I thought it best not to admit that since childhood I'd been prone to thoughts of suicide. I'd been on and off antidepressants, I admitted. The last one made me feel stupid as a cheerleader. I acknowledged taking home a trick who dosed me and made off with my laptop. And against my better judgment, I shared a secret that was causing me real anxiety. I had a book to be published in the spring by the University of Michigan Press. I was so nervous about it, I kept the proofs locked in my briefcase when I wasn't making changes. It was a risky business, publishing the book: several essays were sure to gall, if not outrage, Bigelow and the industry bigshots whose checks kept the doors of the museum revolving. Without my other job at NYU and the likelihood of tenure (Hugh Maynard, the chairman of the Media Studies Department was in my corner) I might never have had the courage to publish the book at all and jeopardize my paycheck from the museum.

"You should write what you feel."

"I know. That's what I'm doing."

"What's it called?"

"The Trouble with Frasier: The Network Sitcom and the Status-Quo."

"You don't like *Frasier?*"

"No, I do. That's the point."

I told him my thesis—that even the best shows like *Frasier* are betrayals of comedy's mission to subvert the powers-that-be.

"Uh-huh."

I explained that sitcoms—with their round-trip stories beginning and ending in a cozy living room or office—were sapping the American spirit and contributing to, among other social ills, the decline of the union movement and disregard for the poor.

"You're blaming *Home Improvement* for all that?"

"Yeah."

"Cool."

He asked me to dinner the following night. I hesitated. After all, if it weren't for my screwball videos and the little pink and white pills that put me to sleep every night, I might already have been found by the super with my head in the oven like Emmett's other boyfriends.

His apartment was minuscule and charming, full of art books (Klimt, O'Keefe) and theater posters *(Angels in America, Into the Woods)* and the phonograph albums of guys who had died of AIDS which he found in Chelsea thrift shops. He opened a shoebox and showed me pictures of his parents pushing a lawnmower, his brother sailing in Chesapeake Bay.

"Are you in touch with your family?"

"Not if I can help it."

We had that in common. He had more to confess about his drinking and drugging: he had once come out of a blackout on the checkout line at Gristede's, eating a frozen pork chop. The morning after watching a PBS broadcast of the *Judy Garland Christmas Special,* he had awakened to learn from his answering machine that he had pledged—in another blackout—to give the station $30,000.

"You must really love Judy," I said.

"Not *that* much."

"They didn't make you pay."

"How could they?" he said. "I didn't have a dime."

In the weeks before he entered AA, he had had an affair with a Broadway composer who tied him to a barber chair and pissed on him.

"Really?"

"Are you into that kind of thing?"

"No," I had to admit. "I can't say I am."

"Neither am I," he said. "To be honest, I was hoping he'd put me in a show."

"But he didn't."

"I didn't even get to opening night."

"Do you act?"

"At Maryland, I did," he said. "I should be taking classes. But my sponsor says, 'Take it easy, you're eleven months sober. One day at a time.'"

"You've had quite a life."

"Yeah, right."

"I just feel like a dumpy, balding, middle-aged man."

"You're not balding." He smiled.

I loved his sense of humor. It was like hearing Oscar Wilde or maybe Oscar Levant—when you pulled the string—coming out of a teddy bear.

That weekend, we went out to the Pines with his AA sponsor, Trey, a man my age with a body twenty years younger, highlighted hair, and a diamond in the piercing just above his belly button. He was a producer, he said, though apart from investing in *Thoroughly Modern Millie*, his work seemed confined to booking entertainers for trade shows, corporate galas, and cruise ships. It bugged me to see Emmett's hands kneading Trey's big ripped shoulders as he rubbed in suntan oil.

"I don't get it." Trey pointed to a man, a mile up in the sky, in a paraglider attached to a motorboat.

"What?" Emmett looked up.

"That guy up there. It looks so boring."

Emmett thought it over a second. "Not if you bring a book."

We saw a lot of Trey. He had tickets to everything—dress rehearsals, benefits, sneak previews, dance parties. He was ground zero for who's-gay gossip. Mr. Fashion, he wore the latest silver sneakers and leather pants and pec-hugging T-shirts. When he wasn't dressed like a Vegas hustler, he was got up as the glossy WASP dad in a Ralph Lauren ad, rugged and effete, serene and superficial: I couldn't stand him.

Emmett and I got together almost every day but he refused to sleep with me. Not till he had celebrated his one-year anniversary in AA. (Getting into a relationship, your first year in the program, is frowned upon, and Emmett was determined to follow the rules.)

I went to an AA meeting with him, the day before Thanksgiving. Trey was "qualifying"—recounting his years of drunkenness and his roundabout path to redemption. Little he said—or so it seemed to me—had much to do with alcoholism.

"My first lover—I don't know what he saw in me," Trey recalled with unconvincing modesty. "He was an architect. A famous architect. His house in the Pines was on the cover of *Architectural Digest*. He was good-looking, almost too good-looking. He had muscles for days. A washboard stomach."

I saw Emmett nodding off.

"He was six-foot-three. Austrian. An aristocrat. An athlete. An expert horseman. He had a great sense of humor. He was good in bed. Everything you could ask for. Maybe he was a little cold."

"Mmmm." Emmett's eyes opened in interest.

I jabbed him with an elbow.

"What?"

"Would you like me better if I were colder?"

"No. I don't think so," he said. "You're cold enough."

Twenty minutes into his spiel, Trey was just getting to his "bottom."

"There I was in first class: I'd had champagne, God knows how many martinis, hors d'oeuvres, nuts, a white wine with snapper soup, a little salad, lobster thermidor, a cheese course—"

Emmett whispered, "There's always a cheese course in this story."

"What? You've heard it before?"

"Verbatim."

Emmett came to watch me teach at NYU. I showed a clip from the documentary *An American Family,* in which the mother, Pat Loud, comforts her teenage kids in the wake of their father's leaving home. One of my students, a shy Jewish girl from Mexico, started to cry. I followed her into the hall. She had just lost her father. I hugged her awhile and convinced her to return to class.

"You were great," Emmett said.

"I'm good in a crisis," I preened.

"Yeah," he said. "It's all the rest of the time you're inadequate."

"Fuck you." I had to laugh.

"I'm only kidding."

"You don't think I'm inadequate?"

"No, no," he said. "You're adequate."

The night of his AA anniversary, we slept together for the first time. He was nervous; he hadn't had sex in a year. And he'd never once had sex sober.

"This is a mistake." He got up from the bed.

I pulled him back. "We can just spend the night together."

"I'm sorry."

"Don't be sorry."

"I'm so fuckin' crazy."

"No, you're not," I said. "You're just nervous."

"It's too soon."

"Okay. Stay. Spend the night. We've got time."

"I'm a basket case."

"Would it help if I said I love you?"

He started crying.

"What's wrong?"

"You're so good to me."

"No, I'm not. I love you."

"Why?"

"'Why not?"

"I'm such a nothing," he said.

"Bullshit. You're smart. You're funny."

"I'm so fucked up."

"Everybody's fucked up."

"Not like me."

"Everybody in New York."

He laughed. "You should see Maryland."

"They're fucked up too?"

"Worse." He turned away.

"Come 'ere."

"I need a tissue." He blew his nose. "Are these down?"

"What?"

"The pillows."

"Oh. Maybe."

"I'm allergic."

I tossed the pillows off the bed. "Here."

"What?"

I pulled his head down on my chest. "How's that?"

We lay awhile. I could hear the doorman on the street talking basketball with the super. I started to feel sad. "Maybe you don't love *me?*"

"No, I do. Really."

"You do?"

"That's the problem."

"Why is that a problem?"

"I don't know."

"Why?" I said.

"You're gonna leave me."

"No, I won't."

"You will."

"No, I won't. Why should I?"

"I don't know."

"You're not in the Mafia, are you?"

"No," he said.

"Shit."

"What?"

"You're straight."

"Right. Yeah, I'm straight."

"So, what's the big deal?"

He stroked my dick. "You like that?"

"Uh-huh." I returned the favor. Suddenly, he was hard and desperately ardent, a castaway clinging to a deck chair on the sea.

Some weekends, we just stayed in bed, making love, or lay on the sofa, listening to music. He'd point out a clutch in Bonnie Raitt's voice that touched him or expound on the effortless way Rosemary Clooney dramatized a song. His worries vanished. Eyes closed in concentration, he'd touch my knee as the singer approached a phrase he wanted me to love as much as he did. I didn't always get what he was so excited about. But I loved to see his rapture, his body riveted in anticipation like a hunting dog. He had coffee-table books of lyrics by Cole Porter and the other masters. He'd make me read them before he played one of his favorites.

So if it's raining, have no regrets
Because it isn't raining rain, you know
It's raining violets

He found a temp agency that sent him out a few days a week to do word processing in French for banks and fashion houses. At night, he went over to the Brownstone and entertained. I'd never felt so peaceful. Life wasn't a contest. He didn't mind that I was on no one's short list for the national academy of anything. He didn't toss and turn in the middle of the night, as I used to, trying to spell eleemosynary, and losing the spelling bee to a Korean girl. He just wanted to be happy. And all that took was letting his Higher Power handle the big questions, while he focused on the things around him: a new rug for the bathroom, fresh basil, friends you could count on to give you a surprise party.

Before I knew it, shopping bag by shopping bag, Emmett had moved in and let go of his own apartment. I'd never lived with anyone before. He slipped into bed in the early morning, after his shift at the Brownstone, and we made love. We had dinner on trays and watched *Biography* before he went to work. He came to parties at the museum and afterward bragged to his friends about meeting Carol Burnett and Drew Carey. He got me to a gym a couple of times a week. I was surprised how much I could lift. We went to London and saw some mediocre musicals. Everybody told me they'd never seen me so happy.

I *was* happy. With Emmett waiting at home and tenure looming at NYU, I put up with Bigelow's guff a lot less meekly than I had before.

"What's wrong with *The Gallagher Report?*" he asked me, one day, as he pulled down his pants and stepped into striped trousers for some black-tie benefit.

"Jesus. It's the worst news show on TV."

"You think?"

"It's not even news. It's just bullshit attitude."

"It gets ratings. People like it."

"Yeah, people in the Klan."

"He's not that bad," Bigelow said. "He's had a book—two or three books—on the best seller list."

"Did you read them? They're crap. Self-serving crap."

"We've got to do something for Rupert."

"Again? We put two Fox shows in the summer festival."

"He'll sell tickets."

"Gallagher? I *know*. But how low do we go here? We've gotta have *some* standards."

"I don't appreciate that." He hooked a paisley cummerbund over his gut.

"And I don't appreciate having my name put on tributes to assholes like Gallagher."

"All right, all right. Let's talk tomorrow."

I sprinted out of the room on such a high, you'd think I'd won the Oscar pool. I'd stood up to Bigelow. He'd do as he pleased. But at least for once I'd stood up to him.

I took Emmett out to dinner to tell him what a ballsy guy he had for a boyfriend. He brought Trey along.

"You don't mind, do you?"

Trey had just returned from an all-gay, "clothing optional" cruise in the Caribbean. A porn movie was shot onboard. Several lucky passengers—who paid extra—got their big break, getting screwed on camera by the pros.

"Did you get a part?" I asked him.

"In the movie? Honey, I was too busy with the crew."

"Of the movie, or the ship?" Emmett asked.

"Which night you talkin' about?"

I never got around to telling Emmett of my little triumph with Bigelow.

"You light up when he's around." I bitched about Trey later that evening in bed.

"Do I?"

"You do. He makes you laugh."

Emmett curled up closer. "David Letterman makes me laugh. I don't want to fuck him."

"I didn't say you were fucking him."

"Well, I'm not."

"I just mean, you're on the phone to him twice a day—at least."

"He's my sponsor. I've got to tell him everything. It's against the rules, anyway."

"What is?"

"Hooking up with your sponsor."

"Oh, and you're such a big stickler for rules."

I wish I could say I had no idea what Emmett saw in this pumped-up old pretty boy. But to be fair, Trey had one saving grace—a sense of humor about his own narcissism.

"He's lost weight," I said to Emmett—about Nathan Lane—as we came out of a matinee of *The Producers*.

"No, I haven't," Trey said.

"We're not talking about you." Emmett turned to him.

"Why *aren't* you talking about me?" He looked hurt. Then laughed.

I was jealous, of course. And it pained me to be jealous of Trey of all people. But I'd never been in love before—I'd never been *happy* before—and I knew something would fuck it up.

It was two nights before Christmas when things really started to unravel. In the fifteen years I'd lived in Manhattan, I had never seen a snowstorm like it. Why the building remained open to the public, it was hard to imagine. Maybe Bigelow, who decided matters large and small, could not be reached on his safari in Kenya with the president of Viacom. Except for two ladies napping at the front desk, a couple of guards, and a handful of college students who ushered visitors through the museum, the staff had fled home hours ago.

I stayed behind—ostensibly to review clip tapes that Marissa, my assistant, had assembled for an *American Idol* seminar. I had something much more exciting to do. The galleys of my manuscript had just arrived. It was my last chance to reread the copy and make corrections. In its gray paper cover with the sticker, REVIEW COPY: NOT FOR SALE, *The Trouble with Frasier* was virtually a book. I felt proud. It wouldn't be long now before the tenure committee met at NYU and I slipped out from under Bigelow's thumb.

Tired of reading, I took a stroll through the museum on my way to Bigelow's office to drop off the *American Idol* tapes. There were fewer than a dozen people watching shows on little monitors in the library carrels.

There was no one on Bigelow's floor. His Rothkos glowed in the waiting room. I went into his office: windows on every side, it was like stepping into an ice cube. A pair of opera glasses hung from the coat tree. On his desk, atop a pile of papers, was a printout from the University of Michigan Web site announcing publication of my book. Above a picture of the cast on the set of the sitcom was a banner: DUE IN JANUARY: *The Trouble with Frasier,* A LEADING HISTORIAN OF TELEVISION TAKES ON THE TV ESTABLISHMENT.

There was a pink Post-It stuck to the printout: "Have you seen this?—Marissa."

Marissa, my own assistant.

Shit. How long would it be before Marissa—or some other ambitious bitch—dropped the book off on Bigelow's desk?

I took the printout. I was scared shitless. I was much too wired to go back to my office. I should've known: you can't work for the Emperor and tell him—in print—he's got no taste, no standards, and no fuckin' clothes on.

In each of the museum's three big screening rooms, two stubborn patrons remained slumped in their seats viewing one of the programs selected for the eve of Christmas Eve: a *Bing Crosby Christmas Special,* with guest star, David Bowie, joining Bing for "The Little Drummer Boy"; *The Television Interview,* our non-Christian offering; and Truman Capote's *A Christmas Memory.* I sat awhile, watching Geraldine Page play little Truman's wacky old aunt. I couldn't help wishing I'd been raised by an aunt who doted on me and sent fruitcakes to FDR. I cursed my parents: they didn't love me; all they loved was a good report card.

When I got back to my office, the telephone was ringing. It was Lillian, the assistant to Hugh Maynard, my chairman at NYU.

"I have bad news."

"What? Lillian. Are you all right?"

"It's Professor Maynard."

"What?"

"He had a stroke."

"Oh no."

"He was in the car," she said. "On the LIE."

"Oh God. How is he?"

She was crying. She couldn't say it.

"Oh Lillian. I'm so sorry."

"There'll be a service on campus, in the Catholic Center. Some time next week. I'll call you."

Now, I loved the man. Professor Maynard was a first-rate scholar and a total mensch. But I hardly gave his death—or his widow—a thought. I was scared to death about my own future. Hugh was my champion in the department. Without him, my chances for tenure (they'd boot me out if I didn't get it) were slim. As treasonous as my book was sure to seem at the museum, it was nothing incendiary in academia. Old-fashioned, it was short on theory, long on specifics. Not the kind of thing the ideologues on the committee were very likely to look kindly on.

Why the fuck had I written it? I banged my fist against my forehead. What the hell was I thinking? In one shot, now, it could cost me my job at the museum and at NYU too.

It was a short walk home from midtown to my apartment in the East Sixties. A cap tugged down over my eyebrows, an umbrella jousting against the wind, I climbed the snowbank at each corner, unnerved by the familiar avenues narrowing into toboggan runs, the little avalanches snapping the awnings of stores.

I tried to convince myself things were not as bad as they seemed. My book was good. There were guys on the committee who could not fail to see its merits. If worse came to worse, I could find a job *somewhere*. Find a cheaper apartment. One day at a time.

The farther I got from the museum, the less panicky I felt. I began to notice the six-foot snowdrifts, the mannequins in bikinis, the hotel doormen in red-braided uniforms bargaining with the last cabbies brash enough to brave the snow. The book was good. Anyway, it was done. My fate was sealed. It was almost Christmas. I couldn't wait to see Emmett.

As Basil, the manager—"Hey"—acknowledged my entrance with a wink, the Brownstone bellowed laughter. The joint was jumping. A Christmas tree shed its ornaments as the well-dressed throng pressed against its branches. The few guys I recognized, like myself, lived right nearby; they hung out at the front, without checking their coats.

"You seen Emmett?"

"I think he's on."

I had a drink at the bar in the back, without letting Emmett know I was there. (I didn't like him to see me enjoying a drink when he couldn't indulge in one himself.) Between the elbows of two heavyset guys in suits, I could just make him out, playing the piano. He wore one of the oxford shirts I had had monogrammed for him, the sleeves rolled-up over red-haired forearms. His voice was sweet and easygoing; he let the lyrics do the work.

> *The weather is frightening*
> *The thunder and lightning*
> *Seem to be having their way*
> *But as far as I'm concerned it's a lovely day*

A skinny queen kept interrupting Emmett to travesty the lyrics ("It's just the queerness of you." . . . "Good morning, hard-on"). I hated to see Emmett having to abide any drunk who dropped a tip in his cognac snifter. But Emmett didn't mind, or at least he didn't let on. When he was performing, it seemed nothing could fluster him. Not the old-timers who took the microphone to brazen their way through "You'll Never Walk Alone." Not the hunky young Broadway wannabes demanding attention with doleful ballads from *Miss Saigon*.

When his set ended, I got up from the bar to go see him. I was intercepted by a short, cute, chubby guy with a mustache.

"Don't you work at the TV Museum?"

"Uh-huh."

"I heard you on that panel about the blacklist."

"Right, right," I said. "That was years ago."

"I had no idea about Jerome Robbins."

"No?"

"What a prick."

"Absolutely."

"It was *very* interesting," he said.

"Thanks."

"What's your name?"

"Frank."

"Robert."

He had an accent. "Are you from Cuba?"

"No. Brazil."

"Are you a teacher or something?"

"No. A banker. Why?"

"Oh. I just wondered why you're interested in the blacklist."

"I'm not. I mean, I wasn't—till that seminar," he said. "I took my kids upstairs to that thing where they put on a quiz show."

"Oh, the Nickolodeon thing."

"Right. While they were doing that, I checked out the seminar on the blacklist."

I was about to tell him, 'Well, nice to meet you, Robert, but if you're cruising me, thanks, but you're barking up the wrong tree,' when I saw Emmett getting tugged down onto somebody's lap. It was Trey, of course.

"You want a drink?" Robert picked up my empty glass.

"Oh, no thanks."

"You live around here?"

"Yeah. Sixty-Second."

"You?" I said.

"Roosevelt Island."

"You've got kids."

"Yeah. Two. Ivan and Maria. They're with my wife. They've gone home to Brazil."

Trey had one hand on Emmett's shoulder, the other on his knee. It pissed me off. But it didn't surprise me. Part of Emmett's job, like a dime-a-dance girl, was flirting with the customers. It wasn't unusual for him to get a backrub or a pat on the ass from a horny old regular, let alone his "sponsor," Trey.

"I haven't been to the museum in ages."

"I don't blame you."

"Now they've got everything I want in the video store."

"Like what?"

"Brideshead Revisited."

"Oh, right."

"Jewel in the Crown. All the BBC stuff."

It was Granada stuff, actually, but I didn't correct him. Trey was rubbing his hand up and down Emmett's leg.

Robert caught me staring. "He's the piano player."

"Oh. Him. Uh-huh."

"They should get a room."

"Oh, they're just flirting," I said.

"They've been at it all night."

"Really."

Trey was telling a joke. Emmett was laughing and wagging a finger at him. Trey grabbed his tie and tugged it up like a noose.

"What's going on at the museum?"

"Oh. *Everybody Loves Lucy. TV and the Presidency.* The same old shit."

"You sound a little bit . . ."

"What?"

"I don't know . . . cynical?"

Emmett rested his head on Trey's shoulder. Trey kissed him on the forehead.

"Fuck."

"What?"

"I just remembered something."

"What?"

I'm an asshole.

"Are you all right?"

"I left the oven on."

"Oh." He looked crushed. He didn't believe me. "You better go."

It was snowing harder. Who was I kidding? Emmett didn't love me. I was just his life raft. If he loved anyone, it was fuckin' Trey.

I would never be loved. I was used to the idea before I met Emmett, the little bastard. Now it caught me off guard, a vet awaking in a wheelchair, expecting to walk to the fridge for juice.

I could barely put one foot in front of the other. I think I was crying. A taxicab kept honking. I didn't give a shit if it hit me.

I passed one of those old guys with no fingertips in his gloves and a shopping cart overloaded with trash bags full of empty cans to return for the five-cent deposit. I wondered what gave these poor devils the will to go on. And why the hell did they? What was the point?

I hated Emmett. But I couldn't really blame him. I was that least sexy of creatures, an academic—a soon-to-be-unemployed academic—a brain on a wobbly stalk. For all his glitz and mousse and bullshit, Trey was a vertebrate, funny and successful, with a full tank of testosterone—all the attributes to which the gay male of the species is attracted.

In my lobby, I tripped on the wire to a plastic menorah of yellow lightbulbs.

"Frank."

I recognized the voice. "Perry."

"Hi." He looked thin, unshaven, haggard in his beautiful suit and shoes.

"What are you doing here?"

"I've got an appointment tomorrow."

"Oh. How are you?"

"All right."

He looked worse than I did. "What is it?"

"I've been better."

"What's wrong?"

"Can I come up?" he said.

"Well . . . yeah. Sure."

"Were you doing something?"

I was going to stick my head in the oven and chug-a-lug some propane, but as long as you're here. "No, no. Come up."

He didn't speak in the elevator. It was scary. I was used to him brimming with stories which alluded to, but never quite trumpeted, his latest accomplishments in law and journalism.

From my kitchen table, you can see the Fifty-Ninth Street Bridge. The traffic was barely moving in the snow. "How'd you get in?"

"What?"

"Isn't the airport closed?"

"Oh. I got in yesterday."

"What's up?"

"I've got an appointment," he said.

"Uh-huh."

"Oh God."

"Perry, what is it? Is something wrong? You want a drink?"

"No."

"You're not sick?"

"Well—"

"What?"

"I'm sick in the head," he said.

"Oh. What's wrong? You're depressed?"

"Yeah. I guess."

"It's not Elaine?"

He tightened his eyes to hold back tears.

"Did something happen?"

"We're separating."

"Oh no."

"It's not her fault."

"No."

"I'm depressed," he said. "I'm . . ."

"What?"

He shook his head.

"Have you seen a doctor?"

"Yeah."

"Did he put you on drugs?"

"No."

"Why not?"

"I don't want them."

"Why not?"

"I don't want them."

" 'Cause of your career?"

He looked baffled.

"In ten years, there won't be politician or a judge who's *not* on Prozac."

"What are you talking about?"

"I saw it in *Time*: they said you're one of the great legal minds of your generation."

"Minds," he snapped, as if he took a dim view of minds.

"*I've* been on Prozac," I said.

"I don't want Prozac."

"You should try it."

"I'll lose everything."

"No, you won't."

"If I lose my faith," he said, "I lose everything."

I must've looked shocked.

"You think I'm crazy."

"No. Lie down. Where are you staying?"

"The Roosevelt."

"Come on. Here. Lie on the couch."

He lay down and closed his eyes. His right hand was shaking. He covered it with his left.

"Are you hungry? I can microwave something."

"No."

With his wet curls and graven cheeks, he looked like a knight on a sarcophagus.

"You just sleep. I'll be here."

"I can't sleep."

"No?"

"I haven't slept for days."

"You wanna talk?"

He tilted his head toward me as if he were going to ask a question. Then he tilted it back.

"Perry. What is it?"

"Do you believe in God?"

"I don't know. Maybe," I said. "Sometimes. I don't think about it."

"You don't?"

"Not really."

"You used to."

"I did?"

"You don't remember?"

"No."

He brightened. "After Sunday School. You'd get pissed off when Daddy'd joke about Jesus in the car."

"Did I?"

"You were very devout."

"When I was seven."

"What happened?"

"I don't know."

"You don't believe?"

"I don't believe in *Jesus*," I said. "I suppose there's *something* out there—before the Big Bang or something—whatever."

"What good is that?"

"What?"

"Believing in a God who doesn't give a shit." He started to cry.

"Perry. What's wrong?"

"I don't know. I'm just . . ."

"What?"

"Scared."

"Scared of what?"

"Everything."

"You're not scared of me?"

His eyes were pleading. "Tell me the truth, Frank. Do you love me?"

"Perry. Of course." I knelt down beside him. "You're my brother."

"So."

"You helped me with my homework."

"I did?"

"When I let you."

"You didn't want help," he said. "You wanted to do it yourself."

"Not when *Mary Tyler Moore* was about to start."

He pressed his hands like a vise to his head.

"Perry. What?"

"I used to think it must be so hard for you."

"What?"

"Being gay."

"Yeah, well. You get used to it."

"You've got a boyfriend?"

"Yeah. Sort of." I checked my watch. He was due home soon.

"You know what I think?"

"What?"

"It's a blessing. Being gay."

"How's that?"

"You always had your own world. Even as a kid. You were off to yourself."

"You think that's a blessing?"

"You weren't like doing everything Mom and Dad wanted."

"Yes, I was."

"No. They didn't want you watching TV."

"Oh, right."

"They didn't like your friends," he said.

"Nobody did."

"You played loud music. You smoked marijuana."

"So did you."

"No, I didn't."

"You didn't?" I couldn't believe it.

"I was too fucking scared."

"Of what?"

"Disappointing *them*. Why weren't you scared?"

"I was scared."

"Not like me. You stayed out late."

"I already *knew* I disappointed them."

"Lucky you."

He was right. "We should smoke a joint." I got up from the floor. "No."

"Fuck them. Let's smoke it. I've got one in my desk. It's like five years old."

The joint smelled of mint from the Altoids tin.

"I can't believe you got through Harvard without smoking." I took a drag and handed him the joint.

"It wasn't easy." He raised his head on the arm of the couch and reached out for the joint.

"God, you can't win," I said.

"What?" He inhaled.

"You *never* disappointed Mom and Dad, you feel like shit. I *always* disappointed them, I feel like shit."

"You feel like shit?" He held onto the smoke in his lungs.

I didn't. Not then. Amazing. "Some days."

"You were great."

"What? When?"

"When we were kids," he said. "You were the only one who didn't expect things from me."

"Really?"

"Yeah."

"Thanks."

"I should've said something."

"About what?"

"The way they treated you," he said. "Like a stepchild. I can't believe I'm still fuckin' scared of her."

"Mom? You're kidding."

"I'm afraid she's gonna die if I disappoint her."

"Bullshit."

"I'm leaving Elaine. I'm leaving Chicago."

"What's up?"

"I'm going to Texas."

"University of Texas?"

"No. I'm gonna run this campaign against the death penalty."

"Oh."

"You think I'm crazy?"

"No."

"Elaine does," he said. "It's a Christian group."

"What?"

"You know, every Jew I've ever met thinks you have to be really stupid to be Christian."

"Don't you?"

He laughed. "No. Just desperate. You should see them on death row. They're all Christian. Or Muslim."

"No Jews?"

He thought it over. "All the lawyers, pro-bono, are Jewish."

"Except for you."

"I'm getting paid," he said.

"What? Not what you're worth."

"Fifty thousand."

"Shit. Can you do ABC?"

"No. Ssssh. Listen."

"What?"

"The clock is ticking. Listen."

The little travel clock on an endtable sounded loud as a metronome.

"You hear how fast it's ticking?"

"It's not fast. It's just loud."

He thought it over. "So this is marijuana."

We exploded in laughter.

"What's your boyfriend like?"

"He's cheating on me."

"Bitch."

We laughed again. "You never talked dirty."

"I'm gon' be a Texan. I sure better learn to say piss and bullshit."

"And pussy."

"And hooters." He stopped. "God, I'm still like, what if Mom hears me?"

"She's got hooters."

"Stop."

"She's got big hooters."

He threw a cushion at me. His shirt cuffs rose above his wrists. His wrists were bandaged.

"Jesus, Perry. What's with your wrists?"

"Oh. That was weeks ago. Before I figured things out. I won't do it again. I promise."

"When's your appointment?"

"I don't need a doctor."

"Perry."

"There's nothing wrong with pain," he said. "It makes you think about what's important." He drew up his knees and closed his eyes.

"Getting sleepy?"

"Yeah. Sort of."

"I'll put on some music. It's great when you're stoned."

"The Hokey-Pokey?"

"What?"

"You made me do it."

"I did?"

"And 'Alley Cat.' And 'Jingle Bell Rock.' We used to dance in the living room. Till Dad caught us. He said we were sissies."

"Well, he was half right."

"Do you ever miss him?"

I thought it over. "Not really."

"Lucky you."

I grabbed a pile of CDs. "You like Etta James?"

"Who?"

"You'll like it. It's bluesy."

He was asleep when I returned from putting on the CD. I went into the bedroom and sat on the window seat, entranced by the snow and the colored Christmas lights in apartments across the street. I felt incredibly happy. My brother loved me. And he'd rewritten my childhood, my life. I wasn't a loser. I was a tough little tyke, a survivor, who'd stood up to his evil parents.

I checked on Perry. He looked peaceful. We were brothers; we had a common enemy.

I pretended to be asleep when Emmett came in. I didn't want a scene with my brother in the living room. I was through with Emmett, the dim little bastard. Let fuckin' *Trey* commit suicide.

"Frank?" He touched my shoulder.

"What?"

"Who's that on the couch?"

"Perry."

"Oh."

"Did you wake him up?"

"No," he said. "I've got something to tell you."

"Uh-huh."

"I got a job. A good job—for ten days."

"Uh-huh. What?"

"Trey got me a job entertaining on a cruise through the Caribbean."

"Oh."

"I'm so excited. I've never been to Bermuda. I've never been on a ship."

"When does it sail?"

"That's the awful thing," he said. "Tomorrow morning." He looked at his watch. "Three hours from now."

"Oh."

"What about Christmas?" He gave me a look of great concern.

"Oh. Go on. Forget it."

"You don't mind?" He brightened. "Will your brother be here?"

"Yeah. Go on."

"You're sure you don't mind?"

I was glad to be rid of him. "What line?"

"What?"

"What cruise line?"

"Oh. Nothing special. It's not the QEII."

He *was* lying. "What is it?"

"Carnival, I think. Trey was frantic. The guy he booked had to cancel at the last minute."

"What about the Brownstone?"

"I called Leon," he said. "His show just closed. He's gonna fill in."

He turned on the light in the closet. "Can I borrow your suitcase?"

"Uh-huh."

"I don't know what to bring. You're sure you don't mind? We can have our own Christmas, just the two of us, when I get back. Are you all right?"

"I'm just stoned."

"Stoned?"

"We smoked a joint."

"Oh. I'll be quiet. You go back to sleep."

He couldn't help humming to himself as he packed. He was out the door before the sun came up.

The next day, Christmas Eve, I went to church with Perry—St. Jean Baptiste, a Catholic church on Lex. He hadn't settled on a denomination yet. In the meanwhile, the Roman Catholics were hard to beat for ceremony, if not music.

The day after Christmas, he left in much better spirits.

"You'll have to visit."

"Texas?" I didn't think so.

"You'll love Austin. It's like the Village. I'll find you a boyfriend—with cowboy boots."

"You say when."

At the boarding gate, we hugged for the first time since he'd left for Harvard.

Even Bigelow, dropping the axe, couldn't dent my mood.

"What did you expect?" He tossed the book across the desk.

"You didn't like it."

"I didn't read it," he said.

"So, what else is new?"

I had fifteen minutes to put my things in boxes. Guards escorted me out of the building.

Standing on the sidewalk outside the museum, waiting for a cab to pick me up, I heard a familiar voice.

"Frank."

It was Robert, the Brazilian from the Brownstone.

He helped me home with my boxes. "When does your boyfriend come back?"

"The day after New Year's. I'm gonna ask him to leave."

"Yeah, right."

"No, honestly, I mean it."

We made a date for New Year's Eve.

NYU was merciful. The committee was divided about my book. But they gave me tenure anyway. I was a good teacher, they said. I guess I am.

On our way back from dinner on New Year's Eve, Roberto and I dropped by the Brownstone. It wasn't as crowded as it was the night we met. Emmett's friend Leon was at the piano. He tugged the elastic band of a party hat under my chin and asked if I had a request.

"You know 'Corcovado'?" Roberto asked him.

"Which one is that?"

"Jobim."

"I know. But which one?"

"Quiet Nights of Quiet Stars," Roberto gave the English title.

"That's too down for New Year's Eve," Leon said and flipped quickly through his sheet music for something else.

On the way back to my place, it started snowing. Roberto sang the song in Portuguese.

The Wedding Party

IAN

"On or about December 1910," Virginia Woolf famously claimed, "human character changed."

Sure. Fine.

On May 17, 2004, humanity itself became a less exclusive club when the first same-sex marriage was performed in a Massachusetts city hall. Despite the backlash that would follow in the courts and assemblies of the "red states," this legal development brought new rights and dignity to a long-scorned segment of humanity. But for many of the newly liberated, the prospect of getting married quickly proved to be a mixed blessing.

Take Ian Reath.

Head writer of the soap opera *Eden Heights*, Ian Reath knew a lot about weddings. He'd written a wedding, a royal wedding, in the fictional kingdom of San Cristofer; a Midwest wedding, a sort-of barbecue *cum* hoe-down, in the no-less-fictional town of Westfield; and most memorably, at least for the cast and crew, a wedding at gunpoint on the sputtering edge of a not-at-all-fictional volcano in the South Pacific.

These were straight weddings, of course. From bachelorette party with string of male strippers to honeymoon foreplay in the Jacuzzi, protocol was well-established. For his own wedding to Bobby Bayard, a candidate for city council in Manhattan, Ian had fewer precedents to guide him. There were those guys in Massachusetts—you saw them on all the news channels in the week after May 17—who went to city hall in their business suits, signed the necessary papers, and called it a day. And then there were the guys, the chubby guys, who made Ian queasy with their cast-of-Scooby-Doo cummerbunds and long wet kisses on the city hall steps. What Ian *really* wanted to do—if he had to get married—was invite a few friends, make a few toasts, and lie back in a lounge chair, looking up at the moon from the deck of his beach house in Amagansett.

It was not to be.

The trouble started when Ian's father, Trevor Reath, pastor of Gramercy Presbyterian Church in Manhattan, offered to perform the ceremony himself. Of course, the civil authorities in New York—despite all the progress in Massachusetts, San Francisco, and other places—were not yet ready to sanction the marriage of two men. But that was all the more reason, Reath argued, to go ahead with the wedding and protest this injustice.

Now, you might think that any gay man in his right mind would be pleased to receive such an extraordinary show of approval from a parent. But from the moment his father offered to officiate, Ian could see that the reverend welcomed the wedding, not as a chance to get schmaltzy about his only offspring, but as an occasion to stretch his own moral fiber.

His father seldom did anything—from buying a car to promoting a curate—without putting his conscience and his family through a Gethsemane of reflection and struggle. Too young or at least too cautious to board a bus with the Northern clergy who answered Dr. King's call to march in the Civil Rights Movement, Pastor Reath had embraced every subsequent cause from nuclear disarmament to feminism to animal rights with a willingness to suffer that bordered on eagerness. A good-looking man, he began every day—squaring vanity and conscience—by subjecting his scalp to a thousand strokes of a rigid hairbrush. Then, assuming one of the more advanced yoga positions, he read a book of the Pentateuch on Web TV. He never drank. He never ate dessert. He never laughed at an ethnic joke. His marriage to Iris, Ian's mother—happy, in its way—was a shared commitment to reproduction, social service, and the vigorous Christianity of Dietrich Bonhoeffer. That his fancy CV—Groton, Yale, Union Theological Seminary—led him to fancy parishes where poor and dark-skinned souls were seldom numbered among the choir, only fueled his desire to distinguish himself as a servant of the disenfranchised.

His son Ian was a different story. Growing up gay on a Protestant planet without gossip or small talk or irony, he had chewed all the gray roast beef he could stomach by the time he left for Groton. A closet dandy, he ironed his khakis and polished his Topsiders, listening to Noel Coward, Boz Scaggs, and the B52s. At Princeton, he wrote papers on Larry Rivers and Billy Strayhorn and an award-winning senior thesis, "Love Among the Ruins: The Construction of Queer Space in the Gothic Novel." Hoping to please and offend his father in equal measure, he wrote a musical about bisexual songwriter Stephen Foster, *Beautiful Dreamer,* that was (at least in *The Times* review he imagined) simultaneously sexy, sophisticated, and socially concerned. *Dreamer* was workshopped but never produced. Too fastidious to starve in an East Village walk-up, he took a job on a soap as a dialogue writer, then was promoted to writing breakdowns. He became head writer when the lesbian in charge—(Subject for American Studies students: Why are there so many lesbians writing daytime TV?)—ran off with her lover, a volcanologist, to Jakarta.

He was sitting pretty. Nice-looking in a brown-haired, blue-chip law-firm kind of way, he was making good money, terrific money, for a guy in his thirties without a law school or business degree. If he had no time to look for love, he seldom noticed till vacation was upon him. It was on vacation in Palm Springs, two Christmases ago, that his best friend Nathan spotted a guy they'd met at a bar in New York a few weeks earlier. Bobby and Ian hit it off, got it off, and spent the remainder of the holiday sunning, playing baccarat at the Agua Caliente Casino, and talking till sunrise about their favorite books, singers, cities, presidents, and film stars. They'd been together ever since.

It was Bobby's idea to get married. Ian still had his doubts. Living together was better than living alone but far less fun than he imagined when Bobby first unpacked his books, his CDs, and his modest cache of porn. He couldn't tell: was it Bobby or just the give and take of living with *anyone,* 24/7, that made shacking up such a chore sometimes? Bobby talked politics, local politics, and dragged him to dinners where he had to make conversation with business blowhards, high-minded socialites, and gay reporters for newspapers he'd never even heard of. Sex was routine. They bickered over the loud, humorless campaign workers Bobby invited for the weekend. They fought over Ian's drinking—he liked a few vodkas in the evening—and his language (fuck, suck) and whose turn it was to unload the dishwasher. If Bobby seemed ashamed of Ian's work (despite two daytime Emmys), well, Ian was a little ashamed of it too. But it pissed him off that his lover had no idea how incredibly difficult it was to plot three stories—virtually three novels—that intersected in every episode, five days a week, an hour a day, no matter how banal the people in Westfield might seem to highbrows in Tribeca. Granted, Bobby was a sweetheart, dashing to the door before the elderly doorman could spot him and rise from his seat. He never failed to drop at least a dollar in the violin case of a subway recitalist. He couldn't scold his dog with any real conviction, no matter how many shoes were chewed or suits pooped on. He forgave Ian in advance for any hand job in the steam room he might be tempted to indulge: they were in love, what did it matter, a little unromantic nookie? All things considered, they got on, Ian and Bobby, and they cared about each other. On summer evenings, sun setting through the dune grass or the towers of Central Park West, they felt lucky to have each other and familiar pillows to lay their heads on.

Why they had to get married, Ian couldn't quite fathom. Was it the excitement of the Massachusetts decision that had swept Bobby away? Or was he just tired, in the days after the decision, of dodging the question from friends and constituents: When are *you two* going to get married?

Ian drew the line at Provincetown. No way was he going to travel to P-Town, a town he loathed, to get a piece of paper that might or might not be legal back in New York anyway. Disappointed, Bobby gave in. After all, he owed it to his gay constituents to take his stand for justice in his home district, anyway.

It was Ian's fault that the wedding slipped out of their hands and into the consecrated clutches of his father. Before Ian had even thought to urge his father not to make too big a deal of the nuptials, the Reverend Reath had announced to the parish council that he would be performing, not a "civil union," but a wedding, for two gay men on Christmas Eve. Nobody liked the idea. Two Koreans on the parish council informed the regional presbytery. The regional presbytery passed the buck to the Synod of the Northeast. The Synod of the Northeast complained to General Assembly Permanent Judicial Commission. Pastor Reath was instructed to call the wedding a commitment ceremony or a civil union.

"My son is to be married," he insisted with the obstinacy of his hero, Martin Luther, posting his theses on the Wittenberg door.

Before the Commission could officially censure Reverend Reath, his own parish council asked him to leave.

News traveled. The Fifth Avenue Presbyheteros were scolded in the online newsletter of The More Light Presbyterians of New York City. Co-anchor of *Gay USA,* Andy Humm, featured the story on his Gay Cable Network news program that same evening. Within hours, GLAAD, the national Gay and Lesbian Alliance Against Defamation, was faxing word of the firing to its allies in the media. *The New York Times* put the story in the Metro Section and arranged to have Ian's reporter friend, Nathan Branche, work up something a little trendier for Style. *Times* in hand, Mary Verdi, one of the hosts of ABC's kaffeeklatsch, *Take Five,* made the brouhaha a "Hot Topic" on the dishy morning talk show. The show was not off the air ten minutes before its producer, Marla Waters, was on the phone, arranging to interview father and fiances and to film the wedding for an upcoming segment of *Newsline ABC:* "The Pastor Who Gave Up His Church for His Son."

Ian was astonished by all the attention and, at first, he quite enjoyed it. The electronic Japanese on his answering machine would announce as many as "Twen-ty se-ven mes-sa-ges." Buddies he hadn't heard from in years called to say mazel tov or to interview him for the *Princeton Alumni Weekly.*

Clouds had started to gather, however. In the CBS mailroom, the hate mail for Ian was piling up in bundles. A death threat postmarked Indianapolis threatened to shove a shotgun up his anis [sic]. Fans of *Eden Heights* were logging on to Soapsuds.com and other chat rooms to express their disgust for the show's head writer; many refused to watch the program till he was replaced by someone "pro-family." Ian was scared. The network dropped headwriters the moment a show dropped in the ratings. Each morning, he switched on his computer in dread to check the overnights. *Eden Heights* was near the bottom of the heap, as usual. If it fell behind *Passions* or *Port Charles,* he'd be joining his father on the unemployment line.

Bobby was worried too. Vinnie Pagano, his portly campaign manager, feared that all the attention being paid to the candidate's homosexual wedding was proving too much for the reputedly liberal—but often Republican—voters of Manhattan's silk-stocking Fifth District. Pagano had a question about the wedding tacked on to the tail of a telephone poll. Twenty-eight percent of the people who didn't hang up proved pretty queasy about the idea. Bobby's lead was withering, but only two points behind, he remained statistically dead even with the incumbent, an old-timer whose reputation had been sullied by a solid waste management scandal. On the bright side, Bobby had months and money, his family money, to recapture the hearts of the voters. If he was lucky, very lucky, he could have his wedding cake and eat it too.

By the eve of the ceremony, the eve of Christmas Eve, the reverend was rejuvenated; Ian and Bobby were exhausted. They'd worked hard at their careers to counter the flack from freaked-out voters and viewers. They'd pumped hard at the gym to look trim in the photos appearing in *Out, New York Magazine,* and *American Wedding.* They'd spent the few hours their paths crossed arguing over which interviews to grant, which poses to strike in photos (nothing too sexy or groom-and-groomy), which psalms might sound silly in sound bites excerpted from the wedding ceremony.

The rehearsal dinner—there was no rehearsal, just a briefing from Reverend Reath—at the Lotos Club was given by Bobby's father, a retired diplomat, one of whose clubs in Philadelphia, The Union League, had a reciprocity agreement with the Lotos. In his welcoming toast, Ambassador Bayard thanked the guests for braving the snowstorm swirling outside. "*My* pastor asked me," he said with a nod to Reverend Reath, "was I angry with my son for his choice of lifestyle?"

Smiles froze.

"I told him, 'No, I don't think it's a choice,'" he said. "'But becoming a Democrat is.'"

The Reverend Reath looked away. It was no laughing matter, supporting a party that opposed affirmative action, universal health insurance, and saving endangered species.

Ian had never met Bobby's parents. Mrs. Bayard, Bobby's stepmother, was cheerful and spry as Katharine Hepburn in one of her late-blooming spinster roles. "My first boyfriend," she admitted to Ian, "was 'gay.'" She said the word as if it were naughty.

"Oh. He told you?"

"Oh no," she said.

"But you knew."

"Years later."

"How?"

"He turned up at the Devon Horse Show," she said, smiling. "He was the only man who competed in dressage."

As guests arrived for cocktail hour, Ian had his best man, Nathan, to quip with. The only black person in the room who wasn't a waiter, Nathan had been Ian's best friend since college.

"Oh, a Princeton man. Your parents must be proud." Mrs. Bayard patted Nathan on the sleeve.

"Nathan's father went to Princeton," Ian said.

Mrs. Bayard looked puzzled; she squinted: "Oh."

Throughout dinner, Ian sipped vodka sneaked into his wineglass by a waiter he knew from Barracuda. His mother looked pretty in the red woolen suit he'd surprised her with (he was taking no chances) as she chatted with Bobby's campaign manager.

"Bobby has *my* vote," she said.

"But you're not in his district."

"We'll move." She smiled, sipping merlot right under the reverend's nose.

Even the reverend seemed to be enjoying himself, listening to the producer of *Eden Heights* catalog the diseases (Hepatitis C, male breast cancer), drugs (K, X, GHB), and behaviors (internet addiction, spousal abuse among seniors) Ian had used his soap opera pulpit to educate the public about.

"You should be proud of him."

"I am."

Was he? Not since fourth grade, when he won the Young Peacemaker Award at Friends Seminary for an essay opposing bullying, had his father seemed really proud of him.

Winking at Ian from far down the table, Bobby in black tie looked like a thirties movie star. Ian winked back. It was hardly Verdun or Stonewall, but they'd been through a battle together. They'd survived the e-mails from wackos and the goadings of gay activists enlisting them in every cause from same-sex proms to the outing of Academy Award contenders. They'd done their bit. They'd kept their heads. And now their hard work was paying off. Still behind, Bobby was catching up in the polls. In the Nielsens, *Eden Heights* was head to head with *As the World Turns*.

The reverend clinked his glass.

Ian looked up at a bright, bemused-looking portrait of Mark Twain. He'd been a member of the Lotos.

"I want to thank Ambassador and Mrs. Bayard for this wonderful get-together," the reverend began. Then he stopped. A ponderous pause. "Biblical theology and Christian tradition support the basic need of all persons to have a wholesome, intensely affectionate, and long-term relationship with another person."

Ian put a hand over his eyes. Why couldn't his father simply enjoy anything? Why couldn't he be like Ambassador Bayard? *He* wasn't embarrassed to have nice shirt studs and travel first class to places where Christ never trod. Why all this bullshit about the Bible? He and Bobby were *in love.* Or at least, they had been, and would be again, when the bullshit stopped and they could find an hour to smoke a joint and fuck and order Thai and watch HBO.

A glass was clinking. Bobby was speaking. "I'd like to thank the Reverend Reath for his courage in standing up for Ian and me and everybody who gets the wrong end of the stick in this society. I was out campaigning the other day at a subway stop—"

You're campaigning right now! Ian put his hand to his head again.

"I gotta split." Nathan tugged at his elbow.

"Not yet," Ian pleaded.

Nathan was sneaking out to polish a piece for the *Sunday Times.* "I gotta go."

"Let's meet up at the Brownstone."

"I can't."

The bar was on Ian's way home. "One nightcap. It's early. Come on."

Nathan sighed. "I'll try."

"See ya later."

The end was near: Ian's mother looked tipsy; Mrs. Bayard was yawning.

"How ya holdin' up?" Bobby put his arm around Ian.

"All right."

"It's a long day tomorrow."

"No shit."

Bobby took Ian's glass and sniffed the vodka. "You wanna look your best."

"Fuck you."

Bobby covered with a smile. "I've got a favor to ask you."

"I'm meeting Nathan at the Brownstone."

"You can't."

"Just for a nightcap."

"We've got a conference call with my parents," Bobby said.

"What?"

"To my brother. In Santiago."

"I thought Michael was coming." Ian loosened his tie.

"Davey has measles."

"Oh, fuck. You handle it."

"*Ian.*"

Ian reached in his pocket for his coat-check ticket. "I'd only embarrass you."

"Don't be like that."

Outside, the snow was up to his knees and still coming down thick. It felt good to be out among strangers to whom he needn't be polite. Waiting in line to get into the Brownstone, he couldn't help envying the guys out on their own, single guys with dicks jammed into threadbare dungarees, chafing at the bit to get into the bar and stare down their game.

The Brownstone was hopping. With its armchairs and paintings of rabbits and sailboats, it looked like the Lotos Club—in an alternate gay universe. Ian checked his coat. He found a spot at the bar beside a guy who was reading *HX*. He looked like a dad on *Dawson's Creek*. A couple of tipsy Brits were singing an unusually comprehensive *My Fair Lady* medley, from "Wouldn't It Be Luverly" to "I'm Getting Married in the Morning."

Ian tapped the guy on the shoulder. *"I am."*

"Excuse me?"

"I am."

"What?

Ian nodded toward the piano. "Getting married in the morning."

"You're kidding."

"No. I am."

"To a man?" The guy checked.

"Yeah, to a man. What the fuck do you think?"

"Sorry." The guy shifted a chair toward Ian. "So, what are you doing here?"

Ian sat down. "Just takin' a breather."

"Uh-huh."

"Time to chill."

"When's the wedding?" The guy closed his *HX*.

"Noon."

"Where?"

"Gramercy Presbyterian."

"I guess they're pretty liberal."

"Not as liberal as they think they are," Ian said.

"How's that?"

"You can have a 'commitment ceremony' or some bullshit like that. But not a wedding."

"That *is* bullshit."

"My dad wanted us to have a wedding," Ian said. "You can't imagine the stink."

"Your dad sounds cool."

"He's the pastor there." Ian reached for an olive from the bartender's little plastic cupboard of condiments. "I mean, he was the pastor. He got fired 'cause of all the bullshit."

"Wait: I read about this. In *The Times.* He really went to bat for you."

"Uh-huh."

"You really gotta admire him."

"He's a fuckin' saint." Ian signaled the bartender.

The musclebound bartender was wearing a Santa cap. "What can I get you?"

"What are you having?" Ian picked up the guy's drink.

"Absolut and cranberry."

"Two Absoluts and cranberry." Ian reached for his wallet.

"No, that's on me."

"I got it."

"Put that away. It's my wedding present."

"Well, thank you."

"How many have you had? Better make this your last."

Ian got up. "What are you, my mother?"

"Take it easy."

"Fuck you."

"I didn't mean to offend you. I'm sorry. Please. Sit."

Ian settled. "I guess I'm just tense."

The guy reached past Ian for a bowl of potato chips. "Cold feet?"

"What?"

"It's only natural." The guy took a chip and left the bowl in front of Ian. "It's a very big step."

"You're tellin' *me*."

The bartender brought the drinks. "Two Absolut cranberry."

The guy paid him.

Ian raised his glass. "Cheers."

"Mazel tov." The guy clinked glasses. "What's your name?"

"Ian Reath."

"Joe Estrine. Who's the lucky guy?"

"I am."

"Who's the other lucky guy?"

"Bobby Bayard."

"Bobby Bayard?" Joe sounded surprised.

"You know him?"

"Yeah, I know Bobby," Joe said. "He's like a really big deal. In politics. I mean, he's the one respectable—"

"Faggot."

"—gay politician you ever see on TV. Even straight people like him."

"Straight *women*," Ian said.

"This wedding can't hurt."

"The election? You wanna bet?"

"No. Come on," Joe said. "If you were fat or effeminate, it would creep people out. Oooo, two fat faggots holding hands in church. But you two, it's like central casting: two nice young men—"

"Who just happen to suck dick."

"They won't think of that. They'll picture Bobby at home with you making pasta, watching *Newsline*."

"We're gonna be *on Newsline*," Ian sneaked another olive.

"You're kidding."

"Bobby, me, and my father. They shot half the segment already."

"What's she like, Marla Waters?"

Ian shrugged. "She was all over Bobby 'cause she thought he was a Rockefeller."

"He isn't?"

"His brother Michael is married to one of the cousins," Ian said. "She's like the black sheep of the family."

"How so?"

"I don't know. She like gives away money to Art for Animals and these women's colleges that aren't accredited. Get *her*."

"Who?"

"There." Ian pointed to a guy in a green fur coat. "She works for Fendi."

Joe laughed. "She'd better."

Taking in the crowd, Ian zoned out a moment. Joe was asking him something. "Excuse me?"

"Are you having a reception?"

"Just champagne and cake," Ian said.

"Where?"

"Here."

"Here?"

Ian loved the Brownstone. Decorators and queens old enough to know Judy brushed up against club kids with fake IDs.

"What do you do?"

"I'm a writer," Ian said.

"Oh. What do you write?"

"Soap opera."

"Oh, cool," Joe didn't miss a beat. "Which one?"

"Like you watch."

"Which one?"

"Eden Heights."

"Uh-huh."

Nobody watched *Eden Heights.* "What do *you* do?"

"I'm a psychotherapist."

Ian didn't know whether or not to believe him. "You're kidding."

"Why do you say that?"

"I don't know. You don't sound like a psychotherapist."

"No?"

"And I guess it's like I don't expect a therapist to be sitting here at the bar reading *HX.*"

"Why not?"

"I don't know," Ian said. "It's like a bad habit."

"My eight a.m. canceled for tomorrow morning—'cause of the snow."

"You ever run into one of your patients here?"

"Once," Joe said.

"Did he like freak out? 'Ooo, I caught you.'"

"Is that what you'd do?"

"Yeah, probably," Ian laughed.

"You've never been in therapy?"

Ian shook his head. Then he remembered, "Oh, I went twice in college. I couldn't sleep."

"Did he give you drugs?"

"No, no. He was just like, 'Take it easy. It's okay to hate your father. Everybody does.'" Ian spotted a black guy coming in. But it
wasn't Nathan. "So how do you know Bobby?"

"Oh. We were in a group together."

"AA?" Ian slipped. "Whoops."

"No, no. A caregivers group. I was just the facilitator. We all had
friends or lovers with AIDS."

"Oh right," Ian remembered. "Tuesday nights at St. Vincent's. But
you sort-of burnt out."

"Everybody but Bobby."

"Everybody but Bobby." He made fun of Joe's reverential tone.
"He's a fuckin' saint."

"So what's the problem?"

Ian tuned him out. Some guy with a beard—he looked like Josh on
Eden Heights—was stepping up to sing.

"I mean, what are you doing here? On the night before your wedding."

The bearded guy had brought his own sheet music.

"Who's your best man?"

The piano player looked pissed.

"You should call him. To take you home."

"He's gonna meet me here," Ian said.

"I guess you guys are like head over heels."

"Bullshit," Ian snapped. "It was totally over a long time ago."

Joe spoke softly. "I meant you and Bobby."

Ian took a second to replay the conversation. "Oh, yeah, right."

"You had a thing with your best man."

"Years ago. At school."

"But you still kinda like him."

"I 'like' Nathan." Ian said. "I'm not sucking his dick."

"I'm just saying, you sound a little conflicted."

"What the fuck are *you* doing here?" Ian turned on Joe. "Cruisin'
the bars, like some horny teenager."

"I'm looking for a friend of mine," Joe said. "He works here—
Ralph—one of the bartenders."

Ian knew him. He was a fuckin' psycho. "Bandanna Ralph?"

"Right. Have you seen him lately?"

"He's nuts. You ask for an olive, he bursts into tears."

"You don't think they fired him?"

Ian shrugged.

Joe looked awfully anxious.

"So what's with you and Ralph?"

"What?"

"Are you like dating or something?"

"*No.*"

He was *blushing.*

"I just haven't seen him lately," Joe said.

Ian had him. "Come on. You can tell *me.*"

Joe looked at his wristwatch. "It's late. I gotta go."

"Is he one of your patients?"

"Ssssh."

"You're not fucking him, are you?"

"No. I'm just . . . worried about him." Joe got up. "Nice meeting you."

Poor bastard. "Hang on. I'm sorry."

"I gotta go."

"I didn't mean to pry." He took Joe's elbow. "I won't mention his name. Stay. Please."

Joe hesitated.

"You haven't finished your drink."

He hovered a second before sitting down. "What's keeping your friend?"

"Nathan? He's finishing an article."

"Uh-huh."

The bearded guy was singing a song—"Some Enchanted Evening"—with a very long intro.

"I think you've got the wrong impression," Ian said.

"About what?"

"I mean, Bobby. He's perfect."

"I know. Like your father."

The truth of it hit him like a loose floorboard he'd stepped on in a cartoon.

"I mean, it's only natural," Joe said.

How could he be so stupid?

"I'm sure Bobby has his flaws."

He was marrying his father.

"Come on. Nobody's perfect."

"*Bobby* is." Ian started to laugh.

"Bullshit."

"He won't send out for Chinese when it's raining, 'cause the delivery man'll get wet."

"So he's considerate."

"He won't use an EZ Pass 'cause he thinks some poor fuckin' toll-taker is gonna lose his job."

"Let me get you some coffee."

"Get this." Ian brushed tears of laughter from his eyes. "When Buddy makes a poop and Bobby picks it up in a plastic bag, he puts it in *another* bag, so the garbage man won't get poop all over his hands."

"What's wrong with that?"

"Some enchanted evening": the bearded creep was belting out the chorus.

"I am totally fucked," Ian said.

Joe patted his hand. "You'll feel different in the morning."

Ian covered his mouth.

"What?"

He *would* feel different in the morning. He'd lose his nerve.

"Take it easy."

It was now or never. Ian tripped on the foot rail.

"Sit down. Breathe."

How the fuck does it happen?

"It's just a panic attack."

You give up on yourself and they *applaud* you, the whole congregation, for writing crap and settling down with The Stepford Fag.

Joe moved his drink away.

"Give me that." Ian grabbed it back.

"You've had enough."

Ian belted it down. "Where the fuck is Nathan?"

"I've got a cell." Joe reached for his phone.

Nathan never liked Bobby. "At least Nathan's got balls."

"What's his number?"

"He's not like 'What'll people think?' all the time. I mean, he *is*. Everybody is. But then he says, 'Screw 'em, it's *my* life. Fuck you.' "

"What's his number?"

"He's not like 'Cheat on me if you have to; I don't mind. I love you whatever you do.'"

"Who said *that*?"

"Bobby." Ian whistled for the bartender. "He's so fuckin' understanding."

"What would happen," Joe started, "I'm not saying you *should*— but what would happen if you spoke to Bobby and told him: 'Maybe this is too big a step for us to take right now.' "

Ian laughed. "Are you kidding?"

"I'm just asking."

"My fuckin' father lost his job."

"I know."

"Marla Waters is sending a camera crew."

"So what?"

"We're like the fuckin' poster boys for gay marriage."

"Not if you don't want to be."

"Oh shit." Ian held back a sob.

"What?"

He started laughing again. "You know what?"

"What?'

"I should've done therapy. But I never had the money."

"You can always find a therapist who charges on a sliding scale."

"I've got the money *now*," Ian snapped at Joe. "Is that how Ralph does it?

"What?"

"Pay for his sessions—on a sliding scale?"

"It's none of your business."

"He should let you run a tab."

"Ssssh. Please."

"Like for every hour he spends on the couch, you get an hour at the bar. Top shelf, all you can drink."

"Very funny."

Ian spotted a tall black man arriving. "It's about fuckin' time."

"What?" Joe said.

It *was* Nathan. "I gotta go."

Joe reached for his wallet. "Here's my card. You don't have to see *me*. I can refer you to somebody. You should give it a try."

"Yes, sir." Ian saluted.

"Good luck tomorrow."

"Yeah, right."

"I mean it."

Ian bowed. "Thanks for the drink."

JOE

Swiveling on his bar stool, Joe watched Ian run over to his friend and hug him hello.

Good riddance: Joe was glad to see him go.

What Bobby saw in Ian was beyond him. Sure he was clever. But not *that* clever. A good-looking Guppie. A Guppie drunk.

That was it. A nice young drunk would keep Bobby busy. He liked to take care of nice young people.

Mystery solved.

The real mystery was Joe himself. After the weekend he'd spent with Bobby, how could Bobby have *ever* slipped his mind?

"How ya doin'?"

Joe looked up.

The bartender, Eddie, was holding his glass. "Another Absolut cranberry?"

Another vodka might not mix well with the Valium he'd popped before leaving the apartment. "I better not."

"Oh, go for it," the guy next to him said. An old frat boy with grizzled dimples, he was crocked.

"Yeah, why not," Joe said.

Say, I ain't loved but three men in my life.

The angelic-looking white kid at the piano was singing the blues with a creepy conviction.

No, I ain't loved but three men in my life,
My father, my brother, and the man who wrecked my life.

Joe hadn't really loved his father or his brother, but he couldn't deny that he'd been in love with Bobby from the day he walked into the caretakers group at St. Vincent's. Week after week, listening to some dentist or decorator vent his anger at a lover demented with AIDS, Joe had to struggle to keep his eyes off Bobby: even in a button-down shirt he was buff as any naked little trophy boy floating in a coffee table book at Rizzoli's.

"That's six," Eddie brought the vodka.

Joe reached for his wallet.

Eddie sniffed the air. "Somebody's being naughty."

Joe hadn't smoked a joint for almost a year. Not since the weekend he'd spent with Bobby, helping Bobby's friend, Gopal, to commit suicide.

It wasn't something he wanted to do. Not that he had any moral scruples. The guy was half-dead already: just ninety pounds of ulcerated rashes and tumors big as peaches. But still. Drowning a mouse, squealing on a sticky board, was bad enough. Tying a bag over somebody's head and waiting for him to die was fuckin' freaky. No wonder he and Bobby had spent the weekend fucking and drugging like there was no tomorrow.

"Is that for me?" Eddie reached for a couple dollars on the bar. "My shift is over."

"Oh yeah, thanks."

Poor Gopal. By the time it came to die, he was stuck to the bed like a burnt slice of bacon. He could barely raise his head. His eyes searched the bookshelves, the geranium, the *Lisbon Traviata* poster, for an inkling of meaning that might give him some solace.

Bobby counted out the pills. "You're sure?"

Gopal turned to the window. It looked out on a fire escape wound with little Christmas tree lights and Budweiser beach towels hanging out to dry. "I've got to," he said. "It hurts too much."

Bobby tipped his head up and handed him the Seconal.

He and Gopal reminisced a little. They'd grown up together. All Joe knew about Gopal he'd heard from Bobby in the caregivers group.

Gopal nodded off.

They waited awhile. And then Bobby slipped the bag over Gopal's head.

"Fuck."

The bag had handles. A second bag had cardboard in the bottom. Joe found a trash bag under the sink. Bobby got cold feet; he couldn't do it. Joe was pissed, but he took over.

They waited five minutes. Bobby picked up a few photos from the desk. "This is Hammerwood Farm. My grandfather's place. We grew up there." There were photos of Bobby and Gopal at Yale. A few pieces of paper were in the printer. "Shit," Bobby said, "it's another fuckin' play."

Joe tapped him on the shoulder. "We'd better go."

They had to leave so they could come back in an hour and find the body, as if by accident.

They went to Joe's apartment.

Bobby took out a joint. "I hate to say this, but I'm horny."

Joe was hard already. They felt each other up like schoolboys who'd never dared do anything like this before. They came together, convulsing, shouting, then lay awhile, Bobby's head on Joe's knee. Sweaty and dirty, they pulled their clothes on and headed back to find the body.

Bobby took off the bag.

The police came quickly. They had no suspicions, few questions to ask. They lifted Gopal onto the stretcher; he was brittle as a pretzel stick.

On the way back to Joe's, Bobby stopped at a friend's house to pick up some E and some K and a six-pack of beer. The next forty-eight hours, they zoned out to U2, Mary J. Blige, and *All Things Must Pass,* shuffling unpredictably on the CD player. They read randomly—out loud—Blake and Eliot, David Sedaris, *Harry Potter,* and *The Joy of Cooking.* They made love in positions that would have seemed funny or dangerous if they'd had a moment of inhibition. They saw saints in the spaghetti sauce and a rainbow over the showerhead. They told each other the things they'd done on one-night stands and the shameful way they'd ignored the kids in high school who looked *really* gay and couldn't pass.

"I hate to think this'll end," Joe had to admit as the weekend waned.

For weeks afterward, seeing patients in his office, Joe found his thoughts drifting back to Bobby.

Ralph called him on it. "Anybody home?"

"What?"

"You're fuckin' fallin' asleep."

"No, I'm not." Joe sat up. "Excuse me."

Ralph was the first patient in years Joe was really intrigued by. A Cuban refugee, he was the poorest patient Joe had worked with since training at Bellevue with abusive mothers. His curly hair was tied back in a red bandanna. He wore the same silver sneakers, ripped jeans, and sunglasses to session after session. It gave the doorman pause.

"What's he think? Every Latino's a fuckin' cluckhead?" Ralph protested.

"Sorry, 'cluckhead'?"

Ralph enunciated in mocking Anglo, "Crackhead. Crack *user.*"

Ralph wasn't a cluckhead, but his boyfriend Derek, a realtor, was. With his salary as a bartender, Ralph was dependent on Derek for his pad in Chelsea, vacations in Miami, and his entree to the VIP lounges of the dance clubs he went to after work.

"Take off your sunglasses," Joe asked Ralph in their first session.

"Why?"

"I can't see your eyes."

The lid of his right eye was so swollen he could barely open it.

"What happened?"

"I bumped into a coat rack."

He had HIV too.

"You *are* taking your antivirals?"

"No." Ralph sneered. "I'm stupid. I pray to Jesus."

"I don't think you're stupid. I think you're depressed."

Little by little, Ralph's contempt gave way to curiosity. "What the fuck does my father have to do with it?"

"You wanted his attention. You only got it when he beat you up."

He burst into tears.

Joe could've cried too. It was a fifties movie; Freud worked like magic; every insight produced a catharsis. Ralph had none of the dreary defenses of middle-class patients, outwitting themselves with rationalizations and sneak attacks on his professional competence. If Ralph was a little paranoid about authority, well, he'd served nine months in a Cuban jail. His abandonment "issue" was abandonment: he'd been left behind in Cuba to serve in the army as his whole family escaped to the States. His nightmares were not about losing his bonus or the notes for his dissertation. He dreamed of children crying out for help, sinking under the waves in the Mariel boatlift.

By the fourth or fifth session, Joe was writing a story about him. It was the first story he'd attempted to write since he was an undergrad at Columbia. Without telling Joe, a buddy in publishing passed on his story to the fiction editor of *The New Yorker*. With a lot of little changes to disguise Ralph's identity, it was published in an autumn issue with other stories and nonfiction about Latin America.

Presto. The fog of depression Joe had moved in since med school lifted in the breeze of congratulations. He let his roster of patients diminish by attrition and set aside time in the afternoon for writing. For several months, he was downright happy. But inspiration didn't strike twice. Everything he wrote just seemed like crap. He wasn't a writer. He resented his patients for sapping his energy. He didn't date or masturbate. He went back on Zoloft and started on Valium to take the edge off the frustration his life had become.

"He's here." Eddie returned with a coat slung over his shoulder.

"Sorry? Who?"

"Ralph. Weren't you lookin' for him?"

"Oh, yeah, thanks." Joe was scared, all of a sudden. "Where is he?"

"There." Eddie pointed. By that guy in the suit."

Ralph spotted Joe at just the same moment. "Yo. Dr. Estrine."

Joe stood up and held out his hand. "Hi, Ralph." Ralph's arm was in a sling. "What happened?"

Ralph looked pissed. "What are you doing here? You *know* I work here."

"I'm having a drink. What happened? Your arm."

"I fell. I broke it."

Joe didn't believe him. "You fell."

"I fell."

"That's it?"

"I fell on the ice."

"Without any help."

"Fuck you."

"You missed two sessions. You didn't call."

"*Perdóneme.* I no have good manners."

"You're angry."

"*Vete a cingar.*"

"Why didn't you call?"

"I quit." Ralph started away.

"Ralph. Wait. How can you work with your arm in a sling?"

"I no have to work. I've got the rich boyfriend."

"You can't depend on Derek."

"*What is your problem with Derek?*"

"Ssssh. Take it easy."

"You never met him. You don't know him."

"I know what you tell me."

Ralph called, "Hey, Eddie. Bacardi and Coke."

Eddie called back, "I'm off duty."

"One fuckin' drink," Ralph said.

Joe shifted sideways to get his attention. "I thought Derek was moving back to Los Angeles."

"He is. We are. Tomorrow."

"Ralph. No."

"If the fuckin' plane gets off the ground."

"What time is the plane?"

"You are so full of shit." Ralph laughed.

"I've got a cancellation—at eight."

The bartender brought the drink. "What's up, Ralph?"

"I'm outta here, Eddie. I'm movin' to LA."

"No shit," Eddie said. He waved away Ralph's money. "Leave me your number. We gotta keep in touch."

"Thanks, pal." Gulping his drink, Ralph headed off.

"Ralph, wait. We should talk about this. I care about you."

"Oh, *papi,* you do?" he covered his mouth in mock astonishment.

"Why didn't you call?"

He fixed his eyes on Joe. "I read it."

Oh *fuck.* "Read what?"

"Your story. In *The New Yorker.*"

"Oh."

"Congratulations."

"Thanks."

Bolting his drink, Ralph started away.

"Where you going?"

"To take a fuckin' pee. You mind?"

"Come back."

"Okay," he said. "Buy me a drink."

Joe hesitated.

Ralph laughed. "You can write about me but you can't buy me a drink?" With his free hand held in front of the arm in a sling, he headed off through the thicket of men.

"Bacardi and Coke," Joe called to the new bartender.

Joe kept his eyes on the men's room. He was in deep shit. It was a breach of confidentiality, writing a story about a patient. He could be reprimanded. He could be sued. Surely he wouldn't lose his license. He'd changed so much: the Cuban protagonist was unrecognizable to anyone but Ralph. It had never occurred to him that Ralph would get hold of the story. How many bartenders—Cuban bartenders—read the short stories in *The New Yorker?*

He reached in his pocket for a Valium.

"Twist of lime?" The bartender returned with Ralph's drink.

"Yeah, sure."

Ralph was overreacting. The story was flattering. It celebrated his courage and perseverance. Not one other of Joe's patients—with their unresponsive spouses and unappreciative bosses—would have risked, let alone survived, the journey from Mariel to the mainland.

With a different—a dry blue—bandanna around his head, Ralph came out of the bathroom.

Joe waved.

Shit. There was sex in the story, Joe remembered. Sex with Bobby, but Ralph wouldn't know that.

Joe handed him his drink. "Thanks for coming back."

No smile. No thank you.

"How ya doin'?"

"I didn't know you were a famous writer."

"I'm not," Joe said. "Let me tell you how it happened."

With his free hand, Ralph unbuttoned his jacket. "Do your other patients mind?"

"Let me explain," Joe said. "I wasn't writing about *you*. It's just a story."

"It's my fuckin' life."

"No, it isn't. It's fiction. I borrowed . . ."

"My life."

". . . an incident or two."

Ralph was unbuttoning his flannel shirt down to his waist.

"What are you doing?"

"You like?"

He had a big hairy chest.

"Button your shirt."

"I owe two sessions. Here, feel." He took Joe's hand.

"Stop."

"You dream about me?"

"No."

"You want to see my dick?"

"He's just a *character*. Ralph, stop."

"You shoulda fuckin' told me."

"I never thought you'd see it."

Ralph flushed with rage. "You don't think I read?"

"Of course you read."

"You think I watch Telemundo all day?"

"I didn't know you read *The New Yorker*."

"It's in your fuckin' waiting room."

"Not that issue."

"What should I read? *Working Woman*?"

"I kept that issue in my office."

"*Working Mother*?"

"I didn't even submit it. A friend of mine did."

"*Smithsonian Magazine*? Where do you get all that shit?"

"Someone told you about it?"

"I buy it on the corner," Ralph said.

"You bought it?"

"I want to finish this article; part two—about Basquiat. And what do I see? A map of Cuba. *The Boatlift Boy*."

"It's just a title."

"What about the bananas? In the A and P? I didn't fuckin' cry," Ralph shouted. "I *felt like* crying."

"He isn't *you*."

"I sound like a fuckin' *maricón*."

"No, you don't."

"You know what they're gonna think?"

"There's nothing wrong with crying," Joe said.

"They're gonna think those loco Cubanos cry every time they see a banana."

"No way," Joe said. "He's been in Cuba all his life; he's never seen so much fruit."

"You think they know that? Americanos?"

"Well, now they do, if they read the story."

"You don't explain."

"It's obvious from the context."

"Every banana, every mango, every fuckin' shrimp," Ralph shouted. "It's all for export."

"People know that by now. Educated people."

Ralph raised his eyebrows. "Oh, *educated* people. Not the scumbags I hang out with."

"Ralph. No."

"The cop in Mariel; you fucked that up too."

Joe was irked. "Oh, did I?"

"He just takes *Sergeant Pepper* and puts it in his bag. He doesn't say shit."

"He doesn't have to."

"He could be a Beatles fan."

"He is," Joe said.

"A cop?"

"He can't like the Beatles?"

"I got jail time for *Sergeant Pepper*," Ralph grabbed the back of his hair. "They cut my fuckin' hair off."

"I know."

"When he's caught with the tourists . . .?"

Joe's favorite scene. "What? He gets sent to the country to cut sugar cane."

"For three months. It was nine fuckin' months, twelve hours a day."

Joe exploded softly, *"He isn't you."*

Ralph laughed. "You are so fuckin' pussywhipped."

"Excuse me?"

"By the liberals."

"What liberals?"

"Your friends."

"What friends?" Joe said.

"They think we're all scumbags in sweaty T-shirts sayin' the rosary for Elian."

"*I* don't think that."

"And what's the fuckin' problem. You can't spell my name?"

"What?"

"Raphael: R-A-P-H-A-E-L: you can't spell it?"

It took Joe a second. "You mean you'd be happier if I'd used your real name?"

"It's my story."

"No, it isn't."

"Yes, it is."

"In *part*."

"Name one fuckin' part that isn't me."

Joe started ticking them off on his fingers: "His wife. His son. His beard."

"I had a beard."

"He becomes a dancer—a stripper—at the Gaiety Theater."

"You don't think I could be?" Ralph puffed out his chest. "You don't know what I did before I met Derek."

Joe waited as Ralph wiped his nose with a cocktail napkin. He looked feverish. "Ralph, I'm so sorry this had to happen."

"Pardon me?"

"I changed everything I could."

"It didn't *have to* happen."

"I gave him a stutter."

"He sounds like an idiot."

"I just want you to be happy," Joe said. "What the hell are you gonna do in LA?"

"Same shit I did here."

"With a broken arm?"

"It's not broken; it's sprained."

"What happened to school?" Joe said. "Didn't you register at Visual Arts?"

"They have schools in LA."

"What about Dr. Lueck? You've been doing so well. Your T cells are rising."

"Barely."

"Give it time. This new drug . . ."

"Makes me sick."

"You're having symptoms? What?"

"Nothing. I just get . . . shaky."

"Is that how you fell?" Joe got up. "Here. Sit down."

"I don't wanna sit down."

"Did he hit you?"

"No."

"But he's still drinking."

"*You're* drinking."

"I'm not an alcoholic—and a cocaine addict. Are you going to meetings?"

"With the fuckin' housewives?"

Joe tried not to smile. "It's *not* all housewives, Al-Anon."

"You should hear them. Bitch, bitch, bitch."

"What about that gay meeting?"

"At the Community Center? What a bunch of losers."

"What are you gonna do with yourself in LA?"

Ralph reached for his drink. "I don't know: peddle my ass."

"If he asked you to, you would."

"Fuck you."

"He doesn't want you to . . ."

"Better myself? He doesn't think I have to. He likes me the way I am."

"Yeah—dependent on *him*," Joe said.

"Are *you* paying my rent?"

"Get a roommate."

"And move to Queens?"

"There's nothing wrong with Queens."

"When's the last time *you* were there?"

Joe couldn't remember. "You don't know where I live."

"Three-Fifty-Seven East Seventy-Ninth Street," Ralph said, smiling.

Joe shuddered. "Jesus."

"I checked you out on the Web. I pay fifty dollars. I get all your records."

"No kidding."

"There wasn't much. Your address. Your credit rating. You missed a few payments on your car loan."

"Years ago."

"You're a fuckin' Al-Anon case yourself."

"What makes you say that?"

"Who's Maurice Estrine? You live with your father?"

"I did. He died."

"Oh. Too bad." Chewing the last ice cube, Ralph put down his glass. *"Hasta la vista."*

"Ralph."

"I gotta go."

"You think I'm an Al-Anon case 'cause I care about you?"

Ralph looked away shyly. "Whatever. I'll send you the money."

"Forget the money."

Ralph looked relieved.

"Whatever you decide about LA, you're a wonderful man. Don't you forget it."

His face trembled. "No, I'm not." He started to cry. "Oh God."

"Ralph. Here. Sssssh."

"It's these fuckin' drugs."

"Sit down."

"What am I gonna do?"

"You're strong," Joe said. "You'll make it."

"I can't even work."

"We can figure it out."

"I'm fuckin' packed."

"Good," Joe said. "You can move to Queens. Derek's leaving town. You can start all over."

"You changed so much."

"I did?"

"In the *story*."

"Oh. What?" Joe said. "Tell me."

"Why they leave for America."

"Your family."

Ralph reached for a napkin. "They *made* Papi leave—when he got out of jail."

"I know."

"He fuckin' told them: put me back in jail. I'm not leavin' without my wife and kids."

"But they did," Joe said quietly. "They all left without you."

"I was in the army."

"Sssssh."

"They wrote every week."

"I know," Joe said. "It was hard for them too."

"Oh Christ," Ralph covered his eyes. "What am I gonna do?"

"You are gonna do fine. You've been through much worse. You survived. You're here."

He blew his nose in a napkin. "You changed the boat lift."

"I'm sorry, Ralph."

"No. You got it right. I lied—what I told you about it."

Joe knew.

"When it starts to rain," Ralph said, "and the people start swimming from the rafts to the shrimp boat—you know where I was?"

"Where?"

"I was on the shrimp boat. The captain shouted, 'No more passengers.'"

"Ssssh."

"Then he turned off the lights. You could hear them screaming, 'Don't leave me!'"

Joe put a hand on his shoulder.

"This lady held up a baby. 'Take my baby!'"

"What could you do?"

"I could've said *something*. I covered my ears."

"You would've all gone down."

"Oh God."

"Sssssh. It's over. It's okay."

Ralph rubbed his face on his sleeve. "I gotta go."

"No. Sit a second."

"I can't. It's late."

Joe put a few napkins in Ralph's pocket. "You'll be okay?"

"Yeah."

"See you tomorrow?"

"I can't."

"Why not?"

With his good hand Ralph pulled the hood of his sweatshirt over his head. "I meant to call. I didn't know what to say."

"What did you *want* to say? Come on."

Ralph looked away. "I can't. It's stupid."

"Feelings aren't stupid."

"Wanna bet?"

"Come on: you can tell me."

"Don't look."

"Okay."

"Close your eyes."

"Uh-huh." Joe closed his eyes.

"I think I love you."

Eyes closed, Joe smiled. "Wow. Ralph."

"I'm in love with you."

"I'm really flattered."

"I know you don't love me."

Joe opened his eyes. "No. Not the same way."

"Shit." Ralph hit his forehead with the heel of his hand. "I'm such an asshole."

"You're not an asshole. I really care about you."

"What is wrong with me?"

"Nothing. It happens," Joe said, smiling. "People fall in love with their therapists all the time. It's a very good sign. It means some day you'll fall in love with somebody who really cares about you."

"You mean: not Derek." Ralph stiffened. "He's gonna kill me."

"Stay with a friend. Just let him leave."

Ralph looked to the phone behind the bar. "I gotta call him."

"Don't tell him where you are."

"He'll fuckin' wreck my stuff."

"It's only stuff."

"Yeah." Ralph laughed. "Easy for *you* to say."

"Don't call him yourself. Get a friend to call him."

Ralph thought for a second. "I could ask Eddie. I could stay with Eddie."

"Good."

"He's on the East Side."

"Near my office?"

Ralph shrugged. "Sixty-Fifth."

"So, good. I'll see you tomorrow? Eight a.m.?"

"Fuck that." Ralph laughed.

"It's the only opening."

Ralph was shaking. "I don't know."

Joe had never hugged a patient before. "Gimme a hug."

Ralph brandished his broken arm. "Yeah, right."

Joe hugged him. "How's that?"

"I've had better."

"I bet you have."

Ralph smiled. "You're such a fuckin' *maricón*."

"See you tomorrow."

"If I go to bed, I'll never get up," Ralph said.

"So don't go to bed. Watch Telemundo."

"Fuck you." Ralph headed out, laughing.

NATHAN

The seat Nathan found on the Metroliner was next to another African American, an army officer, wearing a Walkman and reading *The Lord of the Rings: Weapons and Warfare,* an illustrated guide to the armor and weaponry of the creatures in the movie trilogy. The guy had a nice smile; he was built like a bodybuilder. But Nathan quickly regretted his choice of seat. He had an article to finish writing for the *Sunday Times,* a stupid piece about rich people's Palm Pilots. It was hard to concentrate with the tinny clatter of dance music—Beyonce?—rattling out of the officer's headset.

"Excuse me."

The officer took off his headphones.

"I don't want to be a pain, but could you turn down the volume a little? It's louder than you realize."

"Oh, sorry, bro," the officer said. "I'm glad you told me. I'm a little deaf."

Nathan was taken by his gentle response. "No problem. I guess combat's kinda rough on hearing."

"I ain't seen *that* much combat." The officer laughed and picked up his headphones.

Nathan scrambled for something to say. "You've got a lot of decorations." He pointed to a medal on the officer's chest, a bar of ribbon with a little gold palm tree in the middle. "What's this one?"

The officer squinted down. "Oh. Iraqi Freedom."

"Whoa. You been there. What's that like?"

He closed his eyes as he slipped on the headset. "Fuckin' hot."

"You don't have to go *back?*"

"You wanna take my place?"

"No, thanks."

Nathan returned to his laptop but he couldn't concentrate. He was nervous about seeing his parents. They shared a policy with the military: "Don't ask, Don't tell." No matter how many male roommates or Provincetown tank tops he accumulated over the years, his father never asked directly, "Nate, don't lie to me. Are you gay?" Nor had Nathan worked up the courage to tell his mother, "I'm not 'playing the field,' Mom. At least, not with women. The truth is, I'm gay." It was ridiculous. His parents knew. He knew they knew. They didn't ask. He didn't tell.

Once upon a time, maybe, Nathan and his parents had had some reason to maintain this fiction. Nathan's father was making his way to the top and he didn't need any dirty laundry trailing behind him. The son of a porter and a nurse's aide, Dr. Branche had become a geriatrician when there were only a handful in the whole country. A former dean of Howard Med and former director of the National Institute on Aging, Dr. Branche had racked up more honorary degrees, board memberships, and invitations to the White House than, at seventy, he could always remember. For the past five years he'd been president of the nonprofit American Institute for Longevity Studies (AILS). From his office near the campus of George Washington University, he presided over a small team of scientists, economists, and experts in public policy attempting "To Make the World Safe for Longevity."

Nathan couldn't stand him.

Twenty years younger than her husband, Nathan's mother, Leila Branche, was head of the education department at the Corcoran Gallery of Art.

He adored her. That is, until six months of psychotherapy made him realize he didn't like her all that much either.

With the best of intentions, Mrs. Branche had raised Nathan and his two sisters to be a credit to her forebears. (They included the first black president of a bank in the District, and the first black journalist admitted to the National Press Club.) She corrected his homework;

vetted his friends; let him wear sneakers only for gym. On weekends, little Nathan was driven to "Jack and Jill" parties in the backyards of black powerbrokers in Georgetown and Foggy Bottom. Summers he spent sailing on the Vineyard with other black Little Lord Fauntleroys. Until he left for Princeton, the only poor black people Nathan ever really got to know were the Dominican maids who helped his mother and the dyslexic kids he tutored at a public high school.

At Princeton, he rebelled. He had secrets to keep. Not just the odd hand job after a mixer with another boy in the English department. He was doing something else equally forbidden: playing volleyball and acting in plays. Sports and show business, as far as the Branches were concerned, were the pipe dreams of boys from the ghetto. Nathan never invited his parents to see him play Wesleyan or Yale, *Macbeth* or *The Elephant Man*. With his friend Ian, he wrote and starred in the senior Triangle Show, a musical travesty of *Driving Miss Daisy*; it won them few friends, black or white. Stung by jeers of the audience at the Triangle Show, Nathan went off to Harvard to study history. He got lucky at Harvard with his thesis on Carl Van Vechten, a white godfather of the Harlem Renaissance. He was chosen to write the slim introduction to a coffee-table book of Van Vechten's photographs of artists and celebrities. He interviewed the surviving subjects: Lena Horne, Gloria Vanderbilt, Christopher Isherwood, Marlon Brando. When the book became a surprise best seller, he was contacted by *The New York Times* to contribute occasional interviews. Three years after getting his PhD, he was assistant Style editor.

But despite his success, Nathan wasn't happy. His mother's fretting and quibbling about his deportment had left its mark. Ten years out of college, Nathan still couldn't do anything—pick up a chicken breast, choose a video, or slip off his loafers on the train—without hearing his mother admonishing him: What will people think? (What will *white* people think?)

Fuck 'em all.

"Fuck 'em all" was the mantra Malcolm, his photo editor on the Van Vechten book, had given him as a going-away present, the last day they got together. It worked. Like a nugget of kryptonite, it humbled the mother and father and disapproving white boogeyman in his head. Fuck 'em all.

He slipped off his loafers.

He was on his way to DC. His father had asked him to fill in for a *Washington Post* reporter in a discussion of The Media and the Older Person. The other panelists would all be experts on the media or the "aging beat."

"I watch *Golden Girls,* Dad." Nathan tried to beg off. "That doesn't make me an expert."

"You write for *The Times*—about people. That's expert enough."

"I just don't have the time, Dad," Nathan pleaded.

His father insisted; the discussion would begin by one. It would end by two; he'd be back in New York for dinner.

Nathan gave in.

He was on a tight schedule. Back in New York, later that evening, he had a wedding rehearsal to go to. His best friend Ian was getting married. The same-sex wedding had become a news story when Ian's father, a minister, lost his parish for agreeing to perform the ceremony. Nathan wasn't looking forward to the wedding, exactly. But Ian had asked him to be best man.

The officer was asleep. Half the train was asleep. Across the aisle, a young brother in a Phat Farm polo shirt was flipping through *Pensions and Investments.* In front of him, a white man with an earring was reading a biography of David Geffen.

Nathan closed his eyes.

Times had changed. But as far as his parents were concerned, it was nineteen sixty-something. It pissed him off. Sure, they bragged about his job on *The New York Times.* But come out of the closet: forget it. He'd be a homo they wouldn't dirty their hands with.

Fuck 'em all.

Maybe it was the snow. He felt sad. When he thought back to Princeton, there was always snow on the ground. He and Ian were walking to the student center to share french fries and write their own translation of the Plautus comedy, *The Menaechmi,* in which they were to star as twins.

He snapped his laptop shut. Union Station. A blizzard. In two hours, thank God, he'd be heading back to New York.

The bland old buildings of the Federal Triangle were up to their porticos in snow. The snow was already so thick on New Hampshire Avenue, it was one o'clock by the time Nathan made it to The American Institute for Longevity Studies.

Outside the AILS townhouse, a half-dozen limousine drivers were napping at the wheel or brushing the snow from their windshields with scrapers and rolled-up newspapers.

Entering the lobby, Nathan brought in a gust of wind that sent the magazines on the front desk flapping. The morning receptionist was a sprightly black woman of seventy-something, her white hair tied in a topknot with a baby's Christmas sock. "I'm Lucille," she said excitedly. "I've heard so much about you."

"And vice versa," Nathan said.

A messenger buzzed. The front door opened. A gust of wind rifled through *People* and *Modern Maturity*. Lucille put a little black Santa riding a sleigh on top of the magazines to weigh them down.

"Where'd you get this?" Nathan scrutinized Santa, a bearded old white man in blackface.

"You like it? Take it."

"Oh no."

"Please. I've got one at home too," Lucille insisted. "And I've got one for my daughter."

"Well, thank you, Lucille."

"You go on up. I'll wrap it." She pointed to the elevator. "They had to start the Men's Group without you. Mr. Mellon has a plane to catch."

"The Men's Group?" His father hadn't said a thing about it.

The Men's Group was a luncheon held once a month, at which a dozen white-haired gentlemen shared their feelings on the tribulations and consolations of growing old. They were an eminent bunch: four-star generals, former secretaries of state, business big shots, diplomats, and counselors to the president. Once featured players on the national and international stage, the old men now had little to do but attend funerals, and keep an eye on their family foundations and grandchildren's birthdays. They were stoic about their suffering, at least in public, but their frailty was impossible to disguise.

Nathan tried to take his seat in the John Glenn Dining Room without causing a fuss.

His father got up and hugged him. "Nathan, my boy."

Nathan stiffened. His father hadn't hugged him since he was six.

"Nathan writes for *The New York Times* on sociological trends."

Well, that was one way of describing the Style section.

"I thought he might give us a younger perspective on some of the subjects we're discussing."

Nathan whispered to his father, "When does the roundtable thing begin?"

The doctor answered him aloud, "Nathan's come down for our Journalists' Roundtable on The Media and the Older Person. You're all very welcome to attend. It begins right after lunch in the Claude Pepper Directors Room."

Nathan took his seat. The old men eyed him with bleary fondness as if he were their own son or grandson. A waiter brought Nathan his salt-free longevity lunch, a slab of fish, a baked potato with something like salsa in the middle, and a beautiful salad with lemon juice dressing.

The subject at hand was heart disease and depression. "Think of all the words that have heart in them," Dr. Branche said. "Heartache, heartbroken, heartsick—"

"Hearty," a hearty old man mused aloud.

"That's good, General," Dr. Branche said. "It's hard to imagine how medicine could've neglected the connection between mental and physical health for so long."

"Western medicine," one fellow put in. The only guy in a turtleneck, he wore a crystal on a chain around his neck.

"Quite right, Austin." Dr. Branche nodded.

One old gent with a paisley bow tie told of the depression—"It was a year to the day after Lily died"—that had preceded his latest heart attack.

Nathan checked his watch. It was one-fifteen already. The old men were still picking at their potatoes. There was no sign of dessert. He had to leave by two fifteen at the latest to make his three o'clock train to New York. The rehearsal dinner for Ian's wedding began at seven on the Upper East Side. He had no time to spare for Suetonius, Galen, Deepak Chopra, and the other worthies his father was quoting to the old men.

"You know what the simplest antidote to depression is?" Dr. Branche asked his guests.

"A bull market," the guy in the bow tie suggested.

"No. Zoloft." Austin laughed.

Nathan knew the answer.

"Walking." Dr. Branche smiled smugly.

The old and healthy were even smugger than the young and beautiful.

"Twenty minutes a day: that's all it takes," the doctor reached for the pedometer on his belt to tout its features to his guests. "I've got one for each of you," he said. "A little Christmas gift from AILS."

Nathan marveled at his father's narcissism. Half the men had *canes* with duckbill handles hanging from the backs of their chairs; one or two were in wheelchairs. But what was easy for his father was easy. It was pitiful, the way these decrepit patricians looked up to their fabulous black paragon. They were like boys at St. Albans tacking up posters of Pele and Earl the Pearl Monroe. And it didn't come cheap, the chance to bask in the beauty and wisdom of Dr. Branche. The old men had made generous gifts to AILS, and their wills provided for even more.

It was one-thirty when a plate of berries was finally placed in front of Nathan and the other guests. Nathan tried to get his father's attention but he was passing out the latest AILS publications, an assortment of beautifully published studies on long-term care insurance, antiaging medicine (a no-no), and safe sex after sixty.

The slimmest of the studies had been written by the Japanese guy, a former head of Toyota, who was the featured guest at lunch. In excellent English he explained that the plunging birthrate in Japan was due to the demoralization of Japanese men. Defeated in World War II, Japanese men had lost their confidence, and feminism had only made things worse. Japanese women today cared only about getting the best jobs and the best-paid husbands.

"Female teachers," Hidaki claimed, "routinely bully little boys and favor little girls."

Nathan looked around. The old men were buying this bullshit. "Excuse me."

"Yes?" Hidaki turned to Nathan.

"I can't help thinking," he started politely, "that Japanese women have a hard time too. From what I hear, they're shut out of government. They're shut out of the corporate hierarchy. Even at home, they're told what to do by their husbands and their husbands' mothers. Isn't that so? Or have I just read the wrong things?"

Hidaki smiled. "Have you ever been to Japan?"

"Well, no, but . . ."

"Perhaps you should visit. Then you can see."

Nathan managed a smile. "I'd love to visit. But when it comes to the facts, the statistics, on who's earning what . . ."

The General spoke up. "Let me tell you something, young man."

"Uh-huh?"

"I was in Tokyo with MacArthur."

"Ah." Hidaki smiled.

"We had a housekeeper. Mrs. Mini, we called her. And believe *me*, she ruled the roost."

The old men laughed.

Nathan tried again. "Be that as it may . . ."

"My granddaughter," Austin said, "doesn't even want children."

"Till she's made her first billion," Bow Tie added.

Nathan started. "This is all anecdotal. If you look at the facts . . ."

"Gentlemen," Dr. Branche broke in sharply, "that's all we have time for." His eyes scolded Nathan as he put down his napkin.

Nathan fumed.

The old men beamed at his father: he could still put a son in his place.

"I hope you can all stay for our panel discussion." Dr. Branche stood up. "Good luck in London, Jim." He shook hands with the bow tie guy.

The door opened a crack. Nathan's mother popped her head in as the guests teetered to the elevator. With her clipped hair, hoop earrings, short skirt, and Armani jacket, she looked like the head of a black modeling agency. "Sweetheart." She took Nathan by the shoulders and kissed him on one cheek and then the other.

"Mom, I'm in a terrible spot here."

"You got a haircut."

She didn't like it.

Nathan checked his watch. "It's ten past two."

"I've got to show you something," she said.

"I've got to leave at two-thirty to get the train back to New York."

"This won't take a second." She dragged him after her down the hall.

"Mom, I don't have time."

"Take a later train," she said sweetly.

"I can't. Dad said this journalists' thing began at one."

"Look." She opened the door to her husband's office. "What do you think?"

Something was different. He didn't know what. "Looks great."

"You like it?"

"Mom, I've gotta go in fifteen minutes."

"What's the rush?"

"It's Christmas weekend. I was lucky to get a seat at all."

"Stay the night. We never get to see you."

"I can't. I'm in a wedding."

She hesitated a second. "All I did was darken the paneling and put down a new rug."

She didn't ask, "Whose wedding?"

"Oh, and the shades are new too," she went on. "See, they're inside the windows."

She *loved* weddings. It wasn't like her not to ask.

"You just press this." She demonstrated the shades.

Every morning she flipped to the weddings in *The Post* before reading the headlines on the front page.

"Now, if your father would keep things a little tidier, I'd be a happy woman." She gathered the magazines on the doctor's desk into a pile.

Shit. She *knew* whose wedding.

"Your father's always been a pack rat."

She'd read about the wedding in *People* and all those other fucking magazines he's got spread around the room.

"I can't keep up with him anymore."

What if he got his picture taken? Nathan Branche, Best Man at Gay Wedding. It could appear in *The Post*!

"You should see your father's sock drawer."

They'd planned the whole thing.

"Can't you stay the night, Natie?"

They'd lured him down for the fucking roundtable. They were keeping him late to miss his train.

"I've got tickets for The Kennedy Center."

Fuck 'em all. "I've gotta go, Mom."

"What about the Roundtable?" She looked stricken.

"He said it would be over by two. It's almost two-thirty."

"Nate," she called after him, "wait."

He passed his father in the hall, greeting the other reporters arriving for the discussion.

"Ready, son?"

"I've gotta go."

"Nathan. Come back here!"

In the lobby, two old millionaires from lunch were inching their way to the door.

"Mr. Branche!" The afternoon receptionist, a natty old gent with a sprig of holly in his lapel, held out the plaster Santa that Lucille had wrapped. "Don't forget this."

Nathan took the package. "Oh, thank you."

"Merry Christmas."

"You too."

"Come back and see us again."

There were no taxicabs to be had in the snowstorm thrashing
Manhattan. Nathan trudged to the Lotos Club on foot. At least the
trip to Washington would make a good story to tell Ian in the cocktail
hour before the rehearsal dinner.

"You're just being paranoid," Ian said. "They can't be that crafty."

"You don't know my mother and father."

"I met them," Ian said.

"You did?"

"At graduation."

"Oh right." The less said about graduation—the weekend he and
Ian slept together—the better.

"Look at him." Ian pointed to his father.

Arms folded, the Reverend Reath was conferring a compassionate
smile on the other bridegroom's parents, the worldly old Ambassador
and Mrs. Bayard.

"He makes me sick."

"Ssssh," Nathan cautioned.

Ian was tipsy. "Who's got a bigger crush on himself. Your father or
mine?"

Nathan had to think about it.

"My father talks to God," Ian said. "Man to man."

Nathan laughed. "Yeah, but can he get him to feel guilty about being white? *And* write a check?"

Ian thought it over. "I guess it's a toss-up."

"My father only came to graduation," Nathan said, "'cause he was
getting an honorary degree himself."

"Oh, you're a baaad brother." Ian tried to sound like *Shaft.*

Nathan laughed. "Asshole. No one says baaad anymore."

"What do they say?"

Nathan shrugged. "How would *I* know?"

Ian spilled his drink, laughing.

This is the only man in the world I trust, Nathan thought, as he
wiped the liquor from Ian's shirt cuff with a napkin.

The other bridegroom, Bobby, came over with a bottle of wine.

He didn't deserve Ian.

"You don't have to do that, Bobby." Ian pulled his glass away. "You're gonna piss off the waiters."

"How ya doin' Nate?" Bobby refilled his glass.

"Survivin'."

"Did you meet my mother?" Bobby summoned his stepmother over. "Mom, this is Nathan Branche, Ian's friend from Princeton."

"Oh, a Princeton man. Your parents must be proud." She smiled like the Queen meeting a scholarship boy.

"Nathan's father went to Princeton," Ian said.

"Oh." Mrs. Bayard looked confused. She looked at Nathan harder. Fuck 'em all.

Ian pulled him away. "Did you see how she looked at you?"

"I know."

"Like, maybe he's from Kenya." Ian mimicked the old lady.

"We *love* Nairobi," Nathan carried on.

"Such handsome people. We brought back a Masai. He's an absolute genius with the dogs."

Bobby was signaling Ian to come over and meet another old guest. "Shit."

"You better go," Nathan said.

Ian pointed to place cards on the table. "Did you see who you're sitting with?"

On his left was Straight Kate, the Children's Ballet Mistress of the New York City Ballet. She loved to gossip. On his right was Gay Kate; she ran a nonprofit agency that encouraged third world TV producers to include family planning information in their soap opera story lines. She loved to talk about sex.

Nathan didn't listen to either of them. He was brooding. There would never be another guy like Ian he could just be himself with, do nothing, and laugh. Fourteen years they'd known each other. They'd not gone a month without meeting for dinner. With a little more nerve, or a little more liquor, a hundred evenings could've ended in bed. The one evening that did, at graduation, they'd gone at it like felons released from solitary. They lay in the moonlight, a tangle of black and white, combined like strands of DNA. In the courtyard below, a quartet of old grads, back for reunions, sang a boozy, doo-wop "Smoke Gets in Your Eyes."

Ian winked from across the table.

It was just like the last day of Princeton: Ian disappearing in the rearview mirror.

"What does Bobby do?" Straight Kate reached past Ian for a basket of bread.

"He's running for City Council," Nathan said.

"Besides that."

"Oh. He worked for some congresswoman."

"How long has Ian known him? He's such a dreamboat."

"Bobby? Like a couple years."

It had taken Nathan just a couple minutes to see what a blowhard Bobby was. All his bullshit about human rights and crumbling schools in the inner city: what a total windbag. Nathan had caught him cheating—in public—at this leathersex club Nathan was dragged to by a guy he got stoned with at Wonderbar.

"I ran into your boyfriend at a conference in Chicago," Gay Kate said.

"My boyfriend?" Nathan bridled.

"From NYU. The professor."

"Oh. Trevor."

Trevor was just another white liberal afraid to dump Nathan *too* quickly lest he seem like a bigot.

"*I* liked him," Gay Kate said.

White guys never told you the truth. Except Ian. He just couldn't resist a good wisecrack.

Another toast. Ian's father was boring the shit out of everyone. Ten o'clock. Time to leave.

Nathan made his way over to Ian. "I gotta split."

"Not yet," Ian pleaded.

Nathan still had to polish his piece for *The Times*. "I gotta go."

"Let's meet up at the Brownstone."

"I can't."

"One nightcap. It's early. Come on." Ian begged like a little boy.

Nathan melted. "I'll try."

Back at home, there was a message on the answering machine. Mom and Dad were "puzzled" by his behavior: "Please call: we're worried about you."

Fuck 'em all.

Nathan made coffee and finished the puff piece on Palm Pilots. It wasn't very funny. If he got up early, before the wedding, maybe inspiration would strike.

He changed into jeans.

The Brownstone was busy. He'd never seen it busier. The storm had lassoed every queer on the Upper East Side and unleashed them on the Brownstone. It was just plain dumb to be despondent, Nathan chided himself, as he scanned the room for Ian. It wasn't like he was never going to see Ian again. He was just getting married, whatever *that* meant.

It was Ian who found Nathan.

"I can't do it," Ian said.

"What?"

"Get married. To Bobby. I can't."

He was drunk. "Take it easy."

"I *can't*."

"Will you fuckin' chill."

"I can't, Nate. I've gotta tell him."

He did this all the time. He quit the soaps, told off his father, moved to Paris—when he was drunk. The next morning, he went back to *Eden Heights* and returned phone calls from his parents.

"Do *you* like Bobby?"

"Get her—in the cashmere." Nathan stalled, pointing to a big black guy in a sky-blue sweater.

"Do you like Bobby?"

"I must be the only homeboy here who doesn't fold sweaters at Bloomingdales."

"Do you like Bobby?"

"I hardly know him," Nathan said.

"That's not true. We've had you to dinner like how many times?"

"I know, but he's shy."

"He's shy?" Ian shouted.

"In private."

"He's never *been* in private. He was born with a mike in his mouth."

Now you notice.

"At Thanksgiving?" Ian said. "He starts lecturing *you* about affirmative action and some fuckin' demo about racial profiling and why the mayor's just a tool of the real estate lobby and I'm like, 'Uh-huh. Uh-huh. Uh-huh. Nathan writes for the friggin' *Times*. You don't have to read him the Metro section.'"

"How many is that?" Nathan steadied Ian's drink.

"Three."

"Not including the party."

"He's a robot. He looks like a robot."

Oh please. "You had a hard-on the moment you saw him."

"Not really."

"At Barracuda?" Nathan reminded him. "After Edmund White?"

"What?"

"'Break me off a piece of that.' That's what you said—when he took off his jacket."

Ian laughed. "Yeah, well, you were mad hot for him too."

"Bullshit."

"Oh, come on, Nate. If he were black, you'd've been all over him."

Nathan was dumbfounded. "Pardon me?"

"You were like, 'Really? Tax incentives—for small and medium-sized businesses? Tell me more.'"

"What do you mean, 'If he were black'?"

"You know what I mean."

Nathan glared. "What do I look like, Louis Farrakhan?"

"Oh, come on," Ian said. "The only guys you ever hook up with—all your boyfriends, they're always black."

Was he kidding? "Except for Trevor."

"Who?"

"The philosopher."

"Who?"

"From NYU. He writes about Vagueness," Nathan said. "You thought he was joking."

"He wasn't?"

"And Ronnie."

"HBO Ronnie?"

"White Ronnie. The dancer. He's in *The Producers.*"

"Oh, her." Ian shrugged.

"And Manny."

"He's Puerto Rican."

Nathan was baffled. "What *is* your problem?"

"Nothing." He looked away shyly.

"What?"

"I just wondered . . ."

"What?"

"You know. I just wondered why we never hooked up."

He was high. "You're on E, aren't you, Ian?"

"No."

"K?"

"No."

"Viagra?"

"No. Remember that once before graduation . . .?"

"Hang on."

"I mean, *I* had a good time . . ."

Nathan marveled at his egotism. "Are you telling me, if a poor wack nigger doesn't fall in love with you, he must be like a racial separatist or something?"

"No, no." Ian laughed. "I just thought—I mean, we both had a pretty good time, didn't we? Christ, you came like a yogurt machine."

Nathan squirmed. "That's attractive."

"Why shouldn't it work?"

It was the vodka talking. "Stop already."

"I'm not saying it wouldn't be weird," Ian said. "We've been friends so long."

He *looked* serious.

"Everybody says, 'You're such good friends, you and Nate, why don't the two of you'—"

"Settle down together?"

"You know what I mean," Ian said. "We don't have to 'settle down.'"

"Oh. Perish the thought."

"What?"

Nathan bristled. "Better we should cruise the bars for a sailor, bring him home and tie him up."

"You like that shit?"

"No, that's your husband."

"What?"

Fuck. "I was kidding."

"What about my husband?"

"I was *kidding*."

"No, you weren't."

"Look, I gotta bounce." Nathan checked his watch.

"How the hell do *you* know what Bobby likes?"

"I don't."

"You just said—"

"I was *kidding*."

"He tied you up?"

"Me?" Nathan said. "No. No way."

"Who, then?"

"I don't know."

"Who told you?" Ian said.

"Nobody."

"You're lying."

"No, I'm not."

"Fuckin A. Oh my God."

"Will ya chill already."

"What did he do? He ties up people? He doesn't like *torture* them too?"

"Fuck no," Nathan said.

"But he ties them up. And pours hot wax on them."

"No way."

"I found this vest, this leather vest in his locker at the gym. And these candles."

"What did he say?" Nathan said.

"He said the candles were for our anniversary. He was making dinner."

Nice save.

"And the vest belonged to this friend of his in the mayor's office—this married guy who doesn't want his wife to know he's like a regular at the Eagle. What a prick," Ian shouted.

People were looking.

"Take it easy."

"He's tyin' up like the deputy mayor and screwing the daylights out of *him*. He's such a bore with me," Ian said.

Nathan wasn't surprised.

"We cuddle; we suck; we set the alarm and turn on *Nightline*."

"See what you've been missing."

"I don't need that shit," Ian exploded. "Christ, he's gonna get AIDS."

"Ssssh. From a rope?"

"That's it. Fuck Bobby. I can't risk that shit. You want a drink?" He headed toward the bar.

"Ian, hang on." Nathan grabbed him. "He was perfectly safe."

"You saw him?"

"You can't tell him I told you."

"What a fuckin hypocrite. Like he's so in love with me he's gotta tie up some stranger in a fuckin' sex club?"

"Ian, promise. I'll cut yo ass."

Ian was staring at something.

"You got a haircut."

He didn't like it.

"Too short?"

"I like you nappy."

"Some Like It Nappy."

"Whoa." Ian snapped his fingers.

"Right, right." Nathan closed his eyes. "*Some Like It Hot* Meets—what?"

"Spike Lee?" Ian said.

"No. Dumber."

"*Color Purple?*"

"Nah."

"*Ain't Misbehavin'!*"

"Right, right," Nathan said. "Two white guys pose as black guys—"

"To escape the mob—"

"Not the mob. The Klan."

"The white guys?"

"Yeah, yeah," Nathan said. "Two stupid crackers—country-western musicians . . ."

"Witness a lynching . . ."

"No."

"Smaller?"

"No. Bigger."

"A bombing," Ian said. "A church bombing. The kids!"

"Jesus Christ." Nathan scowled.

"What?"

"Too fuckin' grim."

"All right, all right," Ian said. "The church is empty."

"Except for a dog."

"A dog and a dream."

They both closed their eyes and concentrated.

Nathan opened his eyes. "They put on blackface."

"Right, right." Ian punched his arm. "And join a gospel choir heading north."

"The Mighty Clouds of Joy."

"No way."

"What?" Nathan said.

"We gotta sell the soundtrack. To finance the picture."

"Right, right. The Temptations!"

"In Birmingham?" Ian said.

"Why not? They're on tour with the Motown Revue."

"Uh-huh."

"And their tour bus, the Klan mistakes it for like this protest bus from the North."

"Right, right."

Nathan closed his eyes.

Ian pounded a hand to his head. "Not the Temps. The Supremes!"

"Are you kidding?"

"They have to do drag!"

"There were *three* Supremes."

"So?" Ian said.

"What, you think Diana's like so into herself she's just not gonna notice that the girls put on fifty pounds and have five o'clock shadows?"

"No, no," Ian said. "She *knows* they're not Mary and Flo. Mary and Flo get sick or something . . ."

"Food poisoning."

"Right, right," Ian said. "At a segregated lunch counter."

Nathan raised his hand, "Gimme five."

"So like Diana—she's not gonna cancel the tour—she needs two girls to back her up."

"Enter Willy-Joe and Joe-Bob."

"In drag and blackface." Nathan smiled.

"They fall in love with Mary and Flo."

"You really hate Diana," Nathan said.

"Mary thinks she's a dyke. Cause she's got the hots for Billy-Bob in drag."

"Ya-da-ya-da-ya-da," Nathan said. "Hilarity ensues. But what do they learn?"

Ian thought for a second. "They learn that racial prejudice is really, really bad."

"What's that sound?"

"What?" Nathan listened.

Ian cupped his ear. "Could that be Oscar buzz I hear?"

"Fuckin' A."

"We really should write this one," Ian said.

"I interviewed Geffen. I could get it to Dreamworks."

"You met David Geffen?"

"On the phone," Nathan said. "For this piece on Diller."

"Dear Mr. Geffen. Please read our script. It's *Some Like It Hot* meets *Mississippi Burning* . . ."

"*Some Like It Burning.*"

"And I'll lick your nuts and fuck you up the ass for a small advance. My friends are right," Ian said.

"What?"

"We should be together. I know I'm drunk. But I mean it. You *know* I'm right."

Nathan's heart was pounding. "You're getting married tomorrow."

"I love you, Nate."

Nathan pushed him away. "Stop fuckin' with me."

"Remember graduation?"

"We were *kids*. I would've poked a camel."

Ian rolled up his sleeve and flexed a bicep. "I don't turn you on?"

Nathan laughed. "Not more than I can handle."

"You saved my life."

"What? When?"

"When that asshole at Rawhide gave me the K. And I thought it was cocaine."

Nathan shivered. "What a fuckin' psycho."

"I'd *still* be throwing up. I'd've jumped out the window if you hadn't stayed all night. I wanted to touch you so bad."

"Yeah right." Nathan looked at his watch. "I've gotta finish a piece."

"So we'll write it together. The way we used to."

"It's bullshit."

"I can write bullshit." Ian brushed his hand over Nathan's buzz cut.

"Don't be such a cunt."

"I was wrong. I like your haircut."

Nathan closed his eyes.

"I can feel your heart through the back of your head."

"I gotta go."

"Give me one good reason why we shouldn't be together."

"You're marrying Bobby," Nathan said.

"No, I'm not. Besides that."

"I smoke."

"That's okay. I don't mind."

"I can never have children." Nathan sniffled, his eyes still closed.

"We can adopt."

Nathan looked away as if in shame. "I'm not really a Negro."

Ian smiled. "Well, nobody's perfect. Oh God."

"What?"

"Guess who's here."

Nathan opened his eyes. Across the room, waving, was Bobby.

"I'll head him off at the pass." Ian squeezed Nathan's hand. "You love me, don't you?"

Nathan couldn't say no.

"Just leave it to me." Ian started toward Bobby.

This is really happening, Nathan rejoiced.

GOPAL

Joe waved to the bartender.

The bartender ignored him. He was opening a Christmas present from the swarthy-looking manager of the Brownstone.

It was time for bed. Joe was already tipsy and his nerves were frayed. He couldn't help worrying that Ralph would change his mind. But that was foolish. Ralph wasn't like that. He was a fuck-up but he was a mensch. He wasn't some greedy paralegal who'd get his rocks off, suing over the story in *The New Yorker.*

"Excuse me!" Joe called to the bartender.

Swirling his new Christmas scarf around his neck, the bartender raised one finger: just a minute.

At the end of the bar, Joe spotted a guy—he looked a lot like Gopal—pulling up a stool and sitting down. He seemed to be enjoying himself. And why not? When you've been dead for almost a year, even the Brownstone would have its charms.

With a chorus of barbershop queens, the piano player was singing yet another Judy Garland song.

You made me happy sometimes, you made me glad,
But there were times, dear, you made me feel so bad

The guy who looked like Gopal was taking in everyone—the boozers crowding the piano, the lechers scanning the crowd like Secret Service agents—with the sweetest eyes.

The bartender came over.

Joe gave him a twenty. "Can you give me some singles?"

"No problem."

Someone tapped Joe on the shoulder.

"My God. It's you," Joe said.

"Uh-huh."

"You're here."

"Ssssh, please."

"This is fucked." Joe slapped himself on the cheek.

"Keep your voice down."

"Gopal, you're dead."

The bartender was looking.

"You're dead."

"All right, I'm dead," Gopal said. "Keep your voice down."

"What did I drink?"

"Don't ask me."

"Somebody slipped me something."

Gopal shook his head. "No, I don't think so."

"I'm decompensating. Shit," Joe snapped his fingers. "I know what it is."

"Willya chill already."

"It's the Valium—on top of the gin."

"What's Valium? An antidepressant?"

"No."

"What is it?"

"It's nothing. Just a few milligrams—for anxiety."

"Oh right," Gopal said. "I couldn't tolerate it. Not on top of the antivirals."

The bartender put the change in front of Joe.

"Thanks." Joe turned back to Gopal. "What are you doing here?"

"Shit."

"What?"

Standing in the doorway was Bobby Bayard.

"Of all the gin-joints in the world," Gopal said.

"I know. He's getting married tomorrow."

"I heard."

"To some TV writer. You heard?"

"You must be jealous," Gopal said knowingly.

Joe dithered a bit. "Why should I be jealous? That's him, Ian, Bobby's fiance—with the black guy."

"He's not that cute," Gopal said. "Who is he?"

"Some soap opera writer."

"You're kidding." Gopal studied Ian. "Surely there's more to him than that."

"I wouldn't know."

"So, what went wrong?"

"What?"

"With you and Bobby," Gopal said.

"Excuse me?"

"You two were pretty hot and heavy there for a while."

"What are you talking about?"

"It's common knowledge."

"What?"

"About you and Bobby," Gopal said. "Jim Taplitz told me."

"Told you what? Jim who?"

"Jim Taplitz. From the Service Station—in Chelsea. He cut Bobby's hair."

"Oh, please. Bobby doesn't confide in his fuckin' hairdresser."

"I know."

"I spent two years with Bobby in that caretaker's group," Joe said. "He didn't say a thing that couldn't be quoted in the Congressional Record."

"He told Vinnie Pagano."

"Who? What?"

"Vinnie Pagano, his campaign manager," Gopal said. "Vinnie told Chris Olmscheid, Chris told Jim, and Jim told me."

"You're fuckin' dead."

"Yeah," Gopal said. "So is Jim."

"Oh. God. Shit."

"Two weeks after you and Bobby put the bag over my head . . ."

"I put the bag over your head; thank you very much."

"Jim was at that jerk-off hotel in the Grove doing hair for some drag queen bullshit. He orders mussels—spaghetti and mussels. He doesn't even puke. He just turns red. Anaphylactic shock."

"What the hell did he tell you?"

Gopal sipped a beer daintily. "What do you think he told me?"

"I have no idea."

"Yeah, right."

"He's a fuckin' hairdresser," Joe said. "They make up crap just to keep you amused."

"We were not amused."

"What the fuck did he say?"

Gopal took a deep breath. "He said that you and Bobby got it on back at Bobby's while you were waiting for me to die. Then you came back to my place. Took the plastic bag off my head. Called the police. Went back to Bobby's and fucked all weekend."

Joe shook his head. "And you believed him."

"Are you still going at it?"

"What? No. None of your business."

"You selfish prick."

"Gopal. Take it easy."

"You know how much I loved Bobby."

"I know. I know."

"You couldn't wait like a friggin' hour till I was dead."

"You were dead. You were blue."

"Did you take my pulse?"

"He gave you thirty Seconal. You were fuckin' blue."

"My heart was beating."

"Bullshit. You went out like a light."

"How long did you stay?"

"We didn't stay," Joe said. "That was the whole idea—put the bag on and go."

"Right away?"

"We had to go—so we could come back later—and like: 'Oh my God he committed suicide.'"

"Was I breathing?"

"When we came back?"

"No, before you left."

"It sure didn't look like it."

"Was I cold? Did you check my hands?"

"No. No. No," Joe admitted angrily. "I didn't check."

"Did Bobby?"

"He didn't touch you."

"He didn't even . . ." Gopal stopped.

"What?"

"Kiss me?"

"With the bag over your head?"

"He could've kissed my hands."

"We said a prayer."

"Yeah, slammed the door and whipped out your dicks in the elevator."

"No way."

"Bobby didn't need you. He could've done it himself."

"Oh, right, please," Joe said. "Bobby wouldn't buy drugs."

"I told him where to get codeine. My next door neighbor had like twenty-five codeine from a skiing accident."

"You were lucky Bobby even showed up."

"He loved me."

"Of course he loved you." Joe tried to calm him down. "But he's a politician. He just can't go 'round killing people."

"I didn't want you there."

"I'm sorry."

"I hardly knew you." Gopal reared back in revulsion. "You didn't even dress. Your T-shirt had stains. Your hair was dirty."

"Are you giving me shit for fucking assisting in your suicide?"

"It would've killed you to shave?"

"I could go to jail," Joe said. "I could lose my license. I only did it 'cause your other friends crapped out and there was no way in hell Bobby was gonna tie that fuckin' trash bag around your head."

Gopal was aghast. "You used a trash bag?"

"The fucking Rainbows and Triangles bag had handles."

"I know. They detach."

"It wasn't airtight."

"What about the other bag?"

"From Asia House?" Joe said. "It had a cardboard bottom."

"Black or white?"

"The cardboard?"

"No, the trash bag."

"Oh. It was white," Joe said. "You know, one of those clean white ones for the kitchen."

"Bobby could've done it himself if he had to."

"Bullshit. He's won't check out a porn movie that might pop up in a background check for the State Department."

"I can't believe he let you touch him," Gopal seethed. "You don't even know him."

"What a crock of shit. I've known Bobby Bayard for over two years."

"Two years." Gopal jabbed two skinny fingers in his chest. "I was his best friend for thirty years. The first play I wrote—you never knew he acted, did you?—at Chester Country Day School, he played Mahatma Gandhi."

Joe tried not to smile. "Bobby Bayard. Mahatma Gandhi."

"When we were kids at Hammerwood, I could throw a paper plane from his window to mine."

"Look, Gopal, I'm sorry we . . ."

"My father was his grandfather's chauffeur. My mother was the cook. He never told you that."

"No shit."

"His grandmother sent me to all the best schools 'cause he refused to go without me."

Joe grinned. "How cool is that?"

"He wouldn't fill out his application for Exeter. He went on a hunger strike. They had to Fed-Ex another application before he'd lift a spoon to his brown Betty. When I got pneumocystis—I don't even know how he heard about it—he dropped out of Oxford."

"He went to Oxford?"

"For a summer course."

"In what?" Joe said.

"Guess."

"I'm not gonna guess."

"*Guess.*"

"What?"

"T. S. Eliot. William Blake."

"Oh, right." Joe remembered. "We talked about Eliot."

"Bobby talked to *you* about T. S. Eliot." Gopal was appalled. "You hardly knew him."

"I know him now."

"Look." He pointed to Bobby. "He's not just another asshole politician."

"Uh-huh."

"Watch. They touch him like he's Bobby Kennedy."

"Uh-huh."

"He's a dreamer. A poet. A visionary. A saint."

"Willya get a fuckin' grip here, Gopal."

"People think he's like plastic 'cause he plays it so safe. You know why?"

"He plays it so safe? Yeah. I do. I think so," Joe said.

"Oh. Why?"

"It's just a guess."

"Fine. Tell me."

"Well, I think his mother—he shows all the signs—couldn't really love him the way he needed. She could only show interest or affection when he behaved like a good little boy and did exactly what she wanted."

"His mother died when he was four." Gopal smiled smugly.

"His grandmother, then."

"His grandmother was like the first fuck-you divorcée on the Main Line."

"Oh really."

"She was a foxhunting champion. She collected wine lists from hotel bars: the Ritz in Paris, the Bombay Hilton—"

"All right, I'm an asshole."

"She taught him to play blackjack." Gopal was enjoying himself. "She taught him to smoke."

"All right." Joe gave in. "It's totally unprofessional to start analyzing someone without sufficient information."

"It only works one way?" Gopal said.

"What?"

"Psychiatry? It only works in hindsight?"

"Fuck you."

"If it can't predict any phenomena, it's not really a science."

"What are you," Joe said, "the fuckin' devil?"

"The reason Bobby is such a Boy Scout—"

"Yeah, right."

"Is that he knows—deep down—he's gonna be senator or maybe even president some day, and he's gotta have a clean slate to run for office and achieve all the things he was born to achieve. And you know why he's so sure he's gonna make it?"

"No, Gopal. Tell me."

"We were nine or ten—fourth grade—serving Easter Mass at St. David's."

Joe was confused. "You mean, you were Catholic?"

"Episcopalian. Father Hewetson said that one day in the future . . ."

"You were like never like a Hindu or anything?"

"No."

"Not even your parents?"

"No, sorry, we're all just high-church house niggers; but thanks for asking."

"Jesus Christ," Joe fumed, "don't be so fuckin' touchy."

Gopal went on. "Father Hewetson said that one day Bobby and me would go on to do something extraordinary. I told Bobby he'd be president. He told me I'd be a famous writer."

Joe tried to break in. "Oh, by the way Gopal . . ."

"And if you don't think Bobby's gonna make it some day, then you have no idea the kind of stuff he's made of. He is gonna help thousands—and millions—of people: gay people, straight people, immigrants, illegal immigrants, people who need AIDS drugs, people who need education, people who need housing."

"I *got* it."

"You think I'm crazy?"

"No." Joe shrugged. "What do *I* know?"

"He believed in me too. He spent his own money—two hundred thousand dollars—to produce my first play at the Actor's Playhouse."

"Gopal, about your writing . . ."

"He didn't have to . . ." Gopal stopped. "What?"

"You're a wonderful writer."

"Thank you," he said tentatively. "Bobby showed you my stuff? What did you read?"

"Everything."

"You're kidding."

Joe tried to soften the blow. "In a perfect world, there'd be some other person to take on the job."

"What job?"

"Bobby had to make me—or hire a total stranger . . ."

"What?"

"Your literary executor."

Gopal looked stunned. "You're joking."

Joe could barely speak. "He doesn't want your plays to just rot in his drawer while he's shaking hands at subway stops."

"What the hell do you know?" Gopal exploded. "A fuckin' shrink—about contemporary theater?"

"I just had a story published in *The New Yorker.*"

He hesitated. "You did?"

"Uh-huh."

"Congratulations," Gopal said grudgingly. "But that's hardly theater."

"I know."

"It's a whole different art form."

"I sent out your comedy—about the transsexual. What's the name of the play?"

"You don't know the name?"

"Wait, wait," Joe said.

"Go to hell."

"*Alter Ego.* I sent it to Playwrights. I sent it to Long Wharf. I sent it to the Manhattan Theatre Club."

"Yeah, right. Like they're gonna do a play by a fuckin' unknown."

"I sent it to The New York Theater Workshop."

"It's not pretentious enough."

"I walked it over myself to the guy who runs the Drama Department."

"I coulda saved you a trip," Gopal said.

"I didn't know it's like a . . ."

"Company."

"Closed shop. And you have to be a member."

"Or fucking a member," Gopal said, "Or somebody famous or fucking somebody famous."

"I sent it to Scott Elliott."

Gopal lit up. "I know Scott Elliott."

"At The New Group."

"The New Group?"

"You're thinking of Scott *Ellis,*" Joe explained. "The musical guy."

"Who's this?"

"Scott Elliott," Joe said. "He's a fuckin' genius. He does those Mike Leigh plays and shit."

"Oh. What did he say?"

Joe tried to sound hopeful. "He said he *really* liked it; they're thinking about it. But it's always a crapshoot."

"What else have they got?"

"For this season? I don't know. He just said they really, really liked it but they only do three plays a year and maybe I should take it to the Public Theater."

" 'Cause I'm an Asian—a gay South Asian."

"A dead gay South Asian," Joe reminded him.

"That should count for something. What about Soho Rep?"

"They passed on it too," Joe said quickly. "But don't get discouraged. You worked your whole life—"

"For two fucking off-off-Broadway showcases with non-equity actors playing multiple parts." Gopal started to wail.

"Bobby said you had talent."

"Oh, God."

"Take it easy."

"My Bobby," Gopal cried. "My Bobby."

"Sssssh, now."

"All I had was him." Gopal pushed Joe away. "And you took him from me."

"Gopal. You were dead."

"What difference does that make?"

"Are you kidding?"

"You don't think the dead deserve a little respect?"

"We were both just nuts," Joe pleaded.

"Why bother with a funeral? Everybody in the hot tub! Lather up your dicks!"

"We were out of our minds. The way Bobby was crying—when we went back to find you—I thought he was gonna blow the whole fucking plan."

Gopal beamed. "He was crying?"

"I told him, 'Bobby, if you don't stop crying, I'm gonna put a bag over *your* fuckin' head.'"

"What did he say? Did he say he loved me?"

"Of course."

"Oh God."

"And he said he only wished he'd said it more while you were alive."

"Oh God." Gopal wiped tears from his eyes. "My Bobby."

"He wasn't sure you ever knew how incredibly much he really loved you."

Gopal stiffened. "Why did he say that?"

"What? I don't know. Can't you read his mind?"

"I'm dead. I'm not psychic."

Joe closed his eyes for a moment.

"I didn't deserve him."

Gopal was still there.

"He was so handsome." Gopal was keening. "I was so ugly, ugly, ugly . . ."

"Stop."

"Ugly, ugly . . ."

"You're making me sick."

"I was a little fly. He was a great white stallion."

"Oh please."

"We were on the bed after soccer—sophomore year. He rolled over and kissed me. Then just kinda smiled. And touched my chin. It was the most wonderful moment of my life."

Joe let him sob. "When you were just lying there on the couch, and we were waiting for the police, Bobby told me that his whole life, every thing he's achieved, was like only made possible by your belief in him."

"Oh God."

"All of his values came from you. All the things you talked about and taught him."

Gopal sat up suddenly. "You've gotta tell him: I *know* he loved me. Joe, please. Please. Tell him."

"Are you joking?"

"There he is. By the Christmas tree."

Taking shit from his fiance. "You gotta be kidding," Joe said.

"No. Do it."

"Oh Bobby, excuse me," Joe tried to show Gopal how stupid the whole idea was, "But by the way, I was just talking to Gopal at the bar and he told me to tell you he does know how much you loved him."

"That's it."

"Are you nuts?"

"You can suck my best friend's dick while I'm dying, but you can't do me this one little favor?"

"We were alive, Gopal. We were horny. We were stoned out of our minds."

"You got stoned? While I was dying?"

"No, no, not 'stoned.'"

"Shit. What drugs did you take? Weed? Hash?"

"Just a couple of joints. We had a whole fucking hour to kill before we went back, and we were both like, shit, this is so fuckin' real, why are we so numb?"

"You didn't do E?"

"No. No."

"What?"

"I told you," Joe said.

"I heard you did E."

"Who told you that?"

"Jim. The hairdresser. Did you?"

Joe was sick of this shit. "What if we did?"

"You made Bobby take Ecstasy? He's a politician. Are you insane?"

"I could be. I'm talkin' to you."

"You're insane."

"That's what we have in common, me and Bobby," Joe said.

"He's not insane."

"No, he's just dissociative and compulsive."

"Shut up."

"We both live in our heads," Joe said, "and kinda wave at people from our fuckin' carriage like the queen. You know our favorite Beatle?"

"George."

"George," Joe said simultaneously. "Is that sick or what?"

"I loved George," Gopal said. "He played the sitar."

"We're just great big heads." Joe spread his hands. "Me and Bobby, with like the latest software for showing sympathy."

"Bobby has feelings." Gopal defended him.

"Not if he can help it."

"He was crying so hard—you just told me—the day I died, he almost blew the whole fuckin' thing."

Joe caught himself. "Oh right."

"Isn't that what you said?"

"I know."

"But?"

"But what?"

"He did, didn't he?" Gopal trembled. "You wouldn't lie about something like that."

"No. No."

"Oh my God," Gopal wailed. "You lied."

"No."

"He didn't even cry?"

"Christ, he wanted to cry," Joe said.

"What is wrong with you?"

"He was crying inside."

"How could you fuckin' lie about something like that?"

"I wanted you to feel better. Right now," Joe said. "That's why I'm such a lousy shrink. I get so anxious. It's the fuckin' system. The HMOs. Who has the time to do real therapy?"

"He didn't cry. Not even on Ecstasy?"

"You don't cry on E. You put on George Harrison and talk about Blake and fuck like puppies, but is that love or just the dread of being a total robot whose mother couldn't love him when he got dirty or angry or scared or had a little hard-on?"

"You *think* you love Bobby. You don't know what love is."

"But you do?" Joe pleaded, "Oh, fuck. Tell me."

Gopal stood up and pushed his chair back. "I want you to go over there right now and tell Bobby I know damn well how much he loved me."

Joe clenched his fists. "Why should I?"

"Tell him."

"What's in it for me?"

"You owe me," Gopal said.

"For what?"

"For giving you this chance to make amends for the scummy way you behaved the day I died."

Joe thought it over. "I'll make you a deal."

"What?"

"You tell me about death. I'll tell Bobby whatever you want."

"So, what do you want to know?"

Joe didn't hesitate. "What's the point of everything? I mean, is there a God? Does he give a flying fuck what we do here on Earth, and all the suffering and bullshit we go through?"

Gopal smiled. "You're not gonna like it."

"Shoot."

Gopal drew his chair closer to make sure no one was listening. "There's nothing."

"Nothing?"

"Just Circumstance and Chance."

Joe was tired. "Speak English."

"Circumstance and Chance are the only deities. They rule our lives. Have you read Zola?" Gopal said.

"No. I started one."

"The point is, Zola and Tolstoy and even Proust—all the old-fashioned novelists had it right."

"Had what right?"

"You just get one go at life. You do your best. There's no after-party."

Joe wasn't surprised.

"You want angels? Read Tony Kushner. You want transcendence? Read what's-his-name? Rilke."

"But what's it like being dead?" Joe insisted. "Where *are* you?"

Gopal shrugged. "It's nothing special. It's like watching C-Span with a joint."

Could be worse.

"Now, get your ass over there and tell Bobby what I told you."

"Right," Joe said. "Tell me again."

"Tell him I always knew he knew how much I loved him."

Joe got up and tucked his shirt in his pants.

"On your way."

"Gimme a second."

"*Now.*"

Joe picked up his singles from the bar. "Fuckin A. The dead are demanding."

BOBBY

On the day before his wedding, Bobby had only one campaign stop, a public forum at the East Side Neighborhood House on a proposal to locate a small homeless shelter on Seventy-Fifth Street between Second and Third.

Bobby loved the Neighborhood House. It was full of five-year-olds in swimming trunks, Alzheimer's patients singing Rodgers and Hammerstein, Arabs and Czechs and Chinese and Dominicans studying

English as a second language. He'd attended AA meetings there in the days not so long ago when his drinking was getting out of hand. And despite warnings from Vinnie, his campaign manager, that his press releases would end up in the trash, Bobby even used the messenger service run by the Neighborhood House: it provided jobs for homeless people.

He was looking forward to the forum. It would be a break from all the endless bullshit about the wedding. Ten times a day, Ian, or Chloe, the wedding planner, called him on his cell phone to decide some ridiculous detail he couldn't care less about. Should the white aisle runner run from the nave of the church or just from the communion rail to the altar? Should the best men, Vinnie and Ian's friend, Nathan, get scuba watches, Swiss Army Knives, or little digital cameras? Which went better with notched lapels, a sprig of holly, a rosebud, or a white carnation?

Details mounted with the snow. As airplane flights were canceled and Manhattan hotel rooms were taken by stranded commuters, the less foresighted wedding guests called for train schedules and the names of bed-and-breakfasts.

As he walked with Vinnie to the Neighborhood House—it was faster than driving through the obstacle course of snowbanks and abandoned cars—Bobby was still fielding calls from Ian and Chloe: Were his buddies from Santa Fe still coming? Did he know of a couch where the man from GLAAD could crash for the night? And what was to be done about Nigel, the florist? He had threatened to thrash the manager of the Brownstone over certain decorations he refused to remove: a string of little twinkling phalluses draped over a mantel; a Santa in chaps presiding over the Christmas tree.

The people who had come to speak with Bobby and other community leaders at the Neighborhood House were not the word processors, salesclerks, and handymen who turned out for debates on rent control. They were the young stockbrokers and attorneys who had bought co-ops in the fancier buildings on the corners of the avenues. They joked amongst themselves, exchanged business cards, and made dates for dinner after the forum, but their cocktail chatter was misleading: they felt threatened; they were out for blood. One by one, they took to the microphone to denounce the "do-gooders" with their "social experiments" who would bring alcoholics, needle-users with AIDS, and the mentally ill onto the streets where their children played.

"How old are your children?" Bobby asked one young woman in knee-high boots.

"I don't *have* children," she seethed. "And I'm not going to—not in this neighborhood—if it's turned into a dumping ground for drug addicts and psychotics."

Her pals applauded.

One polite young doctor was honest. He admitted his fear that the value of his co-op would plunge if a homeless shelter were opened on a nearby block. "We're not the people on Park. We're not the people on Fifth. None of us are billionaires."

"Yet," some guy put in.

The crowd laughed.

The doctor ignored them. "All the equity we have—or most of it—is in our apartments. Can't you find somewhere else—a commercial district—where a shelter wouldn't put middle-class people in jeopardy?"

Bobby liked him. "I don't blame you for worrying. And no one wants to see young people leaving the neighborhood for the suburbs. We need your energy. And to be quite honest, we need your tax money."

"Damn straight," someone shouted out.

"Maybe Dorothy can tell us." Bobby turned to the well-coiffed president of the Family Aid Society. "Have there been any studies—in the neighborhoods where you run your other shelters—of the effect on property values?"

"I can tell you this," she said, "from experience. There's a shelter on my block—just a few buildings away. An overnight shelter, for twenty people, just the size of the new one we're proposing. There's been no crime wave in the East Eighties. There's been no exodus of home owners."

The crowd hissed and hooted.

The catcalls continued as the next citizen came to the microphone, an old nun with grey bangs slipping out from under her wimple. "The homeless people we're talking about here are not criminals," she pleaded. "They're everyday people like you and me." She told of a mother with muscular dystrophy who had three young kids on scholarship in the Catholic school where she was the principal.

"Oh, break my heart, Sister," a red-faced guy in a cashmere sweater shouted through a newspaper cupped like a megaphone.

"Where's the father?" somebody added.

The nun bowed her head. "He's dead."

"From crack," the red-faced guy shot back.

The crowd laughed.

Bobby couldn't believe it. These professionals, with their diplomas from Dartmouth and Wellesley, were just as vicious as the working-class bigots throwing rocks at school buses in South Boston.

"Cut to the chase." A cute young woman with a short blonde bob interrupted Bobby as he tried to set an agenda for the next meeting on the issue. "*We're* your neighborhood. *We're* your constituents. Are you with *us*, or are you with *them?*"

From the front row, the nun beamed at Bobby as she fingered the rosary beads in her pocket.

Next to her, Vinnie was removing the elastic band from a stack of campaign brochures.

Bobby hated his job—he hated himself—at moments like this. "There's one thing I've learned in all my years of public service: you can't *force* people to participate in public policy. It just doesn't work."

The blonde looked pleased.

"There are going to be more hearings on the subject. All of us need more—and better—information."

"*I* don't," the red-faced guy megaphoned.

"You need an hour with Emily Post—or Mike Tyson," Bobby said.

To his surprise, the crowd enjoyed it.

Thank God. "Now we all better get on our way home before we're trapped in here and start behaving like the Donner Party."

He slipped out a side door into the snow. The wind whipped his tie back.

"Good job," Vinnie assured him. "You sure weren't gonna change any minds in *that* crowd."

Count on Vinnie. There were homeless people freezing to death in cardboard boxes on top of subway gratings and Vinnie was complimenting him for saving his political capital.

"See you at the Lotos Club," Bobby reminded Vinnie as they parted ways. He felt like shit. And he had one more awful appointment before the wedding rehearsal.

In the two years they'd been together, Bobby had been unfaithful to Ian no more than a dozen times. Compared to the constant catting about he'd concealed from previous lovers, this was monogamy.

The first time he cheated on Ian was after a fund-raiser in the Pines where, for many couples, infidelity is less criminal than forgetting to turn off the pool lights. Then there were a few trips to seedy sex clubs. When he was pissed with anyone—himself especially—a nasty bout of leathersex was just the therapy he needed. He didn't really count Joe, the therapist from the AIDS caretakers group, among the infidelities he was ashamed of. Their weekend together was a major debauch (Ian was in Atlanta at a soap opera convention) but no court in the world would deem it more than a misdemeanor, seeking succor after their awful experience with Gopal.

And then there was Victor. With his backpack, khakis, and headset, Victor looked like any other hot, young, working-class dude on the subway. But the disc in his Walkman was *Rigoletto,* and when the train stopped between stations, he confounded the other passengers by stabbing a thumb to his forehead and flapping his fingers. It was his way, the Neapolitan way, Bobby would learn, of telling the subway conductor what a fuckin' asshole he was.

A nurse at New York/Cornell Medical Center, Victor dreamed of becoming a doctor, if only to show the bastards who were in charge how medicine really ought to be practiced. His reports from the front on his daily skirmishes with overworked residents held Joe transfixed.

But it was the flashing, aggressive swordplay of his hands that really dazzled Bobby.

"He *says* he gave her five milligrams," Victor said, explaining to Bobby how he had reproached one resident for nearly killing an elderly patient with pseudophedrine and prednisone. Stiffening his fingers and sticking them inside his shirt collar, he loosened the collar, rubbing his fingers against his neck. "He gave her twenty-five. Of *course,* she coughed. This ball of phlegm hits the curtain. Then she flies off the table, holding her heart: 'Jesus, Mary, and Joseph.'"

Victor's fingers: was he illustrating something? Were they a crown, a dick, a guillotine? Victor himself had no idea. They seemed to mean *What an asshole,* or *What a liar,* or *Your wife is fucking somebody right this moment behind your back, you fuckin' moron.*

With Victor's four to twelve p.m. work schedule, Bobby often got to his place before him. Victor would leave the key to his apartment under a loose tile in the hallway. Just after twelve, he'd bound up the stairs with a bag of groceries like a hound with fresh fur in his teeth. "You like ricotta?"

Or, "Bobby, *hold* me." When he was sad, he wept like a schoolboy. When he was scared, he deflected fate: index finger and pinky extended, he made the *mano cornuta* that had shielded his family for centuries in Naples and, for thirty years, in Astoria, Queens.

In bed, he was no less exuberant: "This is mine." He would grab Bobby's dick or chin or foot and kiss it greedily. Locked in a fuck, he'd stare at Bobby in wonder as if he were Napoleon or Jefferson or some other demigod of adolescence who had fallen into his arms and wrapped his legs around him.

Not that Victor was blind to Bobby's flaws. He'd bitch, "You can't pick up a towel?" Or "Boy, *you're* in a foul mood." But even his flaws, like Jefferson's debts and bastards, Victor indulged as the inevitable peccadilloes of an extraordinary man.

Am I in love with him?, Bobby often wondered as he took the train home from Astoria. He *is* energetic. And cute. And amusing. And makes love like he's really making love. But it's awfully easy, he reminded himself, to idealize a kid, an attractive kid, you've only been with five or six times, not even forty-eight hours, total. Husband material, he wasn't. He didn't know Dick Cheney from Dick Clark. What politics he had was a blend of *New York Post* In-God-We-Trustism and gay libertarianism picked up from *HX, NEXT,* and other weeklies he found in bars.

Besides, Bobby was happy with Ian. For two years, give or take the odd fuck on the run, he'd been faithful and surprisingly happy. He'd had lovers who were better-looking, nastier, nicer, but none he'd ever felt safer—*cozier*—with. They could talk about anything. They were a team. With all he wanted to accomplish in politics, it was high time to settle down. After years and years of three-month lovers and weekend flings and one-night stands, he knew he would never meet anyone he got along with half as well as he got along with Ian.

It was time to tell Victor. Well, tell him again. He'd *told* him he was engaged but he'd never let on, not even the last time they met, that the wedding was any day now. Victor found it funny: two men getting married. And taking marriage so seriously. It was no life sentence in the culture he came from. Victor's father—and doubtless, his grandfather—had loved his lifelong mistress as much as he loved his wife. Why shouldn't Bobby?

Why indeed? Until he met Ian, Bobby had always assumed that fidelity, like agriculture, was something women had come up with—an advance, no doubt, but not one that men could adapt to with a whole hell of a lot of enthusiasm. Sure, it was admirable for two men in love to contemplate monogamy but, let's face it, the odds are against them. It's hard enough for straight couples to stay faithful. But when both bedmates have balls, the odds decrease exponentially.

Ian made him think otherwise. Their first year together, Bobby had racked up six months—a personal best—without sneaking out for a quickie on the side. After all, Ian trusted him. He didn't want to hurt him. And when they lay together, recalling their roles in prep school Shakespeare or planning a week in Santa Fe, those songs about you and me against the world and my romance and the nearness of you seemed a whole lot less silly. There was something beautiful about sharing your body, your secrets, with only one person on the planet. Of course, you can't expect perfection, not with a discipline as grueling and unnatural as monogamy, but Bobby was doing pretty well, at least by his own standards, until the evening he met Victor on the train.

The day before Bobby's wedding, Victor was waiting for him at The Infirmary, a little bistro near the hospital where nurses and doctors and expectant fathers grabbed a sandwich. Victor had wanted to get together at the Brownstone after work—they'd had their first date there—but Bobby didn't have time and besides, it seemed unseemly to drop the ax on Victor in the very same room where the wedding reception was to be held.

The Infirmary was crowded. Dr. Rudin, the burly chief of infectious diseases who sat with Bobby on the board of GMHC, was sharing a plate of pasta with his stick-thin wife. She reached into a big blue Tiffany's bag to show him the little boxes of what?—swizzle sticks? key chains? money clips?—she'd bought for his staff.

Bobby smiled.

Rudin nodded.

"Over here." Victor waved.

Why did he have to be so cute? There was a little tuft of black chest hair fluffing up through the blue V-neck of his scrubs. His ID, VICTOR PICCIRILLO, RN, was attached to his breast pocket with a silver guardian angel clip.

"Get this." He put a piece of paper in Bobby's hand before he'd even sat down. It was a chart, a patient's medical chart.

"Should I be looking at this?" He glanced over at Dr. Rudin.

"It's just a Xerox." Victor smiled. "I crossed out the name. Here." He pointed to a handwritten sentence at the end of the doctor's report: "The patient has no rigors or shaking chills, but her husband says she was very hot in bed last night."

Bobby laughed. "It must be Butarbutar." He was the Indonesian psychiatric resident Victor was always talking about. He had diagnosed one patient as suffering from "auditory and old factory hallucinations." He'd sent another patient to the psych ward because she said she had a frog in her throat.

"No, no, it's Schneider. He should know better," Victor whispered, "*Giudaico.*"

"What?"

"He's a Jew. From Crown Heights. You didn't read the best part." He pointed to the last sentence: *"The pelvic exam will be done later on the floor."*

"He's a pisser." Bobby laughed.

Victor was working awfully hard to be charming.

"So how you doin'?"

"All right." Victor vibrated his hand in the air: *così, così.*

It was now or never. "You *know* what I've gotta tell you," Bobby said.

"No, what?"

"I'm getting married."

"I know," Victor said breezily, taking the top off a Tupperware container he'd brought his lunch in. "You want some soup?"

"No, thanks. Victor, I'm getting married right away."

"Uh-huh." He cleaned his spoon with a napkin.

"Tomorrow."

He stopped with the spoon. "All right." He folded his arms and tried to look tough. "So. What do you want from me?"

He looked like a little pickpocket in Naples.

"I just want you to know," Bobby said. "I care about you. And if there's ever anything you need, anything at all, you know you can call me. Just call me on my cell phone."

"Don't worry." Victor tugged his open eye down with an index finger. "I won't call you at home."

He wasn't going to get nasty, was he? Bobby looked to the Rudins. They were twirling their pasta.

"If you're thinking of med school," Bobby said, "I know some people. And I've got a little money put aside, if you need some help getting started."

A Chinese busboy arrived with two glasses of water.

"Or maybe you'd rather get a PhD. In nursing."

Victor drew a thumb across his forehead. "Enough. You don't have to tell me how to live my life."

"You can't eat." The busboy pointed to Victor's soup.

"Yes, I can." Victor tipped the container to his lips. "Here. Watch."

"Victor, stop it." Bobby hated it when people gave waiters and salesclerks a hard time. "Save the soup. I'll get you a burger or something."

"No, thanks." He sipped.

"I get manager." The busboy took off.

"It's cauliflower. Here *mangia*." Victor offered the soup to Bobby.

"No. I'm not hungry. Please. Put that away."

Victor started to cry.

"*Victor*," Bobby took his hand.

Mrs. Rudin was looking.

Bobby drew his hand back.

Victor shook with sobs as he pressed the lid down on the soup. "I gotta go."

"Victor, listen, I'm sorry. You *know* how much I care about you. But what can I do?"

Move in? Make veal loaf and bounce you up and down on my dick while you do your homework for med school? If only.

The busboy returned with a muscular girl in a skintight tube dress: she had the parched tan, bleached hair, and pink lipstick of a professional weight lifter. "Hello, I'm Candy, the manager. Can I help you with something?"

Victor wiped his tears on his sleeve.

"We're just going." Bobby reached for his coat.

Dr. Rudin was looking now too.

"Victor, come on." Bobby grabbed a ten-dollar bill from his pocket and slipped it under the salt shaker.

Victor inhaled: it amplified his sobbing like a death rattle.

The Rudins averted their eyes and grabbed their things to go.

"How'd you like a Sambuca?" Candy patted Victor on the back of the head.

Victor kept crying. "I gotta get back to the ER."

Bobby stood up.

Candy slipped Victor's coat from the back of his chair and helped him on with it. "You're just like me. Christmas just makes everything that much worse."

Victor's nose was running.

"Vic, here." Bobby handed him a napkin.

He blew his nose.

Candy slipped the paper bag with the soup in it into Victor's hands as the busboy cleared the table. "Take care of yourself," she said.

"I don't know what you're crying about, handsome," Bobby whispered to Victor as they headed to the door. "You can do a whole lot better than *me*."

Victor stopped. With his fingers drawn together in a point, he aimed his right hand at his open mouth. "You said you loved me."

He had. He did. "I know."

The tears started again.

Bobby opened the door. "Swear to God, Victor, if there's ever anything you need. Anything at all."

"I could be your mistress."

Oh God. "Victor." He felt like a creep now: a slimy barrister blowing off a shop girl in a Bette Davis movie. "That wouldn't be fair to *you*."

"I don't care."

The snow belted them together. What wouldn't he give to go home with Victor and rub his dick against that plump little butt as Vic did the dishes in his underpants?

Siren wailing, a snow-covered ambulance pulled up to the sliding doors of the emergency room.

"You left your razor in the bathroom."

"Oh. Keep it."

"And your CDs."

"No: they're for you."

"Will you call me?" Victor wiped his nose on the back of his hand.

It was worse to lie. "I gotta go," Bobby kissed him on the forehead.

Victor clutched the paper bag. He looked like a kid left behind at the bus stop.

"Ciao, Bobby."

Bobby didn't look back. He felt like a bastard. But you can't just chuck the life you've been living for some kid from Astoria you hardly know. He'd talk to Vinnie: maybe there was something they could do for the nurses union; no one did more important work for less pay.

On the steps of the hospital Dr. Rudin was giving his wife a quick peck on the cheek.

Bobby checked his watch. There was just enough time to get home and change suits. Waiting for the light to change, he looked back.

Victor waved. Bobby pretended not to see.

The one person Bobby really wanted at his wedding wasn't coming and he blamed his stepmother for it.

Mrs. Nair—Nana, he called her—had been his grandmother's cook. Nana was the only one whose comfort little Bobby would tolerate for long when his mother died of leukemia, the month after his fourth birthday. Nana's kitchen table in his grandmother's house had a padded top that looked just like wood: he liked to press his fingers in it and see the fingerprints and lay his head on it to sleep. The window-ledge above her sink had a little Jesus with his hand raised to say Hi and a happy little god with an elephant head. Nana showed him how to do things: put leftover biscuits in plastic bags, roll out the dough for the latticework crust of a cobbler. She helped him with his jigsaw puzzles and let him leave them on the floor of the sunny room at the back of the house where the servants napped and watched TV. She took him along to Indian movies at International House in Philadelphia and let him eat chapattis and run around the theater playing tag with her son, Gopal.

Little by little, Bobby rebounded from his mother's death. He left the kitchen and started exploring. There were three houses he could hide in or play in at Hammerwood, his grandfather's farm outside of Philadelphia. He lived with his father in a house with a steeple that had once been a Quaker schoolhouse but now had a hot tub and lights under the trees that went on like magic when you stepped on a paving stone. There was a blackboard the length of the living room wall and shelves of heads with blank marble eyes that his father had brought back from India in a diplomat's pouch.

Nana's house was the smallest, the caretaker's cottage, where she lived with her husband, her two daughters, and Gopal. It was crowded and noisy and smelled of incense.

Bobby's grandparents lived in the big house, a fieldstone farmhouse that had metastisized into an English manor with a buzzer under the rug where his grandmother sat at the dining room table and a grillwork elevator to a scary third floor where Bobby's mother and his great-grandmother had died. Mrs. Gladwyn, Bobby's grandmother, did her best to be a mother to Bobby but, bereaved herself, she had to keep busy, planning a new wing of the Paoli Hospital to be named after her daughter, entertaining her husband's clients, and acquiring foxtails with the Radnor Hunt. Bobby's brother Michael, ten years older, came home from prep school in the summers, but he had little time for a kid brother who refused to shoot hoops or keep his mouth shut when Mike sneaked a cigarette in the bathroom.

There were nannies, one after the other, who spoke French or German, played the piano or the recorder, and taught Bobby to make the sign of the cross. They took Bobby to riding lessons in Devon and tried to interest him in his peers, the sons of business barons and descendants of Signers, growing up in nearby splendor. But Bobby wasn't interested in Biddles. He wanted only to play with Gopal. They would act out *Happy Days* and *Star Wars* in a little stone house covered with moss and littered with the beer cans and condoms of teenagers who used it as a trysting place. They picked blueberries, fed the horses, and helped the collies lead in the sheep. They communicated at night by string and Dixie cup from bedroom windows, a stone's throw away.

When it came time for Exeter, Bobby persuaded his grandfather to wangle a scholarship for Gopal too. They both got into Yale. They went their separate ways there and thereafter but stayed in touch. When Gopal got sick, it was Bobby who picked up the Nairs at the little house in Cherry Hill where they'd been living since retirement, and drove them to New York. He had always loved Nana but perhaps never more than on that visit to the AIDS ward at St. Vincent's. With her husband squirming in the background, she admitted to Gopal that Raj, her favorite brother, the family hero who owned three Popular Silks & Saris in New Jersey, was homosexual too.

At first, Bobby wasn't sure it was a good idea to invite Mrs. Nair to his wedding. It was less than a year since Gopal's death and Mr. Nair, slowed by arthritis, was too feeble to accompany her. She might feel out of place with all the fancy guests, and as much as she loved Bobby, a gay wedding would test the breadth of her broad-mindedness. Ian convinced him to send an invitation. It was up to Nana to accept or decline. Bobby called a few days after mailing the invitation and told Nana that his father and stepmother would pick up her in Cherry Hill on their way to New York. She said she'd be delighted to come.

Unbeknownst to Bobby, his parents decided to do things differently. They came to New York two days before the wedding and made arrangements for a car to pick up Nana. They didn't count on the snow.

"Why can't she take the train?" his stepmother asked Bobby as he joined her in the suite at the Lotos Club where she and his father were staying.

"That's not the point," Bobby said. "You told me you were going to see that she got here and put her up in a hotel."

"I made the arrangements." Mrs. Bayard finished her makeup at a vanity table in the bedroom. "She isn't a child."

"She's a simple woman. She's seventy years old. She's never stayed in a hotel. She's not going to check into the Sheraton on her own. That's why she's not coming."

"She'll have the time of her life." Mrs. Bayard refused to be ruffled by reality.

"You just said she's not coming."

Mrs. Bayard smoothed the rouge on her cheeks. "I look like a Chinese opera singer."

Glass of scotch in hand, Ambassador Bayard came out of the bathroom in his boxer shorts. He'd spent the day at the Morgan Library comparing the *Democracy in America* he was donating to Haverford to J. P.'s edition of de Tocqueville.

"We've got *five* minutes, Dad."

"I won't be long," he promised as he took his tuxedo from the closet.

Mrs. Bayard picked up the phone. "I'd better call that woman in Bedford."

"Later, Flora," the ambassador decreed. "Tell Bobby what you're doing."

"With Sheila?"

Sheila was her favorite border collie. Mrs. Bayard was soliciting semen from a breeder in Bedford to artificially inseminate Sheila.

"What's wrong with Sheila?"

"I don't know." Mrs. Bayard sipped a cocktail as she stood up with her back to Bobby. "She's just not a very receptive bitch. Mind zipping me up?"

Her hairspray smelled like apple pie.

"This woman in Bedford says her Bruno's got what it takes. But we need a teaser bitch."

"Excuse me?"

"The teaser's mounted by the male." Mrs. Bayard picked up her pearls, "And then the person collecting the semen sort of swirls it around the petrie dish, or whatever they use."

Ambassador Bayard looked at his wife as if she were the most delightful woman in the world.

Bobby could never tell if she meant to be funny. "Why can't Sheila 'tease' for herself?"

Mrs. Bayard put on her pearls. "God knows, she's tried. But she's just off-putting or *something*. Shep can't stand her."

"Maybe Sheila's a lesbian," the ambassador said.

The old man was trying to sound relaxed about the homo wedding he was dreading.

Bobby smiled. "I thought straight males liked lesbians."

"Only in pairs," Mrs. Bayard said. "Two by two. Like oxen on the ark."

Who *are* these people? In the decade they'd been married, his father and Flora had become so enchanted with themselves, their dogs, their books, their trips to Paris and the Cotswolds, that they seemed to have no sentimental connection to Bobby or to anyone else, for that matter. Aloof in their love, mindful only of their stockbroker and room service, they moved through the world in a bubble of mutual admiration: Nick and Nora Charles without the friends from Hells Kitchen; the Reagans with a splash of education.

"Oh, Michael called," his father said. "Alma's beside herself. Davey has measles."

"Oh shit. Where are they staying?"

"They're home."

"In Santiago?"

"They all send their love."

Bobby was hurt—he didn't even matter to Michael—but it didn't surprise him. Like Prince Phillip, poor pussywhipped Mike's main job was toadying to his wife. A Rockefeller, Alma's primacy had recently been reconfirmed by the rebounding of her assets from the stock market slump that followed September 11th.

Mrs. Bayard was tying her husband's tie.

"Remember," Bobby advised them, "Ian's father is a minister."

"He wants you to behave." The ambassador furrowed his brow as he handed his shirt studs to his wife.

"I don't know *what* you're talking about." Mrs. Bayard slipped in a stud. "My grandfather was a chaplain at Yale."

Bobby missed Nana. And he missed his mother. She used to hug him; that much he remembered. And she showed him how, with a great big windup of the mallet, to whack a croquet ball across the lawn into the driveway. When he heard noises in the night, she read to him from Robert Louis Stevenson.

> *Little Indian, Sioux or Crow,*
> *Little frosty Eskimo,*
> *Little Turk or Japanee,*
> *Oh! don't you wish that you were me?*

When she died, he didn't believe it. Like his shadow, she'd come back. When he felt helpless, no one to hug him, he repeated the poems he knew by heart:

> *How do you like to go up in a swing,*
> *Up in the air so blue?*

Oh, I do think it the pleasantest thing
Ever a child can do!

"How do I look?" Mrs. Bayard put a hand behind her head like a bathing beauty.

"Good enough to eat," the ambassador said.

Hustling his parents downstairs to the dining room, Bobby was glad to see Ian in the doorway, fussing over the guests who'd made it through the brutal snowstorm, several with bags from Bed Bath & Beyond.

"Come here often?" Ian sidled up to Bobby with a lustful look.

"No," Bobby said. "It's my first time here."

"Tuesday nights, they've got go-go boys."

Bobby summoned a waiter and asked him to remove two plates. "My brother and sister-in-law can't make it," he explained to Ian.

"They're not the only ones. There hasn't been this much snow—I heard it on the radio—since seventy-something. Oh, there's Straight Kate." Ian took off to thank his friend for her wedding present: she'd pulled strings to have their seats at City Ballet bumped up from mid-orchestra to within goosing distance of Jock Soto.

The room gleamed with candles and Christmas lilies. Little by little, Bobby relaxed. For all their eminence, the old gents in portraits on the wall were as flawed and human as he was. He expected too much of himself, Harvey, his AA sponsor used to scold him. Harvey's motto was "Progress, Not Perfection" And despite some setbacks, Bobby *had* made progress in the past two years. He'd done drugs on a few occasions but he hadn't had a single drink. He'd cheated on Ian but not as often or as shamelessly as he'd cheated on other boyfriends. For every compromise he'd made, running for city council, he'd done a service to his community. As chair of the Fifth District Neighborhood Association, he'd led the charge to get bikes off the street, control the proliferation of news racks, and monitor the availability of ramps and bathroom grab bars for people in wheelchairs.

Things happen for a reason, Harvey used to say. And although Bobby was hard pressed to think of a reason why his Higher Power would've taken his mother from him at the age of four, he could feel a certain symmetry, a beauty, in occasions like this where people gather in their Sunday best to celebrate love and tradition and the sheer good fortune of being alive. For all his silliness, his father *had* made an attempt to say, "No big deal, your being gay, Bobby. I still love you." And he had friends, good friends, like Vinnie who truly believed he had something special to contribute. Not to mention Ian who *knew* him, who had *lived with him* for two years, and still was ready to say in front of everyone they knew, "I love you, Bobby."

Ian winked.

Bobby felt like shit. What was wrong with him? Betraying Ian for a few lousy blow jobs from Chelsea barflies strung out on coke. Ian could have anyone he wanted. Sure, there were people—stupid people—who weren't crazy about him. But what did *they* know? They didn't know the love, the fun, he had in him. Not even his father, Cotton Mather, could scare the *joie de vivre* out of Ian.

"Champagne?" the waiter offered.

"No, thanks."

From now on—Progress, Not Perfection—Bobby resolved to try even harder to deserve Ian's love. Grabbing a bottle from a service table, he went over to Ian.

"You don't have to do that, Bobby." Ian withdrew his glass. "You're gonna piss off the waiters."

Maybe he was right.

Nathan held out his glass.

"How ya doin' Nate?" Bobby poured the wine.

"Survivin'."

He pulled his stepmother over. "Did you meet my mother?"

Mrs. Bayard held out her hand.

"Mom, this is Nathan Branche, Ian's friend from Princeton."

"Oh, a Princeton man," she cooed like a deb. "Your parents must be proud."

"Nathan's father went to Princeton," Ian told her.

"Oh." She sounded surprised.

Stupid bitch. "Mom," Bobby dragged her away, "Have you met Kate Lavery? She trains the children at City Ballet."

Far from Flora, at the far end of the table, the dinner went smoothly. Ian's mother was having a ball.

"Do you think Mark Twain sat at this very table?" she asked.

"I bet he did," Bobby said, though he doubted it. In Twain's day, the Lotos Club was in a building downtown.

Even the guys in rented tuxedoes looked happy to be there. The women lolled, two fingertips under the chin, streamlining their profiles for, say, *Town and Country*. There was a luster to everything, a warmth, a rightness; Bobby felt fine without wine or weed. Gay Kate looked lovely in her white silk pantsuit. Vinnie looked sharp in a red plaid vest. The candles on the little tree in the center of the table had lampshades like the leathery little lampshades on his grandmother's tree.

He felt downright normal.

Fuck. Who'd've thunk it? How the world had changed in a decade or two. Everybody approved of his marrying Ian. They weren't just faggots. They really belonged.

A candle blew out. Ian leaned forward, sleek as a pointer. His blond hair gleamed as he struck a match.

Bobby thought of Jackie on N Street in a photo from *Life* magazine, lighting the candles for dinner with Senator Kennedy. The grace of some people. It was a kind of miracle. Ian was a thoroughbred like Jackie. Victor was Marilyn: hot and heartbreaking. Who could blame him for dallying with Marilyn? But Ian was something much finer.

People had stopped talking. A cameraman from *Newsline* was hovering on the outskirts of the table.

"Go ahead talk. It's MOS," he said.

"What?" Gay Kate put down her spoon.

"*Mit*-out-sound."

Was he kidding?

Talking resumed. The ambassador's toast was short and funny. The reverend's toast, alas, was a sermon. Bobby felt sorry for him. "I'd like to thank the Reverend Reath," he began a quick toast of his own, "for his courage in standing up for Ian and me and everybody who gets the wrong end of the stick in this society."

The preacher looked pleasantly embarrassed.

"I was out campaigning the other day at a subway stop," Bobby went on, "And this kid, a gay kid, said to me, 'I can't believe how cool your parents are.'"

The guests chuckled.

"I said, 'I don't know about cool, but all of them—the Reverend Reath in particular—have been pretty courageous.'" He raised his glass. "To Reverend Reath."

Soon, the guests were parting.

Ian looked tipsy. Bobby put an arm around his shoulder. "How ya holdin' up?"

"All right."

"It's a long day tomorrow."

"No shit."

Bobby took Ian's glass and sniffed the vodka. Tippling too much was his only flaw. "You wanna look your best."

"Fuck you."

Time for bed. After the phone call. "I've got a favor to ask you."

"I'm meeting Nathan at the Brownstone."

"You can't."

"Just for a nightcap."

"We've got a conference call with my parents," Bobby said.

"What?"

"To my brother. In Santiago."

"I thought Michael was coming." Ian took off his tie.

"Davey has measles."

"Oh, fuck. You handle it."

"Ian."

He was pissed about something. "I'd only embarrass you."

"Don't be like that."

He took off in a huff.

"Ian!"

He was pissed about the honeymoon *still,* Bobby reckoned. Ian had agreed to Guatemala but his heart was set on Paris.

Bobby rushed after him into the lobby.

The ambassador stopped him. "Nice party."

"Yeah. Wasn't it?"

His stepmother was holding the elevator.

The phone call to Chile took forever. Davey's fever was still 101 point something. Alma was freaked. Michael had to hear every last fucking detail of the dinner he hadn't bothered to attend.

By the time Bobby said good night to his parents and made it out of the Lotos Club, the cars parked on the street were mounds of snow.

A homeless woman—a gypsy?—with a gauzy red kerchief over her head was brandishing two little children. Bobby gave her a twenty. He gave a five to a black guy in a wheelchair under the awning of Wrap-N-Run. He needn't feel guilty, he reminded himself, for having a fancy party before a wedding. But these poor Mexican guys selling flowers—and sending their pennies home to Chiapas—it wasn't right; they were working for peanuts while he was making a fortune on pharmaceuticals and Comcast. The least he could do was support the homeless shelter on Seventy-Fifth Street. And give away the espresso makers and carving knives they'd be given as wedding presents.

The Brownstone was packed. There was a long line to the coat room. Half the guys in the bar were singing along with the piano player like GIs in an MGM musical.

I've got a Yankee Doodle sweetheart
He's my Yankee Doodle joy

In the sort-of parlor of the bar, he spotted Nathan—and Ian beside him. He waved.

Ian nudged his way through the crowd.

"What a zoo."

"I can't do it," Ian blurted out.

"Fine," Bobby said. "We don't have to."

Ian looked stunned. "You're kidding."

"No. Guatemala'll be there. I'll give Vinnie and his wife the trip for Christmas."

"Bobby, no."

"Honestly, it's no problem," Bobby said. "My parents have a flat on the Rue de Grammont till the Macklins come back in February."

"That's not what I mean."

"Oh. What?"

Ian took a deep breath.

"What?"

"I can't get married," Ian said.

He was drunk. "Let's go home."

"No. I'm not kidding."

He took Ian's elbow. "This is no place to talk."

"Bobby." Ian pulled back. "I'm not drunk. I mean it."

He'd been drinking since *seven*. "Fine. Let's go talk about it."

"*No.*"

He put his arm around Ian.

"Let go of me." Ian shook free like a puppy that didn't want to be held.

"All right," Bobby said. Ian was shitfaced. "Tell me what's wrong."

"You're not listening. I *told* you," Ian said. "I just can't do it. I'm not getting married."

The shock pulled focus: two old showqueens were kicking their legs up to "The Night They Invented Champagne."

"I'm sorry," Ian said.

"Why?"

Ian dithered. "I don't know. It doesn't matter."

Good. He hadn't made up his mind. "Ian, please. Let's just go home and talk it out."

"I'm not going home," Ian said. "I'm gonna crash at Nathan's."

"Why?"

"It doesn't *matter.*"

Keep him talking. "It matters to *me*."

"What do you want me to say?" Ian clenched a fist to his forehead. "There's just something missing."

"What? Tell me."

"I don't know how to say it." He let out a sigh. "It's like you're not really *there* half the time."

"Uh-huh."

"I mean, you're like talking about Iraq or some shit in the papers, but you're not really there."

"I'm there for you."

"No, you're not. You're like hiding behind Iraq 'cause you're scared of people. Getting close to people."

Shit. It *showed*. "You think I'm a phony."

"It's like you just can't chill. You gotta get on your soapbox. You can't like just be there and relate."

He'd been found out. "What can I do?"

"Bobby, it's too late."

"We could get into therapy—couples therapy."

"Oh, please."

He was hollow. A fucking fraud. "Fine. I'll go alone."

Ian shook his head. "It's too late." He looked over to Nathan. "I gotta go."

Bobby held onto his elbow. "You can't just go. What are we gonna do? They're expecting a wedding."

"You'll think of something."

Prick. "You're not being fair."

"*I'm* not being fair?"

"What?"

"Forget it," Ian said.

"There's something else."

"You must think I'm stupid."

Oh, shit. He *knew*. "What?"

"You don't think I know you fuck around?"

"I don't fuck around."

"Bullshit."

"Maybe once or twice," Bobby said. "And it didn't mean shit."

"To *you*."

"Look, I'm sorry. I'm human."

Ian laughed.

"You *drink*."

"Fuck *you*." Ian waved his fingers as if swatting a fly.

"Ian, wait."

"I gotta go. Nathan's waiting."

Bobby felt faint. "I love you."

Ian disappeared into the crowd.

"Can I get you something?"
The waiter looked like a college student.
"No. Not right now."

How do you like to go up in a swing,
Up in the air so blue?

Someone tapped him.
"Bobby?"
He opened his eyes. "Oh, Joe."
"Are you all right? How's it goin'?"
"What are you doin' here?"
"I had a drink with a friend."
Pretend you're okay. "This is a late night for you."
"Well, you only live once," Joe said. "Or twice."
"What?"
"You look great." Joe tweaked Bobby's bow tie.
"Oh, thanks." "So do you."
"I just met Ian at the bar."
Christ. "What did he say?"
Joe smiled. "He said he was getting married tomorrow."
Hold on. "He did?"
"Yeah."
"When was that?"
"What?"
"When did you talk to him?"
"I don't know," Joe said. "Like an hour ago . . .?"
Shit.
"What? Bobby, what's wrong?"
"Oh fuck."
"Bobby, what is it?"
"I don't want to say it—out loud."
"What?"
"It's so fuckin' . . . *Twilight Zone.*"
"What is it?" Joe tried to make eye contact.
"I don't want to say it."

"Why not?"

"It'll make it . . . real."

"Okay. Take it easy," Joe said. "You want a drink?"

"We're not getting married." It was out. It was over.

"What happened?"

"He changed his mind."

"No way. Tonight?"

"Uh-huh."

"Nice timing."

The church would be full. "I am so totally fucked."

"Bobby."

"I mean, what do I do, call everybody in the morning?"

"I don't know."

"Tell them, 'Sorry. The other bridegroom suddenly realized I'm a pile of shit'?"

"Your campaign guy can put out a statement." Joe pulled out a chair. "Sit down. Let me get you a drink."

"I don't drink."

"Oh, right, right." Joe remembered. "What did he say?"

"I told you."

"No. I mean, why?"

"Is he fucking me over?"

"Yeah. What did he say?"

"He says there's 'something missing.'"

"In the relationship."

"No," Bobby said. "In me."

"What's that supposed to mean?"

"I don't *know*," Bobby threw up his hands. "We've been together two years—and it suddenly dawns on him I don't know how to 'chill.'"

"That's it?"

"I don't know how to 'relate.'" Bobby made quotation marks with his fingers. "What the fuck does he want? The Dali Lama?"

"You told him that?"

"I wish. I said, 'Fine, all right. I'll go into therapy.'"

"What did he say?"

"He fuckin' laughed at me."

Joe shivered. "That's harsh."

"We *live* together."

"You can stay with me."

"For the rest of my life? Three hundred people are coming. Not counting the press." Bobby stopped. "Oh, sorry."

"What?"

"I didn't invite you. I should've."

"No problem."

"I just thought, y'know, it might be . . . awkward."

"No problem."

"I thought about it."

Joe smiled. "One less gift to return."

"Oh Christ. The gifts."

"He doesn't know about us?"

It took a second. "Ian? Oh, no."

"Good."

"No, he's totally clueless. He just thinks—"

"What?"

"I've been fucking around a little."

"Have you?"

"Not much." Bobby scanned the crowd for Ian. "I should go talk to him."

"Why?"

"He could change his mind."

"You think?"

Not really.

"It won't be the first wedding to be canceled."

"It'll be the first gay wedding at Gramercy Presbyterian to be canceled."

"So what?"

"The Belgian ambassador sent us cufflinks. We got shirt studs from the ACLU." Bobby hit himself in the head. "There goes the election."

"No."

"I'll be a laughingstock. I should withdraw. That's it."

"Stop."

"Better to withdraw than to lose like an asshole."

"You're not an asshole."

"What'll I do?"

"You make a simple statement."

"With the rest of my life."

"For Christ's sakes, Bobby. You don't have to decide that tonight."

"No."

"You don't."

"You're right. I don't."

"Can I ask you something?" Joe grabbed the bar stool being relinquished by a poor old sot.

"What?"

"I mean, why aren't you angry?"

Bobby thought. "I'm angry."

"Yeah. At yourself. You should get angry at him."

"You think? You're right."

"Trust me," Joe said. "You'd go a little easier on yourself if you redirected your anger where it belongs."

"Right, right."

"You're not the one who should feel like shit."

"No way."

"This is not your fault," Joe said. "You're the injured party."

"Absolutely."

"He's behaving like a prick."

"A total prick," Bobby said. Then at once he felt guilty. "Oh Christ."

"What?"

"He's not really a prick."

"But he's behaving like one."

"He's just a normal guy," Bobby said.

"And you're not?"

It was hard to explain. "I agonize too much."

"He told you that? Over what?"

Bobby shrugged. "I don't know. Iraq. The minimum wage."

"Good for you. What does *he* care about?"

It took a second. "The Oscars. The daytime Emmys." Bobby laughed. "He won a fuckin' Emmy for an *Eden Heights* about Lyme disease."

"That's what I was wondering."

"What?"

"I mean, I only spoke to him for a few minutes," Joe said, "but it was hard to like picture the two of you together."

"In bed?"

"In love."

"You don't think he's charming?"

"I don't know. He's clever. "

"He's got all this energy."

"You really love him." Joe was testing.

Bobby didn't want to say it. "I was crazy about him."

"Why?"

" 'Cause he's so like . . . fun and I'm so fucked up. He wanted to go to Paris on our honeymoon. Who wouldn't? I booked this place in Guatemala."

"What's wrong with that?" Joe said.

"I don't know. I just thought, why not spend your money somewhere they need it?"

"Good for you."

"I've got too much money."

Joe laughed. "Poor baby."

"I know that sounds bad. But it's true. I'm gonna start a foundation. Y'know, a little foundation. For asylum cases."

"Cool."

"Like there's this bartender at Oscar Wilde's, Muhammed, from Egypt."

"With the buzz cut."

"Uh-huh. He's spent like thousands of dollars on lawyers—'cause like in Egypt they don't have any specifically antigay laws but they throw you in jail for 'immorality.' "

"What bullshit."

"So all the gay boys from Egypt who want to stay here have to jump through hoops to prove they're really in danger."

"That's great," Joe said. "You should do it."

"And AIDS research. I'm on this committee. I should do it full time. Fuck the city council. Look at him."

"Who?"

Bobby pointed to a Latin-American man carrying a big box of Bud to the bar. "He earns what? Five fifteen an hour. If he's lucky. And he's probably got kids at home in Mexico like losing their eyesight from malnutrition."

Joe nodded. "You're right."

Bobby spotted Basil, the manager of the Brownstone. They'd met in September to plan the wedding reception. "What is wrong with me?"

"What?"

"Why do I fucking obsess about fucking Mexicans?"

"'Cause you give a shit."

"Maybe I need Paxil."

"Stop."

"I'm so fucked up."

"No, you're not." Joe shifted his chair around. "Look at them."

"Who?"

"All these faggy assholes in Kenneth Cole. What do *they* obsess about?"

"Their abs," Bobby said. "Their glutes. And their fuckin' shares on Fire Island."

"Fuck Ian. Say it."

Bobby tried it. "Fuck Ian."

"Say it like you mean it."

Bobby laughed. "Fuck Ian."

"That's better."

"Fuck the whole fuckin' bunch of these selfish queers."

"How do you feel?"

It sort of worked. "Not bad."

"Good," Joe said. "Now I've got a message for you."

"From who?"

"Gopal."

"Gopal?"

"He says he knows how much you love him."

Bobby gripped the bar. "What the hell are you talking about?"

"I don't really know."

"Are you tripping?"

"I don't know." Joe looked bewildered. "I saw him. At the bar."

"Shit. You're scarin' me."

"Sorry. I know. It seemed so real."

"What the hell are you on?"

"Just a little Valium—"

"What?"

"And a couple vodkas."

"What did he say?"

Joe leaned in. "He said he knew how much you loved him."

"Jesus Christ."

"What?"

Bobby laughed. "You're fuckin' insane."

"I know."

"I'm not kidding."

"I know."

"I dream about him," Bobby said. "He is on my old Schwinn with the pinochle cards stuck in the spokes."

"I did that too."

"Or he's on Fifty-Seventh. By ICM. Waiting for me to come out with an agent and a theater all lined up."

"I've been trying to get him *something*," Joe said. "I've contacted every agent and theater in town."

Bobby'd forgotten. "That's so great of you to be doing all that. I should be helping you."

"No, no, you've been busy."

Bobby shook his head in admiration. "You're really something."

"Well, thanks," Joe said.

No one spoke for a second.

"Remember, back in March?" Joe said. "When we got together . . ."

"Right, right."

"And I told you about that story I was writing."

What story? "Uh-huh."

"I got it published. In *The New Yorker.*"

"Wow."

"You were so understanding when I talked about my work. We shoulda stayed in touch."

He was flirting. "Uh-huh."

"What happened?"

"I don't know," Bobby said.

"I think we both got scared."

He had a pretty good body. "I guess."

"You were starting the campaign."

And he fucked like a teenager. "I had a lot on my plate."

Joe smiled. "Remember that Hispanic lady?"

"Who?"

"Selling flowers. On Central Park West. She had them all mixed up together. They looked like shit. No one was buying."

"Oh right, right."

"You don't remember at all." Joe laughed.

"I was so fuckin' high."

"We bought the whole lot. And put all the red ones together and the white ones together, and gave 'em back to her."

Now he remembered. "She thought we were crazy."

"I saw her last week. She's got a shopping cart now. She's making a fortune."

"No way."

"We should do it again."

"*Flores por los muertos.*"

"We should do everything again." Joe looked Bobby in the eye. "The whole weekend."

Bobby thought of Victor. "Right."

"It's worth a shot? Don't you think?"

Victor was cuter. "I don't know."

"Why not?"

"I met somebody."

Joe froze. "Who? You were getting married."

"That's why I dropped him."

"Uh-huh."

"He's a nurse at New York/Cornell. He's the union rep for the nurses."

"Do you love him?"

Yes. And no. "He's a pisser." Bobby grinned. "One night this resident tells him, 'Victor, take this lady upstairs and get her an MRI.' Victor's like, 'Sorry, Doctor, I can't do that. She's got a pacemaker. She'll explode.' He saved her life."

Joe looked at his watch. "It's late."

"You're mad at me."

"I've got an eight a.m."

"Don't be mad. I'm doing you a favor."

"And why is that?"

"It wouldn't work. I mean, it would be good for me," Bobby said, "but it wouldn't work."

"Why not?"

"You're a shrink. You'd see right through me."

"So, what would I see?"

Bobby shrugged.

"Come on. What would I see?"

With his thumb and an index finger, Bobby made a zero.

Joe got it. "You're an empty shell. We all feel like that."

"Yeah, right."

"Honestly. *I* do."

"Why?" Bobby pleaded. "Why does everybody feel like shit?"

Joe waved his hand around the bar. "Because for each one of us getting shitfaced in here, there are like ten Mexican guys sweeping up some deli on the corner for not *even* five dollars an hour, so we can throw around money and pick up strangers to distract us from how guilty we feel that all these Mexicans are out there delivering pizzas in the snow."

"You think other people feel that way?" Bobby brightened.

"We pretend not to see them."

"But we do."

"And we don't do shit. That's what my story's about."

Bobby objected. "You do shit."

"For rich people with migraines."

Bobby laughed. "Me too."

"What's that?"

Joe was pointing to his dick.

Jesus Christ. "I'm getting hard." Bobby couldn't believe it.

"You *are* hard." Joe touched his pants.

"Don't do that. I'll come."

Joe laughed. "Does this guilty liberal shit always make you hard?"

Bobby adjusted himself. "It never happened before."

"You're in love with me," Joe said.

"Yeah, right."

"You *are.* Universal health insurance," Joe whispered in a sexy voice.

"Stop."

"Human rights," he cooed.

"Stop." Bobby laughed.

"That's love right there." Joe touched his dick again, "When your *heart* gets hard."

"Enough!" He could be right.

"We'd better go before you blow it." Joe got up.

Why not?

Joe handed Bobby his coat. "You know what I do when I'm in danger of coming too soon?"

"What?" Bobby held the coat in front of his crotch as they headed for the door.

"I think of Barbara Bush."

Bobby laughed. "That's terrible."

"It never fails."

"I say the alphabet backward." Bobby concentrated. "Z, Y, X . . . W . . . V . . . U . . . T . . . S . . . R . . . Q . . . P . . . O . . . N, M . . . L . . . K . . . J . . . I . . . H . . . G . . . F, E . . . D, C, B, A." He opened his eyes.

"Better?"

"Barely."

Joe brushed past a Christmas tree as they squeezed into the foyer. "Don't worry about anything. I'll get you up in the morning."

Oh, shit, Bobby remembered: the wedding.

The cars and newspaper kiosks were covered with snow.

"Let's go to my place."

The cold and the Christmas lights and a big white sheepdog sleeping in the snow were real; the wedding wasn't.

"I must be crazy."

"You think?" Joe was smiling.

He didn't look half bad.

Farewell, My Lover

Maybe you know this joke:

What's Irish Alzheimer's?
You forget everything but the grudge.

If you're Irish, I hope you're laughing. If you're not, let me explain.

Despite their reputation as affable rascals, the Irish are seldom willing to forgive and forget. Every slight, rebuff, betrayal is kept on file. And the file is never closed. The accused may never know the charges against him. The slate can never be wiped clean.

My mother, for example, held grudges against three of her five sisters, most of her neighbors, several priests, and innumerable nuns till the day she died. Her sister Sheila was high up on her shitlist for having seated her at a table near the kitchen at her daughter's wedding. Her sister, Maeve, was on the outs for divorcing a doctor. Catherine's crime was revealing to the family back in Ireland that my brother was wait-listed for Georgetown.

My father, who had very few friends and no close relatives at all in this country, maintained a blacklist of public figures as long and peculiar as J. Edgar Hoover's. No amount of postpresidential good works could pardon Jimmy Carter for opposing Edward Kennedy in the 1980 primaries. Not even the most reverent rendition of "Danny Boy" on *The Mike Douglas Show* could excuse Sammy Davis Jr. for hugging a Republican, Dick Nixon. What my father had against Bob Cousy, David Brinkley, Lee Iacocca, and Maya Angelou, I'll never know.

My own grudges, I used to think, were few, well-founded, and not too intemperately cherished. Who wouldn't be mad at a brother for picking a college roommate to be his best man? Who wouldn't be pissed at a boyfriend for coming an hour late to his fortieth birthday party?

The truth is, I'm unforgiving as any IRA Provo. I can remember the face of a stranger—he looked like Peking Man—who cut ahead of me in line for a Joe Cocker concert in 1978. I remember a woman in a fur-trimmed brocade jacket who balked at my apology when I sneezed in her direction at La Goulue on Valentine's Day, 1986. (It was the first time I met Bucky's, my lover's, parents. They weren't much more agreeable than she was.)

The more painful the wound, the more I pick at the scab. The most painful wounds are the wounds from high school. (Ring a bell?) In senior year, I ran for student council. I came in one morning to find the word "fag" scrawled across every poster I'd put up in the hall. I tore them down. I never put up others. I had no doubt who'd done it: Steve Stockton, the ballplaying boyfriend of my opponent, Carla Witmer. I knew how to get him back. I was going to tell Carla—he was crazy about her—that I'd seen Steve necking with Susie Humm at the Riverhead Drive-In.

I never took my revenge. Why? As the multimillionaire Mr. Hackensacker (Rudy Vallee) says in *The Palm Beach Story,* "It is one of the tragedies of this life that the men most in need of a beating are invariably enormous."

Moreover, revenge gives only momentary satisfaction. A grudge, like a rawhide dog chew, provides months and years of delicious gnawing.

Justice is fleeting. Bitterness abides.

Revenge is vulgar. A grudge is genteel. A grudge provides the kind of sly, luxurious pleasure Sir Anthony Blunt enjoyed, tutoring the Queen on the merits of her Titians, while slipping the Soviets the intelligence to swipe her throne. Had the Russians taken Windsor Castle, Blunt would have won the day and lost his raison d'être.

Living well may be the best revenge. (Whatever that means.) But a grudge is its own reward.

The only time I made the mistake of avenging a blow to my honor—until this year, that is—I had to do it in self-defense. Mr.

Masters, the history teacher I had for both terms of eleventh grade, was a short, round drunk who spent most mornings with his head in his hands, recuperating from the night before. On the odd day when he was chipper, he'd laugh at the wisecracks I made at the expense of our sententious history book. On bad days, he'd explode, "Moore, I'm gonna hang you from the light fixture." At the end of the first term, he gave me a C.

I'd never gotten a C before. Action was called for. But I needed evidence. Our homework papers—Masters never read a word of them— were returned with *Good* or *Fair* or *Carry On!* written at the top. On every paper I turned in during the second term, I slipped this sentence into a paragraph: "When you get to this sentence, please circle it, just to show me you've read the paper."

In June, when grades were due, I showed him the pile of homework assignments he'd returned to me. Never once had he circled the sentence. I told him that if I got anything less than an A this term, I'd show the papers to the principal.

Needless to say, I got an A. I should have been proud of my chutzpah and cunning. I mean, after all, he was grading arbitrarily as a chimp and fucking up my chances of getting into Yale. But the look on his face—he crumpled like a murderer on Perry Mason's witness stand—soured me on revenge for years to come.

The next time I took justice into my own hands, it was a quarter century later and I had a real crime to make somebody pay for. The night it happened—the crime, that is—Bucky and I were on our way home from an opening at the art gallery we ran together. We were talking about the trip to Hawaii we were going to take after Christmas.

Bucky was a little drunk. "The 'big island' is Maui," he insisted.

"Bullshit."

"It's huge."

"The 'big island' is Hawaii," I said. "That's why they call it the big island: so you don't get confused."

Cesar, our young art handler, came running up to us with a plate wrapped in tinfoil. "You forgot the brie."

"I thought they ate everything," I said.

"Keep it," Bucky told him.

"You're sure?"

"We're fat enough."

As Cesar took off, I spotted a poster for the Winter Antiques Show in the window of a supermarket. "Hang on, Buck." We still hadn't decided what we were going to put in our booth at the show.

The rest of what happened I saw out of the corner of my eye.

A big guy with curly hair—he had on a cashmere coat—he looked like a Wall Street trader—had stopped in front of Sergio's to light a cigarette. (Sergio's is this restaurant on Lex that only mobsters and kids from Long Island would ever be caught dead in.)

This homeless guy with a scraggly beard and a purple parka came up to the big guy and asked for change. The big guy got pissed. "Fuck you."

Next thing I know the big guy is asking Bucky if he's got a match.

"Yeah, I do. Somewhere." Bucky reached in his pocket.

The big guy got impatient. "Forget it."

"I got plenty. Back at my place." Bucky must've winked at him or something.

"Fuck you, faggot." The big guy hit him in the jaw.

There was ice on the ground. Bucky slid. He hit his head on a big cement flowerpot in front of the restaurant.

The big guy took off. Everybody took off.

The maître d' came out. "Give him a second. He'll be all right."

Bucky was out cold. The cops got there before the ambulance.

"He just hit him?" this young cop seemed skeptical.

"Yeah."

"What did he say?"

"He said, 'Fuck you, faggot.'"

"That's it? Just out of nowhere?"

"No. I mean, he asked Bucky for a match. Bucky kinda . . . joked."

"What did he look like?"

"I don't know. Black hair. Kinda curly. Big guy. Maybe thirty, thirty-five."

"What was he wearing?"

"A black topcoat. Cashmere, I think."

"Were there any witnesses?

I looked around. "There were. People waiting to get into the restaurant." Then I remembered. "And this homeless guy."

The paramedics could tell right away: Bucky's neck was broken.

In the emergency room, Bucky came to. He was in terrible pain but they wouldn't give him a painkiller. They had to wait to see if he had all his faculties.

Dr. Butarbutar asked him his name.

"Jim Roebuck."

"How old are you?"

"How old do I look?"

Butarbutar was not amused. "You don't know your age?"

Bucky winced. "I'm forty-four."

Butarbutar seemed satisfied. Bucky was moving his fingers and toes.

They let me wait with him in his cubicle. He didn't remember a thing.

"If you told me I'd been hit by a car, I'd believe you."

Dr. Butarbutar said not to worry. It was typical of trauma.

They left us there for hours. Once in a while, Butarbutar would peek his head in. "How is Mr. Roebuck?"

"He's in terrible pain."

Butarbutar seemed pleased. It meant Bucky wasn't paralyzed. "I get you the CAT scan," he told us as he took off.

"Do I look like shit?"

"No, no," I told him. It was true. He just looked sleepy.

"I think there's gook in my mustache."

I brushed his mustache with a tissue. "You're fine."

The one person I liked on the whole fucking staff was this gay nurse, Victor, who kept an eye on Bucky. It was lucky Victor popped his head in when Butarbutar was assessing Bucky's mental state.

"How are you doing?" Butarbutar took a pen from his pocket.

"Fine," Bucky said in his lockjawed Kate Hepburn voice. "I'd like another gimlet."

"What?"

"A gin gimlet. And some more of those warm nuts."

Butarbutar looked worried. He wrote something down. "You do know where you're at?"

"We're in first class. On our way to Nairobi to see Humphrey and Mr. Huston."

Butarbutar pulled me aside. "If the hallucinations continue . . ."

"He's just joking," Victor broke in.

I seconded the opinion.

Butarbutar wasn't satisfied. "I continue to observe."

Two male nurses pulled back the curtain. They had to slip some kind of a mat under Bucky to heave him onto a stretcher.

In the X-ray room, they had to lift him off the stretcher and slip him into the CAT scan machine. They put this silver blanket on him. He looked like a baked potato in a big toaster oven.

"You should go home. This could take hours," he told me.

"What am I gonna do at home?"

They got me out of the room. I watched through the glass.

"Want one?" The radiologist had a bag of onion rings.

"No, thanks."

They read the scan right away. Bucky'd fractured three vertebrae but his spine was untouched—except for a tiny splinter.

Back downstairs to the observation room. I hear this beeping. It's Bucky's cell phone.

I got it from his coat. "Hello?"

Bucky said, "Who is it?"

I couldn't believe it.

"Who is it?"

"It's Verizon. You can get twenty percent off your monthly rate if you sign up another customer."

"Let me speak to him."

I put the phone to his head. "It's Tanya."

"Hello, Tanya."

She must have resumed her pitch.

"What are you wearing?"

That's when Dr. Ho came in. I hung up.

"How are you feeling?" he asked Bucky.

"I could use an enormous Darvon or something."

"It's on the way. I can operate on Tuesday, if that's okay with you."

"Not till Tuesday?" I said.

"Who are you?"

"I'm Bucky's partner. And medical proxy."

He looked us over. He'd met queers before. "Oh." He took an X-ray out of an envelope and clipped it to Bucky's chart. "This is what we're going to do. We're going to remove the tiny bone fragment from the spine. And then we'll fuse C-four, C-five, and C-six."

"Uh-huh."

"We'll put in two plates to straddle the lateral masses bilaterally."

"He should be an art critic," Bucky said when he left.

I tried to get him a room of his own. There was nothing. They stuck him in Neurology with three other patients. This poor old guy with his head bandaged and his bony ass sticking out that kind-of apron-thing they make you wear in the hospital kept inching by, pushing his walker.

"I'll get you out of here."

"No, I'm all right."

A nurse hunched down beside him, feeding him soup through a bent plastic straw. "*Little* sips."

"What do you want from home?"

He couldn't move his head. He couldn't read. He had to pee into a plastic bottle. "I don't know. My toothbrush?"

"I'll get your shaving kit."

"How 'bout my Walkman?"

"Right."

"Gimme a kiss," he said.

The nurse looked disgusted.

"I'll be right back."

It was freezing outside. I couldn't find a cab. I had to walk home. I called the gallery. I called my travel agent: so much for Hawaii.

On the corner, near my apartment building, there's a flower shop. I asked Dimitri, the florist, for a dozen red roses. I'd be back in fifteen minutes with a vase.

I grabbed Bucky's razor and toothbrush and shaving kit. I looked in his bureau for his Walkman. No luck. I checked his closet. Way in the back, on the floor with his broken umbrellas, was a gay guide to Europe with an envelope sticking out of it.

The envelope had Hotel Wales written on it. It's this little hotel on Lex where Bucky and I put up our parents when they come to town. Inside the envelope was a pipe cleaner and half a dozen Polaroids—pictures of Bucky, naked, in a bed, on a sofa, in a bathtub.

I hadn't taken the pictures.

In one picture, he had no mustache—it had to have been taken two years earlier, when he shaved off his mustache for a day or two. This other picture had been taken recently. He was wearing the reading glasses I'd just given him for his birthday. Each picture had a little lame witticism printed by hand on the back: "The mind is a terrible thing to waste"; "Playgirl's Man for November"; "The love that dare not speak its name."

On my way back to the hospital, I heard Dimitri shouting, "Mr. Moore. The roses!"

I pretended not to hear.

My cell phone rang. It was Doctor Ho, telling me to hurry.

By the time I got there, Bucky was dead.

"Yeah, right." I didn't believe it. I pulled back the curtain. The bed was empty.

Ho took me down to Intensive Care.

Bucky lay there, eyes closed, a sheet up to his neck. He'd vomited the painkillers and the soup and the hors d'oeuvres we'd had at the opening, the night before. He'd choked on his vomit—he couldn't move his head—and suffocated.

Dmitri caught me as I crossed to my building. "Mr. Moore!" He handed me the roses.

I gave him two twenties.

"Stay. I bring the change."

I stuck the roses in the back of a stroller when the nanny wasn't looking.

The police did their best. They showed me mug shots: the guys didn't look much like Bucky's killer. They had a sketch artist do a composite. Detective Manfredi—he looked like a bulldog—and his puppy partner, Detective Beard, took me for a ride in their patrol car. They promised to do all they could, and to keep in touch, but they didn't sound hopeful.

I dreaded the funeral. I'd never been to Alabama. Freddy, the manager of the gallery, went with me. I wouldn't have made it through without him.

There was this long cortege of black limousines. Freddy and I weren't assigned a limo. We followed along in our rented Lexus.

Temple Beth Or is this fifties-modern thing right near the Montgomery Country Club. Mrs. Roebuck wouldn't look at me. Mr. Roebuck had to sneak away from her to say, "I know what you're going through."

"She hates me."

"Why?" Freddy asked.

"Well, first off, she's pissed that *The Times* listed me as Bucky's survivor."

"Fuck that."

"Not to mention the will. The only thing Bucky left them was an oil painting by Ida O'Keeffe."

"Ouch."

"Not to mention the insurance. And the wrongful death suit. They'll get zip."

"You're suing the hospital?"

"They came to me. The next day. They want to settle before it hits the papers."

"Shit. You're rich."

I was going to be. You'd think it would soften the blow a little. It only made things worse. I didn't go to the gallery. I didn't see friends. I did nothing but pee, stick my glass in the ice machine, pour the scotch, and wonder who Bucky'd been fucking.

I couldn't sleep for more than a few hours. I kept having these awful dreams. We were at a carnival, out in the Pines, I think. It was time for our knife-throwing act. Bucky was strapped to a wheel.

"Go ahead," he'd insist.

"I can't."

"Just do it."

"I'll hit you."

"I'm *dead*."

"You're not dead."

"Throw it!"

I'd wake up before it hit.

Back in New York, on the day of Bucky's memorial service, I took the Polaroids to the gallery. I compared the writing on the back with the writing of the guy I suspected—Cesar. Bucky had hired him when I was in Houston. He had no experience. He was just this cute art major from Hunter. The handwriting looked very similar.

I didn't lift a finger to plan the memorial. Freddy did everything. Bucky's last show of landscapes by Alfred Thompson Bircher and his Hudson River School friends still hung on the walls. The whole place was crowded with little round tables. There was a buffet on the receptionist's desk. Cesar and Freddy had rolled over a baby grand piano from the Romanian consulate next door. The piano stayed shut—it was like this big coffin—till lunch was over. When the waiters began serving coffee, some guy in a navy blazer played songs by Stephen Foster and Richard Rodgers.

"Hang in there, handsome."

It was Bob Russert, the good-natured fop: he used to edit *Art and Auction*. He was on a cane.

"Where's Buster?"

"You didn't hear?"

"Oh no."

He nodded. "I had to put him down."

"Oh, I'm sorry."

"It was just one tumor after another. No word from the cops?"

"Oh. No."

"Any leads?"

"Not really. How you getting home?"

"I've got a car waiting," he said.

"Good."

"You hang in there."

"I will." I smiled, though it pissed me off that the really old people were now treating me like one of their own.

I didn't feel old. Not until Bucky died, anyway. I still had a chin and a good head of hair.

"You need an opinion on something, you call me," said Wallace Burns, the art consultant.

"Thanks." Why did everyone presume I needed help?

I had started the business myself, and had made a pretty big fucking success of it, almost a decade before I met Bucky. Granted, in recent years, Bucky may have been the more visible partner. He brought in the ladies from Houston with their diamond brooches and the Wall Street barons with their soft black briefcases. He was a good old boy—a good old gay Jewish boy—hearty with men, naughty with women.

"You work too fuckin' hard. Live a little. It's only money." He'd press the husbands.

"Oh, buy it, honey. You've lost weight, haven't you? You look fabulous. Don't tell me you don't deserve it." He'd flatter the wives.

In the photo of him that Freddy had placed on a Sheraton candlestand, he looked like Hemingway, with a woolen tie and a woolly mustache.

"I've got an idea."

It was Mike Kassegian, a rival dealer. In his puffy gray down coat, he looked like a walrus.

"Uh-huh?"

"Amanda Shetterly."

"Who?"

"From Phillips."

"Oh. Right."

"She'd be perfect. And believe me, she's ready."

"For what?"

"Replacing Bucky."

"Oh."

Fuck you. What was the rush? I had learned everything Bucky had to teach me about painting. I'd written catalog essays on John William Hill and William Merritt Chase. (Bucky had never dared write about my specialty, American decorative arts.) In terms of sales, my federal tables and Wedgwood vases and silver soup tureens brought in just as much money as Bucky's Bierstadts and Currans and Cassatts. I had the respect of every significant curator in the country's most important museums. And I was a much better businessman than Bucky, who had squandered hundreds of thousands of dollars, buying second-rate works by first-rate painters, giving discounts to friends, publishing expensive catalogs of mediocre shows, and lavishing luncheons and parties, raises and bonuses, on the people now mourning his passing.

"How ya holdin' up?"

"Oh, fine."

My sister, Colleen, had yet another hairdo: this time, it was frizz to frame her face. She had driven in from Long Island with her husband, Donnie.

"You want a fruit basket? Drop by later. I've got like dozens in my apartment."

"You *are* coming for Christmas?" She looked concerned.

"Uh-huh."

"How's the show doing?"

"Pretty well. Lots of red dots."

"What are red dots?" Donnie asked.

"Look on the cards beside the pictures," Colleen pointed. "The red dot means 'sold.'"

The show *was* selling well. It would be enough to keep the gallery going another couple months. But the show to follow this one—Bucky's exhibit of plein air sketches by California "impressionists"—was ill-conceived. The only collectors tempted to buy a painting of a peacock by Jessie Botke or a landscape by Maurice Braun were the Californians who'd never recovered from the dot.com bust.

"I gotta go, Neil." Someone clasped an arm around my shoulder. "It's a blizzard out there."

It was Morris Sumner, the dealer who'd given me my first job in the business. He looked extraterrestrial; he'd had some more work done; his baggy eyes were now sleek as rose petals.

"Thanks for coming."

Sumner squeezed harder. "You take it easy."

"I will."

He grabbed my other shoulder and looked me straight in the eye. "Call me."

What did they want me to do? Throw in the towel? Work for Christie's or Sotheby's?

Of course, there's a lot less pressure, working for an auction house. You can pull down a nice fat paycheck without worrying about the rent or the payroll or where your next Winslow Homer is coming from. But you have to travel—all the time—to do appraisals. And you can't do shows of little-known silversmiths or genre painters you've discovered—rediscovered—yourself. You have to play ball with your colleagues, jockey for attention, suck up to the brass. And once your name is off the door, people forget you.

"Remember Phuket?"

"Oh, yeah."

My doctor, Louise Feinberg, had brought photos of the trip she and her husband had taken to Thailand with Bucky and me almost ten years ago. "I look like a pig."

"You were pregnant."

"You look like Gardner McKay."

"Who?"

"*You* remember: that TV show, *Adventures in Paradise.*"

"Oh. Yeah."

"You should exercise," she said.

"I know."

"For mood, I mean."

"What's wrong with my mood?"

"Nothing. I just mean, it won't be easy." She'd lost her husband. "It took me years."

I gave her a hug.

"You should come in and see me. How's the blood pressure?"

"I feel all right."

"I'm gonna call you." She handed me the photos.

The pictures were blurry: Bucky, bowing and squinting like Katharine Hepburn in *Dragonseed* on the steps of a Buddhist temple; Bucky steering our canoe through a dimly lit sea cave. We looked happy together. But I couldn't help wondering, was he screwing a bellboy while I was out snorkeling with the Feinbergs?

"How do you like him?"

"Sorry?"

Cesar—fuck him—looked terribly cute in his four-button suit and spiky hairdo. "Ain't he slammin'?"

"Who?"

"The piano player," Cesar pointed.

"Oh, he's great."

"You want to meet him?"

"Not now. Where'd you find him?"

"He works at the Brownstone."

"You go to the Brownstone?" It wasn't exactly a hip downtown bar.

Cesar shrugged. "I crack a brew on my way home from work."

"Oh. Where do you live?"

"Chelsea."

"Isn't that expensive?"

"I've got four roommates."

"Oh."

With four roomates, he and Bucky would have had to go to a hotel.

"He's a singer too, Emmett."

"Oh, is he?"

"He's like totally ruthless on all that old shit."

I reached into my pocket for an envelope. "You know what's in this?"

"What?"

I hoped he'd think it was the photographs. "Guess."

"What?"

"*Guess.*"

He looked nervous. "I don't know."

I gave him the envelope. "Can you slip this to Emmett? I don't want to forget to pay him."

"Oh. No problem." Cesar took off.

"Neil."

"Uh-huh?"

Freddy looked concerned. "Check out the snow."

"Oh. Wow." It was still coming down.

"People are leaving."

"It's been two hours."

"Don't you want to say something?"

"No. I've spoken to everyone."

"Still," Freddy insisted.

"What?"

"I just mean, you could say 'Thanks for coming.' Something like that."

It didn't really seem necessary. "I'd rather not."

"People are expecting it."

"No, they're not."

"They want to say things too."

Group therapy. "I hate that."

"You want me to get the ball rolling?"

"I don't know."

He wouldn't let up. "I can do it."

"No. Shit." I gave in. "I'd better do it."

The piano player let his tune waft away before lifting his foot from the pedal.

I stood by the piano. "Excuse me."

They put down their forks. They screwed their necks round all at once, like blackbirds.

"I just wanted to thank you all for coming. And for being such good friends to Bucky and me for so many years."

They wanted more.

"He packed a lot of life into his forty-four years."

"Hear, hear." Someone clinked a glass.

"If anyone would like to say a word or two, well, I imagine Bucky wouldn't object to a little gossip."

They laughed.

"I was on the elevator in the St. Regis, the first time I met Bucky." This collector from Goldman Sachs, Roberta Siegel, started the ball rolling. "We'd both been at the same wedding but we hadn't met. He introduced himself. I said, 'My name is Roberta, but my friends call me Robin.' 'Why, honey,' he said, 'do you have a red breast?'"

The funny stories I enjoyed. The stories about Bucky, The Large-hearted, I could barely muster a smile for. Only that morning, I'd discovered in a cubbyhole of Bucky's desk yet another thick roll of unpaid bills. (The desk itself—by Philadelphia architect, Frank Furness—Bucky was several payments behind on to the Westchester Hunt Club.)

"He picked up the check for every lunch," a pretty curator from the Amon Carter recalled. "He paid for every cab. Did you ever take the subway with him? We were going to the Brooklyn Museum to see the Rembrandt Peale show. He insisted on using his Metrocard to pay for me."

Bucky, the chef. Bucky, the dancer. Bucky, the Katharine Hepburn stalker. He was a "character" to them. They loved him. But they didn't really know him. They didn't know the pain his mother caused him with her pamphlets from Parents for Morality, offering to make him a happy ex-homosexual. They didn't know the fear he felt, trying to hold his own on any subject other than painting. They didn't know how much effort—how much blood, sweat, and tears—went into that Bucky joie de vivre. He'd come home from a gala like a soldier stunned by a raid in which he'd lost several of his comrades. Stretching out on the couch with a Kool and a martini, he'd watch the Discovery Channel: giraffes, hyenas, leopards: how peaceful the Serengeti seemed after Sotheby's.

Colleen was the last to speak. In her clingy acrylic pantsuit, she looked like a waitress. "The last time I saw Bucky, I asked him, 'Bucky, what's the secret of *your* marriage? I mean, Donnie and I, well, we're stuck with each other.'"

Donnie didn't looked pleased.

"Bucky said, 'I don't know: love? I just love the guy.'"

It was my cue to cry. Or not cry bravely.

"Thank you all for coming." I got up and put my arm around Colleen. "Look at the snow. We better get rolling before we all get snowed in."

When I was a little boy, seven or eight, I used to come home from school for lunch with my older brother and sister. My father worked for the city. He came home for lunch too. We'd start on our sandwiches as my mother let the soup cool a little before pouring it into our bowls.

One day, the doorbell rang. There was a telegram. I knew what that meant. Somebody had died in Ireland—one of our dozens of distant relatives. This time, as she returned with the telegram, my mother did not look relieved. My father took the telegram from her hand. She reached for the pot to refill our bowls.

"What is it, Daddy?"

Colleen said, "Ssssh."

No one said a word as my mother portioned out the last of the chicken noodle and put the pot in the sink. "I'll be right down." She headed upstairs.

"Daddy."

"It's your grandfather," he explained. "Your mother's father."

We'd never met him.

"Shouldn't you go up?" I said.

"I'll give her a few minutes."

The lesson? Don't let 'em catch you crying. Better yet, don't cry.

I learned. I don't. Chances are, I wouldn't have cried at Bucky's memorial, even if he hadn't been unfaithful.

I stayed on at the gallery after the service. By the time I'd signed the paychecks and locked up, the sun was setting. The brass poles of the canopies on Park could've blinded you with glare. Cesar insisted on coming along with Freddy and me to carry the photos of Bucky and a few little gifts people had brought me.

Cesar had always been obliging. He hauled paintings in and out of the inventory room as fast as you could say John Singleton Copley.

The sideboards and secretaries he packed for shipping could have survived a shipwreck without a scratch. The youngest on the staff, he was the first one we all turned to when our computers went on the fritz. But walking the boss home—this was beyond the call of duty. Maybe he felt guilty.

One by one, he dissed his roommates. One girl made mosaic portraits of dogs and cats out of styrofoam packing peanuts. She dyed the peanuts in milk cartons and then stuck them to the canvas with dabs of Crazy Glue.

I tried to picture Cesar in bed with Bucky. Filipino, he had beautiful skin; he glowed like a chestnut.

"We can take it from here," I said when we reached my building.

Freddy took the stuff from Cesar's hands.

"I'm really sorry about Mr. Roebuck," Cesar said.

I was still in a shitty mood, but I managed, "Thanks."

Upstairs, Freddy tried to snap me out of it. "Nobody is *saying* you can't run the gallery without Bucky. They just want to help you."

"They think I need help."

"Everybody needs help," Freddy said.

"I should close the place."

"I know what *you* need." He reached into his backpack.

"What?"

He held up a little hash pipe. "It's time you got stoned."

"Oh, Christ."

The dope helped. We talked about Bucky as if he were away on vacation.

Freddy remembered a show of paintings by Marsden Hartley that Bucky had taken pride in.

"My Favorite Marsden," I said.

"What?"

"That's what he wanted to call it."

"Did he?" Freddy looked in his wallet. "He never told me that. I've got the review."

"You're kidding."

He looked in every compartment of his wallet. "From *The Observer*."

"Let me see."

He couldn't find it. But he remembered the typo Bucky loved. "Don't miss the photos of Hartley and his circle in the latrine by the receptionist's desk."

"*Vitrine,* she meant."

"I know," Freddy said. "But what a dweeb. Why couldn't she just say 'cabinet'?"

"Bucky sent it to *The New Yorker.*"

"Did he?"

"Yeah," I said. "And they printed it—with his title: East Side Galleries Hard Pressed for Exhibition Space."

Toking on the pipe, Freddy almost choked.

I got him a glass of water.

Freddy calmed you down and cheered you up; he was so good-natured, you had to love the guy. He could solve any problem: find fresh leis for a Hawaiian party; fix a CD player; make salad dressing out of vinegar and thin air. He not only managed the gallery; he managed just about everything Bucky and I did for fun in the Pines or for charity in the city. And yet he had his own life, his own hyperactive sex life, with pals on the Net and twenty-something young studs in the bars. He was quite the stud himself, bald and muscular. On the worst days at work, Bucky and I got a laugh, a vicarious kick, out of his latest fling with a cop or a chorus boy he'd met at Splash.

"I don't know what I'd do without you," I said, apropos of nothing. (I was pretty stoned.)

"Bullshit. Look at all the other friends you've got."

He was talking about the bouquets—the apartment was full of them. Half of them I hadn't even opened yet. The dining room table was crowded with fruit baskets wrapped in that weird yellow cellophane.

"Take a couple fruit baskets when you leave," I told him.

"You should give 'em to the homeless."

I meant to do something.

"They've got a soup kitchen at St. George's," he said.

"Where?"

"On Second Avenue. We could take all this shit to them."

"In the snow?"

Freddy was undaunted. "You got a wagon?"

I did—a housewarming present, too big to fit through the gates to the house in the Pines. "Maybe tomorrow."

"I can do it." Freddy got up.

"I'll go with you tomorrow."

"Tomorrow's Christmas Eve. I can do it myself."

I was feeling a bit better. "No, I'll go with you."

We brought up the wagon from the basement. Loading the wagon reminded me of summer on Fire Island. A bag in each hand, Bucky would come out of the Pantry in the Pines: "You won't believe who I met at the meat counter."

Freddy held up the hash pipe. "Let's knock this off before we go."

"Okay." We stepped back into the hallway.

"You got a pipe cleaner? This thing is clogged."

I turned.

"Wait. I think I've got a box." He grabbed his backpack. He opened a little pouch and pulled out a thin box of pipe cleaners.

I didn't want to believe it.

I picked up the backpack. There was a label hanging on it from a plane trip. *Frederick Agee, 175 Thompson Street, NY, NY* was printed by hand. It looked just like the writing on the Polaroids.

"I gotta pee."

"Neil?"

I ran to the bathroom.

"Are you all right?"

I was gonna throw up. "Yeah. Gimme a second."

"Don't worry. It's just the hash."

I should explain something. When I was a little boy, like many an Irish Catholic boy, I wanted to be a priest. Years later, I found out that the other boys I thought were my friends were comparing pricks and whacking off together and having all kinds of unholy fun I wasn't included in. There was something wrong with me, I couldn't help feeling. Not even my closest friends—not even Freddy—were friends at all.

I'd had enough. "Bucky told me everything."

"What?"

"About the two of you."

Freddy stonewalled. "What?"

"He showed me the pictures."

"Of what?"

"The Hotel Wales."

That got him. "Oh."

"Yeah. 'Oh.'"

"It was nothing. Honestly."

"Uh-huh."

"It just kinda happened."

"In a hotel."

"We'd just seen off his parents. He was feeling like shit. You know what parents are like."

"Right."

"He made too much of it." Freddy shook his head. "He would never have left you."

But he was *thinking about it?*

I'm afraid I wailed. "Oh, God. Oh, God."

"Neil. Please. It was nothing."

I pushed him away. "Leave me alone."

The intercom rang.

"I'm not home. Whoever it is."

Freddy got it. "It's your sister. She's coming up."

"Go."

"No. Let me get you a soda or something."

"*Go.*"

He looked around for his backpack. "You'll be all right?"

"Just go."

I was sitting on the edge of the bathtub when Colleen arrived.

"What's wrong with *you?*"

I was too embarrassed to tell her.

She sat down next to me. "I miss Bucky too."

"I'll be okay."

"Come home with Donnie and me."

God forbid. "Not tonight."

She put her hand on my hand. We sat for a while.

"I don't want *all* those fruit baskets," she said.

"Oh. They're not for you. I'm taking them to St. George's. They've got a soup kitchen or something."

She clapped her hands together like a Girl Scout. "I'll go with you. Let's do it."

"What about Donnie?"

"He won't mind." She tugged me up.

"We should wait. Till they plow the streets."

"No, it'll be fun." She got her mittens from the sink.

You know that song by Joni Mitchell? She's right. You don't know what you've got till it's gone.

I had no idea Freddy meant so much to me till I found out that he was the one who'd betrayed me.

I could have taken revenge. I could have fired the bastard. I didn't. I just racked up another grudge.

Donnie went off to buy Lotto tickets; Colleen and I took the wagon to the soup kitchen.

St. George's had two flags over its little Gothic nave: a white flag with a red cross on it, and a smaller rainbow flag. Outside its red doors, a bulletin board framed with frost listed the Coming Events for January:

HARRY POTTER, A SPIRITUAL PERSPECTIVE
THE DISCOVERY SERIES: HOW ANGLICANS READ SCRIPTURE
VESTRY NOMINATIONS

"You go to church here?" Colleen looked hopeful.

"Are you kidding?"

The kitchen was in the basement. The soundtrack of an old movie grew louder as, walking backward, I carried my end of the heavy wagon down the steep stairs.

"You okay?"

"Fine." I caught my breath. My back was killing me.

"You sit. I'll find somebody in charge."

Cloaks for the Christmas pageant on their laps, little Mary and Joseph, the Three Kings, and a host of shepherds and angels were watching a videotape of *The Bells of St. Mary's* projected on a screen pulled down from the ceiling. In rows behind them, their parents and a handful of homeless men watched too.

Colleen tiptoed up to a hefty man in the front row. A clerical collar stuck out above the red collar of his reindeer sweater.

I took a seat. I knew the picture by heart. The guy who played Mr. Bogardis—the ailing realtor who held the fate of St. Mary's School in his hands—was the same guy who played the angel in *It's a Wonderful Life*. He looked less curmudgeonly, colorized. As Colleen unloaded the wagon, I watched Bogardis succumb to the charm of Bing Crosby and the prayers of Ingrid Bergman. The school is saved. But Sister Benedict has TB. She'll have to leave St. Mary's.

"That's it." Colleen returned.

"I just wanna see the end."

The priest can't kiss her. He can't even hug her. "Just dial O for O'Malley." He tells Sister Benedict to keep in touch. Her face glows with love as she bids good-bye.

When the lights came up, everyone was crying—the kids, the parents, the homeless men.

"You okay?"

My head was about to explode.

"What's the matter?" Colleen pressed my head to her breast.

The Magi giggled.

"Neil, honey. What's wrong?"

My head was throbbing. "It's just my blood pressure."

The priest in the reindeer sweater came up, pulling the wagon. "Are you okay?"

I started for the door.

"Your wagon," the priest called after Colleen and me.

"Keep it," I said.

Outside in the cold, the panic passed.

"Want to go to the hospital?" Colleen suggested.

"I'll be okay."

A father and son were strapping a Christmas tree to the roof of their BMW.

"You're sure you're okay?"

That's when I saw him, the homeless man in the purple parka, opening the gate to the little courtyard of St. George's.

I called out to him. "Sir?"

He looked like a prospector who'd got lost in the Rockies.

"You remember me?"

His scraggly beard had snow—or dandruff—in it. "Carl?"

"No," I said. "I was with my friend, outside of Sergio's, the restaurant. This guy in a cashmere coat—he shoved you—then he hit my friend."

He took a second. "How is he?"

"He's dead."

He didn't look surprised. He turned to go.

"Hang on." Colleen grabbed his sleeve.

"Who the fuck are *you?*" He pulled away from her.

"I'm Neil's sister."

"Colleen, let go."

He rubbed his arm as if Colleen had hurt him.

"Would you recognize the guy?"

He thought it over.

"Black hair. Kinda curly," I reminded him. "Maybe thirty, thirty-five."

"He works at Babes."

He sounded certain.

"What? 'Babes?'" I said.

"That strip joint."

"On First?"

"He's like the doorman or something."

"You know him?"

"I don't *know* him," he shouted. "I seen him around."

"What's your name?"

He started away.

"Please. Where can I reach you?"

He sort of apologized. "I take meds."

"What's your name?"

"Mark Twain."

"Your real name."

"Sam Clemens."

"Sir, this is important," Colleen said.

"Wait." I reached for my wallet.

He stood his ground. "I ain't gonna talk to no cops."

I gave him a twenty. "Here's my card. You get in trouble; you need money; you know where to find me."

He stuck the card in his pocket.

For years now, Upper East Siders have been doing everything they can to get Babes closed. There's been at least one murder there, several beatings, and countless charges of money laundering, prostitution, and public lewdness. And yet, Babes remains open, a mecca for rap stars, bankers, prizefighters, brokers, frat boys, and date rapists of all ages.

At the door of Babes—I recognized him immediately—was the guy who killed Bucky. His job was unhooking and hooking the velvet rope to let people into the club. His frilly tuxedo shirt could barely contain his pumped-up chest. His curly hair looked like a perm. He knew the guys getting out of their limos by name. He greeted the strippers hopping out of their cabs as if they were Oscar nominees. He was so full of bonhomie and self-lust, I could've killed him myself. I called Detective Manfredi.

Colleen kept an eye on the guy as I waited at the corner for Manfredi and Beard.

"You're sure it's him?" Manfredi checked.

"Absolutely. I'd stake my life on it."

Manfredi nodded to Beard. "Let's take him in."

It was out of my hands now. "What do *I* do?"

"Stay in town," Manfredi said. "We'll call you tomorrow."

"It's Christmas Eve," Colleen objected. She was counting on me to spend the night.

"I'll be here," I promised the cops.

As Manfredi and Beard slipped behind him and grabbed his elbows, the killer bridled with indignation. The crowd heckled the cops. The killer bowed to his buddies, strutting to the car like a teflon don. A red-haired stripper pulled up her skirt and mooned the patrol car as it took off.

Donnie had been waiting for us outside St. George's for over an hour. "Where the hell were you?"

Colleen said, "You won't believe it."

He was trying to keep his windshield free of snow. "What are we gonna do?" He threw up his hands. "We can't drive in this fuckin' blizzard."

They left the car and took the subway to the Long Island Railroad.

I didn't want to go home. I was high as a kite.

I had to walk by the Brownstone. The joint was jumpin'. The snow had stranded people in the city. They were partying hard.

I hadn't been in the Brownstone in a couple of years. The same guys, a bit grayer, were whooping it up at the piano. The same out-of-towners sat in the same wing chairs, eyeing the kids in baseball caps.

I wanted to tell somebody what I'd done—caught a killer—but there was nobody there I knew. There were a few new paintings— yacht races and hunting scenes—the same old crap, but over the fireplace was an oil that intrigued me. It was a portrait of four young and muscular gents—circa 1930?—posing around a motorbike at the seaside. It was snobby and sexy and funny: it *looked like* a Bruce Sargeant, the Anglo-American painter whose work, overlooked in his lifetime, was now fetching big prices at auction. But the surface was so yellowed with varnish, it was hard to judge without a good cleaning.

"Neil. How are you?"

It was Joe Estrine, this old friend of ours from the days when Bucky and I raised money for the counseling service at the Community Center. He's a psychoanalyst.

I told him about Bucky and catching the killer.

"That's a lot to handle," he said, tilting his head sideways in a show of sympathy.

"So, how are you?" I tried to change the subject. I felt so good, I didn't want him raining on my parade.

"I can get you a referral if you want to see somebody," he said.

"I want to see somebody hang."

He looked worried. "That doesn't sound like you."

"So what brings *you* here?"

He was looking for a bartender. I think he had the hots for him.

Emmett, the piano player from the memorial service, came over and hugged me. "Life goes on," he said.

I told him what happened: I'd caught the killer.

He slapped me on the back. "I've got a medley for you."

They were all revenge songs: "Cry Me a River." "Goody, Goody." "I Will Survive."

I put a ten in his tip bowl.

Manfredi dropped by the next morning. They had to let the guy go. It was hard to believe. "I *know* it's him."

"We've got nothing to go on but your I.D.," he explained. "His wife says they were home, watching videos."

"His wife? He's *married?*"

"He's got a kid too."

"Did you check for the coat?" I remembered. "The cashmere coat?"

"Yeah."

"You searched his house?"

"He let us look."

They hadn't found it.

"Now what?"

"We're gonna keep an eye on him," Manfredi promised.

"That's it?"

He didn't look hopeful. "We can work on the wife. If she's lying, she's—"

"What do you mean, *if* she's lying?"

He finished, "She's an accessory after the fact. And when she finds out how many other girls he's nailing, she may change her tune."

"Christ."

"We're talking to his buddies at Babes. At the gym. He's not very bright. He probably said something."

"Who is he? What's his name?"

His name was Angelo ("Angel") Cucciniello. He lived in Brooklyn, Carroll Gardens, and kept a studio apartment near Babes for entertaining the ladies. When he wasn't manning the velvet rope at Babes or training weightlifters at the Pumping Iron gym, he acted small parts in movies.

"Like what?"

"He's starting something now." Manfredi checked his notes. "Fiedler Films."

"Is there a title?"

Manfredi laughed. *The Pit Bull and the Pendulum.*"

"Where are they located?"

"Midtown. Forty-Sixth Street."

"Does he have a record?"

"Nothing that stuck," Manfredi said. "He was picked up for assaulting a guy outside of Babes but the charges were dropped."

Manfredi told me to go spend Christmas with my sister. I told Colleen I had to stay in town. She offered to bring Christmas to me. I declined.

That night, in my dream, it was Angel strapped to the wheel. Bucky cheered me on. I aimed the knife for Angel's chest. It missed. I woke up before it hit Bucky.

Bucky and I had always spent Christmas somewhere warm. I know a lot of gay guys who do. It spares you the Christmas service at the gay-hating church; the parents who introduce your lover as a friend from New York; the cousins who bridle when you bounce their six-year-old boy on your knee. It was doubly weird being in New York for Christmas, without Bucky. People called. I didn't answer the phone.

Christmas Day, there was a knock at my door.

"I know you're in there."

It was Freddy. I let him in.

He lectured, he yelled, he pleaded: Don't be so fucking rigid. So Bucky fucked around a little. He was human. Christ, it's not like he shot your dog. (We didn't have a dog.)

"Yeah, but what about you?"

"*Fuck* me," Freddy said. "I don't matter. You just can't think he didn't love you. He did. You know that. You're just pissed. I don't blame you. But you've got to get over it. For your own sake."

I could tell he was right. Not that I forgave him.

"I better go."

"No, stay," I insisted.

You can harbor a grudge without stooping to rudeness.

Freddy'd brought turkey sandwiches. We watched *White Christmas.* (It was too soon to watch *Philadelphia Story* without Bucky.) During the commercials I made Freddy fill me in on his latest conquests: a tiny gymnast who had parallel bars over his bed and an Alvin Ailey dancer.

When he left, I made a drink and went on the Net. It didn't take long to find what I was looking for.

> With several projects in the works and more in the writing stages, Fiedler Films is becoming an important contender in the entertainment industry. Our slate now consists of features, music videos, television pilots, etc. This is a wacky business, and we're just getting started, and it looks to be a wild ride.
>
> Our first feature, *Rue Morgue,* attracted the attention of critics and distributors.
>
> Our second feature, *The Pitbull and the Pendulum,* begins shooting in New York in February. It stars Brad Theroux, Josh Zito, Angel Cucciniello, and Darcy Forsythe.

There was a profile of Fiedler's founder.

> Like everyone else in the business under the age of forty, head inmate at the asylum, Larry Fiedler, was inspired by *Star Wars* and Scorsese and the endless possibilities afforded to filmmakers in the modern age, if you use the technology and don't let it use you.

Fiedler brings years of experience from the music business to this new playground. He also brings the bitterness and determination to succeed that comes from producing over 1,200 live shows with over fifty bands and having very little to show for it. He now exercises his artistic urges as a script supervisor, screenwriter, director, producer, actor, and anything else it takes to get the film in the can.

The day after Christmas, I made an appointment to meet Fiedler. He shared his office in the Actors Equity Building with a woman, Melanie—a hard-looking old babe in sweatpants—who licensed the logos of Broadway shows to T-shirt manufacturers and a guy who booked out-of-town dates for cabaret acts.

The receptionist, Miles, was a middle-aged hunk with a Julius Caesar haircut. The baseball jacket on the back of his chair read AS-PECTS OF LOVE. Barely looking up from *Teen People,* he called, "Larry, you got company."

Fiedler was a likeable guy, a little sleazy, maybe thirty-five, and as big as a bear. He sat under a mock-up poster for *The Pitbull and the Pendulum* which featured a busty girl menaced by a snarling dog and a swinging ax.

"How did you find us?"

"Oh. Word travels."

"You know a lot of filmmakers?"

"A few," I said. "They're always looking for money and, well, I've got a little to spare, now and then."

"What else have you invested in?"

"Nothing major." I'd done my homework. "A few things for Gramercy and Good Machine."

"Really?"

I got up from my chair and walked around the room, the way heavy rollers do in the movies. "When I heard you were doing Poe, I thought, well, shit, that makes good business sense—he's every teenager's favorite author—and good artistic sense too. I mean, maybe I'm just an old teenager, but I love those stories."

"Let me show you the script." He reached for a copy.

"What's your budget?"

He sounded tentative. "Two hundred and fifty thousand."

"Including postproduction?"

"Oh, no," he said. "We wait—get together like half a rough-cut—and show it to guys like you who can help us with the finishing money."

"What about the cast? Have you got reels I could see?"

He looked embarrassed. "Everybody's nonunion." He reached for a sheaf of head shots. "These are the principals. What kind of money are we talking about here?"

"Let me read the script."

I took it back to the gallery. Freddy was relieved to see me; there were dozens of phone calls and letters to deal with. I ignored them. I read the script. I've never liked horror movies. I didn't like this one.

Freddy tried to interrupt me. He'd built a wall of shelves in the inventory room to stack the smaller paintings.

"I'll check it out later," I brushed him off.

I told my accountant I was going to invest in a movie.

She couldn't believe the title. "Why throw away money on crap like this?"

"It's my money."

"I know, but Neil . . ."

I didn't bother to explain. With all the money from the suit and the insurance, I could piss away a small fortune.

Freddy nabbed me at the door. "Mike Kassegian has a buyer for the Fitz Hugh Lane."

I got confused. "Which Fitz Hugh Lane?"

"The seascape. *Gloucester Harbor*," Freddy looked at me funny. "It's the only one we've got."

"Good. Fine."

"He'll split fifty-fifty anything over six hundred thousand."

"Fine." I hurried out.

"You want me to make the deal?"

"Yeah," I said. "You're in charge."

"I am?"

Besides Fitz Hugh Lane, Kassegian's other favorite, I recalled, was Bruce Sargeant. I asked Freddy to run over to the Brownstone and buy the painting over the fireplace.

He thought I was crazy.

I didn't have time. "Just buy it."

"How much can I offer?"

I thought about it. "No more than five."

"Five thousand dollars? For some crap from the Brownstone?"

If we offered more, they'd start to suspect it could be valuable.

I went back to Fiedler. He had a new suit on. It still had dots of thread on the sleeve from where they'd sewn the price tag. He'd had his hair cut too: with the sides buzzed, and a silver hoop in his ear, he looked downright gay.

I said I could put in fifty thousand.

He did the pacing this time. "Why not a hundred?"

I opened the folder. The photo of "Angel" was on the top. "This guy gives me the creeps."

"He's supposed to."

"Who is he?"

"He plays this thug—this sadistic thug."

"I know. But he's too—"

"What?"

"Pretty boy. Pumped up. I see someone leaner," I closed my eyes.

"I gotta tell you now, Mr. Moore."

"Call me Neil."

"Neil. I don't give creative control to my producers."

"But you listen to suggestions."

"Of course."

"If I'm putting a hundred thousand dollars into this flick . . ."

He stopped pacing.

"I don't want to be blowing it on some guy who looks like he should be on the cover of a romance novel."

"But don't you see? That's the idea. He's like an evil Fabio."

I got up. "Well, I'll think about it."

"You wanna meet the guy? He's a decent actor. And he's very sexy."

"I gotta go."

"Hang on." He reached for another folder. "What about this guy?"

He looked like Kiefer Sutherland. "That's more like it."

Fiedler still seemed reluctant. "Well, he *is* a fine actor."

I took out my checkbook.

Angel was out.

"And please," I said, "let's keep this to ourselves."

"What?"

"My involvement."

"Uh-huh?"

"I've got enough tax people on my ass."

He shook my hand. "No problem."

I looked so pleased with myself when I got to the gallery, Freddy pulled me aside. "You look like you just got laid."

I told him about Fiedler.

"No way."

"Cross my heart."

He couldn't hide his glee. "You're fuckin' nuts."

"How are things here?"

He'd been to the Brownstone. The owner wasn't there. He'd made an appointment to see him later that week.

"Terrific."

He thought I was crazy to be buying the painting. "What makes you think it's a Bruce Sargeant?"

I didn't know. "Intuition? We'll see."

Sally Winston, the art advisor to Citibank, was browsing the Birchers.

"She really likes the show," Freddy said.

I felt up. "I'll go speak to her."

By the end of the day, I'd sold two paintings, caught up on phone calls, and approved the catalog for the upcoming show.

That night I went to bed at eleven. But I couldn't sleep. What good is revenge if you can't see it?

I went back to Babes. I was dying to see Angel without his grin. He was nowhere to be seen.

I went into the club. It was a vinyl Vegas of coked-up ex-ballplayers and realtors in T-shirts and sports jackets. Hands full of twenties, they shouted at the girls in their g-strings like Mexican peasants betting on a cockfight.

"Angel here tonight?" I asked a bartender. He was kind of a smaller black version of Angel.

He shook his head. "He's out layin' pipe."

"Oh." I must've looked confused.

Biting his lip, the bartender thrust his crotch forward and back as if he were banging his dick into a very tight virgin.

"Oh. Laying *pipe*."

"Can I get you something?"

Before I could answer, he shouted, "Hey, Crystal."

On her knees, a lap-dancer with big hard tits was bobbing her head on the crotch of a Japanese guy.

"What?"

"You know what. Fuckin' chickenhead," he cursed under his breath. Then he turned back. "Can I get you something?"

"No, thanks," I bolted my drink and made for the door.

The next day at the gallery, I was too restless to concentrate. Freddy had a lunch date—a sex-date—with his gymnast. I made him break it. Someone had to hang the California impressionists.

I had other fish to fry.

There was only one Angelo Cucciniello in the Manhattan phone book. His apartment, right near Babes, was across the street from a diner. I sat in a booth and watched the door.

It was one of those old red-brick walk-ups. From the look of the slackers and hunch-backed ladies in head-scarves going in and out, it was rent-controlled. There was construction going on. Workmen carried up a sink and a toilet and lowered big buckets of rubble from a third-floor fire escape.

I went to the door and checked the names on the buzzers. There it was: CUCCINIELLO: 2B. From the layout of the first floor, it was clear that 2B was the second-story window facing the street.

"Can I help you?"

A guy in a suit—he looked like one of the cops on *Dragnet*—confronted me in the narrow entryway.

"You live here?" I asked.

He put his key in the door. "I'm from Rutland-Roberts."

I knew the name. It was on my maintenance bill every month. "Oh, you manage this building?"

"We do."

"Any vacancies?"

"Not that I know of. But there should be one in a couple months when they finish construction." He took a card from his pocket. "Call Yorkville Realty."

"Thanks."

I was already down the front steps when I had the idea. I ran back and banged on the glass.

"Yeah?" He didn't bother to open the door.

"I was wondering. I really like this building."

"Yeah?"

"My friend Angelo lives in two-B. I mean, he really lives in Brooklyn but he hangs onto this place to crash in when he's working late."

I could see his mind working. If 2B wasn't Angelo's principal residence, he had no right to a rent-controlled apartment.

"Angelo who?"

"Cucciniello. Two-B. If there's anything I can do to get first dibs on an apartment—"

He shook his head. "Call Yorkville."

I reached for my wallet. "You're sure?"

"We should have one or two units here in a couple of months."

"I'll be in touch."

The paintings were hung when I got back to the gallery.

Freddy wasn't satisfied. "You don't think they look crammed?"

I told him what I'd done.

"I don't believe you."

"I got him fired from the movie. Now he's getting evicted."

"You don't know that."

"Trust me. They're dying to fix up those old apartments and hike up the rent."

"You're fuckin' nuts." Freddy reached for the phone." I'm gonna call your sister."

"What? Stop."

"You're *scaring* me."

I took the phone from his hand. "You don't think he deserves it?"

"Of course, he deserves it. I'm just afraid—"

"What?"

"Of what the fuck you'll do next."

After losing the election in 2000 (well, winning the election and having it stolen from him by the Supreme Court), Al Gore grew a beard: remember? Every asshole on TV had to give him grief: What's got into *him?*

All my life I'd been Al Gore. I'd done the right thing. I'd been a good little grownup. And what did it get me? A closet full of Bucky's clothes.

I could've grown a beard. I could've suffered in silence. Instead, I got pissed and everybody got scared.

Freddy called Colleen.

She came to my apartment. "Neil, you've got to stop."

"I've done nothing wrong."

"You've got to see somebody."

I just flipped through my mail. "I've done nothing illegal."

"You've been through so much."

"You think I'm crazy?"

She put a hand on my shoulder. "I think you're very upset."

"I feel fine. I feel *good*."

"That's what I mean."

To shut her up, I agreed to see Joe Estrine. I wasn't sleeping. Maybe Joe could give me something.

He had a nice little office not far from my place. The guy who had the session before me was this hot Latin hunk with curly hair tied back in a red bandanna.

"It's nice to see your practice isn't all middle-aged queers," I told Joe as I sat down in the seat across from him.

He wasn't one to waste time on small talk.

I told him what I'd been up to: screwing Angel.

"You're in mourning," he said.

"So. Isn't that normal?"

"But you're acting out."

"Oh, please." I hated that kind of jargon.

"You're not?"

"That's what people call it when they disapprove of what you're doing."

"I don't disapprove."

I had to laugh. "Yes, you do."

"I'm concerned."

"Yeah, that I'm not just taking it lying down like a good little faggot."

"You know the whole idea of analysis is," he said in this patronizing voice, "If you put things into words—"

"I *know*."

"—You don't need to act them out."

"I *want to* act them out."

He asked me to think of other people in the past I'd ever had hostile thoughts about.

My mother and father—*quel surprise*—came to mind.

When I told her I was gay, my mother burst into tears: "What did I do wrong?"

I wanted to say, "I could give you a list. But it had absolutely nothing to do with my being gay."

"Why didn't you say it?" Joe asked.

I should have.

My father never admitted he was wrong. Like I'd ask, who was the black singer Eleanor Roosevelt arranged a concert for at the Lincoln Memorial?

"Mahalia Jackson."

"No, it wasn't," I'd say.

"Yes, it was."

I'd get my history book and point to the picture. "It was Marian Anderson."

"That's just what I said." He'd lie without flinching. "It was Marian Anderson."

I could've killed him.

"What kind of revenge *did* you plan for him?" Joe asked.

"I had a little tape recorder. I wanted to catch him at his bullshit."

"Why didn't you?"

I had to admit. "I didn't have the balls."

He checked his watch. "Have you heard of bipolar syndrome?"

What bullshit. "Yeah."

"You go back and forth from depression to elation."

"Manic depression."

He nodded. "Have you felt restless lately?"

"A little. I guess."

"Trouble sleeping?"

"Yeah. Now and then."

"Have you been drinking more than usual?"

"No," I lied.

I agreed to get tested.

I had to act quickly.

The Pumping Iron Gym was not the sort of gym I was used to. It was a hard-core gym for the kind of hard-core weightlifters who get up in the morning, eat four skinless chicken breasts, and then race to the gym for a couple hours of pumping one body part to Popeye perfection.

Lately, however, it seemed that Pumping Iron was seeking to expand its clientele. There was an ad for the gym in one of those papers they hand you at the Food Emporium: it showed a normal-sized guy and a girl in a sweatband watching TV while riding stationary bikes.

I took my gym bag with me when I went to the door.

"Excuse me?"

The guy in dreadlocks behind the desk was human-sized. "Peep this."

"What?"

He showed me *The Post*: MOTHER DROWNS FIVE KIDS IN BATH-TUB.

"How fucked up is that?"

"Jesus Christ."

He went to a computer. "What's your number?"

"I don't have a number."

"Oh."

I told him I was thinking of joining and I wanted to try out the gym for a day.

"Angel," he shouted.

"What? Wait."

I could see him through the glass.

"Oh shit." I didn't want to *talk* to him. "I forgot something."

"Angel!"

He was squatting with a barbell on his shoulders. His little shorts strained against his big hard ass.

"I'll have to come back later. I forgot my sneakers."

The desk guy pressed a buzzer. "What's your name?"

"Ron."

He beckoned me through the turnstile.

"Angel. Show Ron around."

From the look on his face, I thought for sure he recognized me.

I grabbed the turnstile.

"What's so fuckin' good about the Twins?" Angel shook my hand.

"What?"

"They ain't worth shit," he said.

"Who? What?"

"Joe Mays. He's a spaz."

"You think?"

To be honest, I don't remember the conversation exactly. I only pieced it together later when Freddy pointed out to me that the T-shirt I was wearing (with two baseball bats crossed like swords and the word *Twins* written on it) might suggest to a heterosexual that I was a supporter of a baseball team, the Minnesota Twins. All I knew was it fit well, looked butch, and the ten dollars I paid for it in a Chelsea thrift shop went to people with AIDS.

"So, what brings you to Pumping Iron?"

"Oh, I just thought I'd look around."

He looked me over. "What are you hoping to achieve?"

"I haven't given it much thought."

"How flexible are you?"

"Oh, I can come any time."

"No." He laughed. "Do you stretch?"

"Oh. Not enough."

His voice warmed up as he led me around the place, pointing out the machines, reaching down to pick up dumbells and replace them on the rack.

"How old are you?"

"Forty-five," I admitted.

"You're in pretty good shape."

It was hard to believe that this affable hulk was the guy who'd killed Bucky.

"How's the market?" Angel stopped to ask this behemoth in cut-offs lying on the leg machine, pressing hundreds of pounds.

"Don't ask."

"Not even biotech shit?"

The guy shrugged. "Maybe in the long run."

"What do *you* do?" Angel asked me.

"Oh. I sell . . . furniture."

"No shit." He lit up. "I need a new couch. Can you get me a discount?"

It took me a second. "Office furniture."

"Oh. You ever worked with a trainer?"

"No. You think I should?"

"You get a free session when you join."

"With you?"

"Uh-huh. Let me show you the lockers." He led the way.

It was like a porn movie. Musclemen in jockstraps and little white towels.

"Hey, Ang'," a black guy called from the shower. "How's the chihuahua?"

Angel didn't like the question. "Haven't seen her lately."

"Yeah, right."

Angel reached in his pocket and took out a Palm Pilot. "I could see you tomorrow, if you want to get started."

"Uh-huh."

"Work out today. See how you like it." He took a card from a sleeve of the Palm Pilot. "I'm free from ten to one tomorrow."

"Okay. Who's that?"

There was a photo slipped into the Palm Pilot with his business cards.

"Patricia. My wife."

"God, she's pretty."

She was brunette and slim, with bony shoulders and pert little breasts snug in a sundress.

"You bring a lock?"

"Oh, shit. No."

He put his gloves and Palm Pilot down on the bench. "I'll get you one."

"Oh, thanks."

The second he left, I put the Palm Pilot in my pocket.

"Don't I know you?"

"Sorry?"

This thirty-something hunk with his hair combed forward was getting dressed. "I know you from somewhere," he said, picking up his jacket: ASPECTS OF LOVE. It was Miles, Fiedler's receptionist.

I looked at my watch. "Oh, shit. The time." I ran out.

Angel was standing at the desk.

"Forget the lock," I started to say.

He was screaming into a cell phone. *"Bullshit.* You promised me. We shook on it."

I backed out. "I gotta go to the office."

He kicked the desk so hard, a stapler bounced into the laundry bin. "Fuck you, asshole."

Through the window, I could see him ripping the wires out of the computer and hurling it at a freezer full of energy drinks.

When I got to the gallery, Cesar was hauling a Bierstadt out of the closet. Freddy was showing it to the Tatlins, big collectors from Santa Fe.

"Neil." Joe Tatlin shook my hand. "What's the provenance? I hear it's from the Morgan estate."

"I can't talk now."

I dragged Cesar upstairs and gave him the Palm Pilot. "You know how to work this?"

"Yeah. What?"

"It's got a calendar, right?"

"Yeah," Cesar said.

"November thirtieth. Check."

"Last year?"

"Uh-huh."

"I can download the whole thing."

"Just fuckin' do what I say."

Cesar shivered. "Dude, that's severe." With a little pencil he tapped the screen to November thirtieth.

"What's it say?"

He showed me. "7:30 p.m. PB and P."

"No way." I laughed.

"What's so funny?"

I was still laughing when Freddy came in. He'd sold the Bierstadt to the Tatlins for a million-two.

"What's so funny?"

I showed Freddy the Palm Pilot.

"PB and P?"

I'd broken the code. "*The Pitbull and the Pendulum.* The night Bucky died, he was auditioning for the movie."

"Hang on," Freddy said. "Whose *is* this?"

"Angel's."

He covered his mouth. "What the hell did you do? Break into his apartment?"

"I found it. At the gym." I started out.

"Where you going?" He tried to stop me.

We sort of wrestled in the doorway. I ripped his shirt.

"Fuck you."

"Fuck *you.*" I was laughing.

"Neil, wait."

He followed me down the stairs and hopped into the taxicab beside me.

"Where we going?"

"To see Fiedler."

"Why?"

"He can break Angel's alibi; he wasn't home with his wife."

"Neil, listen to me." Freddy got right in my face. "This is not fuckin' *Columbo.*"

"Take it easy."

"Leave the cop shit to Manfredi."

"He's a moron."

"No, he isn't."

"What's he done that I didn't do better?"

Freddy tried another tack. "Look, I don't mean to be down on you. But, Christ, Neil, face it. You're not yourself."

"I know."

He started ticking off my faults. "You don't do squat at the gallery. You treated the Tatlins like shit."

"You made the deal."

"No thanks to you. Ask anybody: you haven't been yourself since Bucky died."

"Good for me."

He grabbed me by the shoulders. "Good for you? You're a fuckin' lunatic."

Apparently, this pissed me off and triggered a tirade. I don't remember what I said. But according to Freddy, I invoked Nietzsche, D.H. Lawrence, Jackson Pollock, and several other worthies to argue that my new Alpha-maleness expressed a healthy scorn for the pussywhipped, sissywhipped, man I used to be. I would not be one of those gays lining up for the gas chamber with my clothes folded neatly in a pile. I would not be one of those Christians, turning the other cheek, so homophobes could take a swat at it. Life isn't a pool party. It's a fight to the death. If the law didn't do its job, I had a perfect right to take the law into my own hands.

I remember Freddy's face. He looked terrified. The cab driver took out his earphones and kept an eye on me in the rearview mirror.

My blood pressure was soaring.

Freddy apologized about Bucky. He told me he'd been in love with Bucky forever, since the very first day we all met in the Pines. He'd done everything he could, he'd admitted, to wrest Bucky from me. Twice, they diddled. Only twice, he said, and it didn't mean diddlyshit to either of them. Bucky loved me. A million times he'd told Freddy how he couldn't imagine his life without me.

None of this got through.

For some reason, Forty-Sixth Street was cordoned off with sawhorses. I offered the driver a hundred dollars to drive through them. He declined. Freddy paid the driver and ran after me.

There were more sawhorses and a phalanx of police outside the Actor's Equity Building. A crowd had gathered.

"What's up?" Freddy asked a hot dog man.

"Somebody's holding somebody hostage."

"Who?"

The hot dog man shrugged.

Across the street, I saw Fiedler's receptionist.

"What's up, Miles?"

He couldn't place me. He was frantic. "Who are you?"

"I invested in *Pitbull*. What's going on?"

He was shaking like a leaf.

"Take your time," Freddy said.

Poor Miles was scared shitless. "This actor came into the office. I don't know what he was on. He just hit him and hit him."

"Mr. Fiedler?"

"Yeah, shit." He looked back to the building.

"How is he?"

"I don't know. He was bleeding. I ran."

"Did you know the actor?" I asked.

"Yeah. He was pissed. Mr. Fiedler'd just fired him."

"Angel?"

"That's right," Miles said. "I think he's on steroids. He's out of his mind. That's his wife." He pointed to a young woman with a baby stroller. She was huddled with the police near the entrance to the building. She had a cell phone wedged between her shoulder and her ear as she opened a bag of potato chips for the little boy in the stroller.

"What's *she* doing here?"

"She's trying to talk him down," Miles said. "He took Marjorie hostage."

"Who?"

"The T-shirt lady. She shares the office."

Freddy said, "Let's get out of here."

I couldn't move. My head was pounding.

The cops shouted, "Get back!"

We hid behind a car.

Angel came out the door, holding Marjorie in front of him like a shield.

The cops didn't wait. The gunfire hit Angel in the head and the shoulders. Patricia screamed. The boy dropped his potato chip.

I was a basket case for weeks.

Fiedler came to visit me at Payne Whitney. One of his eyes was bandaged and his neck was in a foam-rubber brace.

I didn't want to see him. "Who let you up?"

"How's the blood pressure?"

I buzzed for the nurse.

He had a business proposition. He thought the story of Angel would make a great little film noir. Or maybe a TV movie about the dangers of steroid use.

I buzzed again.

He had a title, *'Roid Rage.*

I had another, *Casting Couch.* At the inquest, Freddy told me, Miles had raised the suspicion that Angel had been obliged to perform sexual services for Fiedler to get a part in the movie.

"That was bullshit," Fiedler said. "That little loser Miles made it up."

It explained why Angel had been so pissed when Bucky flirted with him on the street.

The nurse finally showed.

"You *call* me." Fiedler took off.

The tests ruled out bipolar syndrome. My doctors opted for "major depression with hypomania."

Joe said I was in good company.

"Who?"

"Hamlet, Hedda Gabler, Medea."

"No shit."

Freddy came to see me every day. He brought little tea sandwiches without the crusts from Swifty's and my favorite soup from RSVP.

"You know that painting at the Brownstone?" he asked me.

"Oh right. The Bruce Sargeant. Did you get it?"

"No. We'd have to buy the whole bar," Freddy said. The owner had lost his lover and was moving to Florida, soon as he could.

"How much does he want?" I asked.

Freddy slapped me like Cher in *Moonstruck.* "Snap out of it."

"Why?" I laughed. "You could run a bar. You could make us a fortune."

"What do I want a bar for?"

"What else?" I said. "Boys."

"Hmmm." He scratched his chin.

That night I had a dream. Only this time it was me strapped to the wheel. Angel's son reached up from his stroller to hand his mother the knives.

"You can't blame *me*," I screamed. "He killed my lover."

A knife zinged my trousers.

I woke up peeing myself.

They let me out of Payne Whitney after a couple of weeks. The antidepressants—or my visits from Joe—had snapped me out of fetal position. He told me I'd be fine when I found it in my heart to forgive.

"Everybody?"

"Forget your parents. I'm not asking for miracles."

He meant Bucky and Freddy.

I started with Freddy.

I told him to meet me after work at the Brownstone. I got there early. There were quite a few cuties sitting at the bar between older guys in olive suits from the Men's Wearhouse.

"You did *what?*" Freddy couldn't believe it.

I waved my hand around the place. "I bought you the Brownstone."

He put down his drink. "No way."

"Not the bar. Just the lease." I took it out of my briefcase. "It's only got one year left on it."

"You're nuts."

"You'd have to go to grad school to be my partner at the gallery. I don't want the ADA saying I hire guys off the street."

"What makes you think I want *this* dump?"

I could tell he was delighted. "You've got too much talent to be my girl Friday. You need a little fiefdom of your own."

There were tears in his eyes.

I couldn't take the tears. "You run the place. We split the profits, fifty-fifty."

"Yeah," he said. "What about the losses?"

That's when I lied. I told him the painting over the fireplace *was* a Bruce Sargeant. Worth a million five.

So take it easy, I told him. If the Brownstone lost a million dollars, we'd still be in the black.

Of course, the painting wasn't worth a thousand. It was a fake. It wasn't worth the money I'd spent to have it cleaned. But I didn't want Freddy to feel beholden. And to tell the truth, I didn't want to see him every day in the gallery. I wanted Bucky all to myself.

I told you about my mother, how she couldn't let us see her cry when her father died. I forgot to tell you what happened, three weeks later. We were watching TV when Walter Cronkite took off his glasses and said that President Kennedy had died in Dallas. She started crying. She cried for three or four days straight.

Granted, Katharine Hepburn didn't avert a nuclear war or start the Peace Corps or introduce any important civil rights legislation. But when TCM commemorated her death with an all-day marathon of her movies, it finally hit me. I cried all day long as they re-ran *Philadelphia Story* and *Bill of Divorcement* and *The Lion in Winter*. If you'd known Bucky, well, you'd know what I was crying about. He had his faults. But he was one in a million.

Last Call

His last day as manager of the Brownstone, Basil Batsakis showed up at 3 p.m., as usual, to let in Ivar and Vicente, the cleaning crew, and the delivery boys from The House of Spirits. It was Fat Tuesday, Mardi Gras, and Basil had already been down to Pizzazz Party Supplies in the toy district to pick up earrings and beads for the patrons, masks and jester caps for the bartenders. He was determined to put a good face on his firing. It wasn't his fault. The bar was changing hands and the new owner wanted his own man, Freddy, to run the show.

Basil punched in a code to switch off the burglar alarm and flicked on the lights. The room wouldn't miss him. It was impartial as a hospital room.

The delivery boys brushed by with their hand-trucks and crates of beer. Basil pushed back the curtains and opened a window.

In the winter light, the room was a real estate ad: brass well-polished, armchairs empty. On the bar was a stack of ashtrays Basil had designed himself: he'd borrowed the big blue B from a monogrammed matchbox left at the bar by a Brit who worked at Brown's Hotel. Basil still used the ashtrays—to hold condoms and toothpicks—but no one would miss them.

He slipped two ashtrays into his backpack. Someday—who knows?—he might look back on his nine years at the Brownstone without the grief he was feeling today.

"Mr. Baz?" Vicente had something wrapped up in tissue paper. "My wife, she make."

"For me?"

It was a cap with long earflaps, an alpaca cap of many colors, the kind you see Bolivians selling on bedsheets in the subway.

"It's beautiful. Thank you." Basil pulled on the hat.

"You get new job?" Vicente looked worried. He knew what if felt like to be expendable.

"Yeah. I'm workin' on it," Basil said. "Please thank your wife. It's a beautiful hat."

There was a lot to do. Somewhere among the CDs was a collection of Dixieland and zydeco. Basil could hang the garlands himself but he'd need help blowing up the balloons. Then, finish the notebook: he was preparing an instruction manual on how to manage staff, calculate sales, keep track of inventory, keep the IRS and the health department at bay. Freddy had asked him to put it all down on paper. And what was the point of saying no? The new owner had been generous with his severance check. How could he not be? He couldn't afford to have Basil badmouthing him and Freddy to the regulars.

"Hey, Baz."

Speak of the devil.

"I let myself in. I hope you don't mind."

In a tight black sweater, Freddy looked like the handsome bald dance captain of a Bob Fosse troupe.

"I wanted to check out the place—without people—to see how the furniture's holding up."

Basil stiffened. "I had the upholsterers in two years ago. There's nothing *too* shabby."

"Except for the bar stools downstairs."

Fuck you. "Oh, right."

"Can I help you with something?"

Basil drew a balloon from his bag and handed the rest of the lot to Freddy. "You've got better lungs than I do."

"I don't know about that."

Basil blew. The balloon just sputtered.

"I heard you're an actor." Freddy smiled.

"I was."

"My friend Ian writes *Eden Heights*. He can get you an audition. He's gonna drop by. I hope you don't mind."

"No. Great. Thanks," Basil managed. It was a bitch to feel beholden.

"You should do commercials," Freddy said. "You've got a great look for dads."

Basil laughed.

But it was true. For all the good it would ever do him. Not quite forty, Basil looked like a nice, lenient dad in an ad for Progresso or Olive Garden. Tall and broad-shouldered, his hairline had receded but his waistline was holding its own. With his two-o'clock shadow and big Greek nose, he was still sort of sexy, if not handsome. In younger days, he got plenty of auditions, but callbacks were few and far between. Lacking the swagger to play an "ethnic," he was too swarthy to play much else. Mild and well-spoken, he was never *told* he was too gay, but eventually he got the message. He played nerds and fops, little parts, Off-Off-Broadway—till he stumbled into the Ridiculous Theater.

Only once before, in a college rip-off of *Forbidden Broadway*—*Forbidden Fordham*—had he ever done drag but, with his height and his nose, he was a natural. He made a fine Valkyrie, a plug-ugly Mrs. Bluebeard, and a memorable housemaid at Mandacrest. He was never a star—he was always a bit-player—but he got his laughs, and he was part of something. High on weed, he painted scenery. He handed out programs. He partied till dawn. He woke up on strange couches, pulled on his pants, and rushed off to his day job at the Burlington Coat Factory. When rent and AIDS finally closed the Ridiculous, Basil's talent for travesty opened few doors and closed quite a few more. At the Brownstone, at least, he felt appreciated. Having grown up in the Piscataway Acropolis, his father's diner, he found himself taking charge of the poorly run Brownstone without ever really intending to.

Freddy's cell phone rang.

"I bet that's Neil." Freddy tied a knot in his balloon and stepped out of earshot.

Neil was the new owner. Basil had never even met him.

Brian and Chad, the first shift of bartenders, burst through the door.

"He's a *pilot*." Brian swung his gym bag.

"Bullshit. He's a space waitress. For like Air Jamaica."

They were twins from Atlanta. Cute, muscleboy twins. Guys came to the bar from all over town just to check them out.

"Hey, Baz." Chad stuffed his peacoat under the bar. "Is that what we're wearing for Mardi Gras?"

Basil still had the hat with the earflaps on. "Oh, no." He reached for the bag from Pizzazz.

"You look like Rocky." Chad laughed at Basil.

Basil didn't get it. Sylvester Stallone?

"Rocky and Bullwinkle."

Of course. The squirrel.

Brian and Chad tried on their three-petaled jester caps. Brian's had pom-poms; Chad's had bells.

"You know what *you* look like? A pair of jacks. In a deck of cards," Baz said.

"A pair of jack-offs." Chad whipped off the hat.

Ivar switched on the vacuum cleaner.

Basil took a seat at the mahogany bar in the back to finish his notebook for Freddy. The back bar was his favorite, a big long room with tall windows, good moldings, gilt mirrors, potted trees, and a grand piano. It was the room where he'd first tended bar and where he'd hung out, most nights, for the last nine years. He'd drink espresso with Ralph, his favorite bartender, and poke fun at the patrons with their gift bags from the GLAAD Media Awards and their shopping bags from Barneys. Ralph knew all the latest rumors about which film star was seen at the baths, which TV news reporter was a closet case. On slower nights, they'd play Desert Island: What five Motown singles or junk foods or historical figures would you want with you if you were stranded on a desert island? Ralph was the one person he would really miss. Who else would settle a desert isle with Freud, Velasquez, Cervantes, John Lennon, and remix master, Junior Vasquez?

Basil stopped himself.

It was morbid—it was *stupid*—to get sentimental about leaving a shitty job. It was time to move on. He'd let the fuckin' Brownstone distract him from his real vocation for far too long. Some day, Off-

Broadway, taking a bow, he'd look back and say that getting fired was a blessing in disguise.

In the fourteen days since the ax had fallen, Basil had spent only one night, the first night, in despair. He sat up, smoking, drinking, and assessing himself ruthlessly. He was almost forty. His classmates at Fordham were lawyers and brokers with children and Volvos and 401-Ks. He wasn't even a barkeep. He was ridiculous—a stupid showqueen—to think he'd ever make it as an actor. He had no credits worth shit. He had no real talent. A hundred actors make a living. The rest fall through the cracks and land up in suntan parlors, wiping the sweat off fluorescent beds.

In the morning, thank God, the sun came out. Basil rallied and leapt into action. He signed up at HB Studios for acting classes; they would start in the spring on Tuesday and Thursday nights. He found an afternoon workshop at the Learning Annex on Auditioning for Commercials. He renewed his membership at Crunch and read *The Ross Reports* on the stationary bike. He padded his résumé with performances he'd never given for theater companies that had folded. A classmate of Ralph's at the School of Visual Arts took pictures of Basil for a head shot. The eight-by-tens were already printed; the postcards would arrive next week.

"Mr. Baz?"

It was Vicente again.

"Uh-huh?"

He was pointing to the front window. "The lady with the dog."

Fuck. Not today. Basil went to the window. The lady with the dog was the last thing he needed.

Right below the window, just a foot from the stairs leading up to the door of the bar, was Yuri, a Russian sheepdog, big as a motorcycle, lying flat on the pavement. Standing guard over the shaggy carcass was Imogen, the dainty middle-aged lady who lived in one of the two apartments over the bar. Pedestrians had to step into the gutter to get around the stubborn dog and the frail little lady in the belted raincoat.

Every day this happened, two or three times a day. Right in front of the Brownstone, the dirty white dog stood snarling or took a siesta in the middle of the sidewalk. Too big to be budged, too mean to mess with, Yuri just lay there for hours as Imogen stood by, a scarf pulled over her head, like the Virgin at the foot of the cross.

The year before last, Basil had had it with Yuri; he took Imogen to court. Yuri had scalped a cocker spaniel, killed a stray cat, and bitten through the workboots of an out-of-town closet-case slipping into the Brownstone for a nightcap. Basil had assumed that the judge would do the right thing and order the dog be put to sleep. But Imogen's attorney, a pro bono hotshot from Cravath, Swaine, and Moore (*someone* in her family had pull) had brought in her psychiatrist to testify. All one hundred fifty pounds of Yuri, it seems, were needed to anchor Imogen's precarious sanity. "Connecting with" Yuri—her "attachment to" Yuri—was all that stood between mistress and mental meltdown. Poor Imogen suffered from something called "schizoaffective disorder," which didn't mean she was schizophrenic, but didn't mean she wasn't, either. The judge spared Yuri's life, requiring Imogen to keep her dog muzzled whenever she took him outside to pee.

Saying something in Spanish, Vicente was grabbing his nose and pointing to the dog. Yuri didn't have his muzzle on!

Basil ran outside. "Where's Yuri's muzzle?"

Imogen didn't even look up. "He doesn't need it."

Basil reached for his cell phone, "I'm calling the police."

"Go ahead."

"You know damn well he should be wearing his muzzle."

"Not anymore." Imogen knelt down beside the dog and brushed the mop of hair from his bleary eye. "The year is up."

"What year?"

"The court order. It expired yesterday."

She was serious.

"That's ridiculous."

She was fuckin' nuts. "I'll take you back to court."

With a paper towel, Imogen sopped up the drool running down the rust-colored valley of hair that hinted at Yuri's mouth.

"This time the judge won't be so lenient."

Imogen didn't care.

"Did you hear me?"

She was connecting with Yuri. "Come on, lad. I've got a wee slice of liver for you upstairs."

"Hey, Baz."

It was Chad—at the window.

"What?"

"Phone for you."

"Who is it?"

"Some kid. Reggie, from Absolut. He wants to know when he's supposed to be here."

"Hang on. I'll talk to him."

Imogen was humming "We Are the World."

Fuck Imogen. Fuck Yuri. They were Freddy's problem now.

Basil ran back inside and brushed past Chad. "I'll take the call in my office."

His office was a corner of the stockroom with a metal desk, a laptop, a phone, and a corkboard covered with Polaroids.

"Reggie?" Basil picked up the phone.

"Basil?"

"Sorry to keep you waiting."

"I was about to hang up."

Asshole.

Basil told Reggie to arrive at six. He would roam the bar—in a skintight turtleneck, no doubt—with a tray of thimble-sized Mardi Gras drinks. The promoter had already sent the vodka. In his desk, Basil found the recipe for Ragin' Cajuns: 1¼ oz. Absolut Peppar Vodka, 5 oz. tomato juice, 2 dashes salt, cayenne pepper to taste.

"Brian." Basil spotted the friendlier twin grabbing a bag of lemons from the freezer.

"Yeah?"

"We're gonna need tomato juice and pepper. He handed Brian the recipe.

"No problem."

Basil reached for his wallet. "Here. Bring me the receipt."

"Chad's alone up there." Brian was pissed. "Isn't Ralph supposed to be here?"

Basil stalled. "Let me check."

The twins hated Ralph. He was always late or calling in sick. "We'll be busy tonight," Brian warned. "We're already busy." Basil nodded. "I hear you." "He didn't call?" "I'll *handle* it." Brian headed off, fuming. "That dude is worthless." If someone had asked him why Ralph was his one great buddy at the bar, Basil would've been hard pressed to say. Of course, he was handsome—all the bartenders were handsome—and he was fun to play Desert Island with. But he *was* irresponsible; when he wasn't sick with some side effect of his AIDS drugs or hungover from clubbing till dawn, he played hooky at least once a week and didn't even bother to make up an excuse. He dressed like a hoodlum in a hooded sweatshirt, a red bandanna, and silver sneakers. You could say he had talent—he could draw a decent portrait on a cocktail napkin—but he was hardly David Hockney. He had a terrible temper with testy patrons. And just last night, he'd been behaving so weirdly, Basil had sent him home to get some rest. He kept zooming around the bar like a speed freak, clearing people's drinks before they'd even finished them, and talking a mile a minute. "What's wrong with *you?*" Basil had to ask him. Ralph just grabbed him by the waist and began to conga.

He was high on coke or meth or *something*, Basil had no doubt. Though who could blame him for needing time off from reality? He'd been through hell since arriving from Cuba. He was losing T cells; he'd just lost a boyfriend. He had no one but Basil to buck him up. It was probably for the best that Basil had never hooked up with him, though he was tempted to, at closing each night. The guys Basil took home, he seldom saw again. The guys he saw again, he saw for a month or two, tops.

"Baz, am I bothering you?"

"No, no."

Freddy stepped into the office and perched on stack of Budweiser boxes. "I've got an idea."

"Uh-huh?"

"I mean, as long as I'm here, why don't I do the job tonight—y'know, take over—and you hang around, so I can ask you, like where does *this* go or where's the key to the bathroom? Whatever. When I get fucked up, you can set me straight."

"Fine."

"You're sure?"

"Good idea."

Freddy got up. "Oh, by the way, do you have a résumé? My friend, Ian, just called. The guy from *Eden Heights.*"

"Oh, right. I'll look."

Freddy left.

It was over. He was history—already. *Kaput.* He didn't matter to a living soul. Even Yuri had Imogen to wipe off his drool and drag him inside when it started to rain. He could lie on the street in front of the Brownstone and they'd just step over him with their Prada shoes and Barneys bags.

He'd felt like this before—when?

On the day he left Fordham. The stairs creaked indifference to his fate.

Worse was the day he was kissed off at Kennedy.

What was *wrong* with his parents? What was wrong with the Greeks? What other people would even *think* of leaving their flesh and blood behind? And for what? To play pinochle on Patmos with other retirees from Piscataway.

It was no wonder he'd never had a boyfriend. He'd never had parents. Just a bullshitter and a hostess with plastic menus and a plastic smile.

That was why he loved Ralph. Ralph was too crazy to bother with bullshit, too proud to smile for a five-dollar tip.

Basil got up.

On the corkboard was a portrait of him Ralph had sketched, one night before closing. It was a pretty good likeness, down to the chicken-pox scar on his forehead and the rings under his eyes. He unpinned the portrait and rolled it up tightly.

"Is this *too* Mardi Gras?" Chad hustled into the room, wearing a vest without a shirt, a cascade of beads on his hairless pecs.

"Ask Freddy."

"Mais oui." Chad hustled out.

The corkboard was a yearbook page of the patrons Basil would be leaving behind at the Brownstone. Most Popular was Chito, the medical claims processor, who brought chicken wings and stuffed mushrooms to Happy Hour. Most Artistic was Lenny, the opera educator, who broke the filters off his Camels before stepping outside to smoke them. The bow tie was Darius, the actuary, who won the Oscar pool every year. With his eyes closed was Krish, the radiologist, who blinked every seven seconds. Mitch was a blow job virtuoso, former Mormon, and defender of the "Judo-Christian" tradition. Big Jim was a florist; Little Jim was a Jets fan; Craig designed high-priced paper plates. Singing with Emmett around the piano were the guys from 405 East Fifty-Sixth (known as "Four out of Five" for its wealth of gay tenants): Kieran, the doorman; White Bill, the CUNY professor; Black Bill from Bloomies; Brad, Phil, and Toby, the entertainment attorneys who were Silverman, Curran, and Silverman.

Did even *one* of them give a shit he was leaving? Their world was the bar. Out of sight, out of mind.

Where the hell was Ralph?

Basil picked up his notebook. He had one last piece of advice for Freddy: "Read the cash register in the middle of each bartender's shift to discourage theft and overpouring." He'd never done this himself. But it pleased him to think how unpopular this would make Freddy with the staff.

The red light was blinking on his answering machine. He pressed Playback.

The caller was scared. "This is Joe Estrine. I'm a friend of Ralph's. He's in Metropolitan Hospital. He's very ill." A long, choked pause. "He asked me to call and say good-bye."

When somebody's dying, and it isn't you, even Starbucks is beautiful: the laptops glow. Old people at bus stops, kids filching the coin returns of phone booths, are Vermeers. The pretzel vendor hauling his

cart across First Avenue is a hero. A guy in a T-shirt sliding a board
into a pizza oven can move you to tears.

It was over for Ralph: the tail lights, the toddlers in snowsuits,
Today's Earlybird, Pad Thai, $9.95.

It wasn't fair.

Henry Kissinger was dressing for a cocktail party. Dick Clark was
gluing on his toupee.

"Metropolitan Hospital?" the cab driver checked.

"That's right."

"You wannna try First Avenue?"

"No. It's rush hour." Baz figured. "I bet First is just as bad."

Only twice—now Basil regretted it—had he ever seen Ralph outside the bar. The first time he was summoned by Eddie, another bartender, on whose couch Ralph was crashing, having just split from his
last nasty boyfriend. Eddie couldn't wake him. Ralph was breathing,
but Eddie was afraid he'd overdosed on something. When Ralph
came to, he looked disappointed, as if he'd hoped to have escaped his
life for good.

The other time was when they went to see *Les Miz,* already in its
tenth year on Broadway. A friend of Ralph's had given him two tickets. Ricky Martin was playing Marius. Not yet "Livin' La Vida Loca"
in the States, Ricky was already a superstar in Puerto Rico. His Nuyo-
rican fans stormed the barricades outside the theater with no less fe-
rocity than the counter-revolutionaries would storm the barricades
onstage. Mothers held up their babies for Ricky to bless as he waved
his way from his limo to the stage door. Inside, the "Taking of photos
is strictly forbidden" announcement was repeated in Spanish—to no
avail. When Eponine died in Marius' arms and he sang his farewell,
Ricky's fans shouted out, "We love you, Ricky."

Ralph was embarrassed by his Latino brethren.

"You should see a Greek funeral," Basil reassured him.

They went to dinner at Joe Allen's. Al Pacino was there. With a
scruffy beard, long hair, and a coat down to his shins, he looked as
hounded as Jean Valjean.

Basil and Ralph were both surprised by how much they'd enjoyed
Les Miz.

"The plot turns—I mean, it's unbelievable—but boy, can Victor Hugo tell a story," Basil said.

Ralph didn't see what was so unbelievable.

And fuck, why should he? His life was Dickens with a side of black beans. A teenager, he'd been imprisoned in Cuba for owning a Beatles record. Released from jail, he was drafted into the army. By the time he got out, his whole family had left for the States, taking advantage of one of Castro's odd fits of largesse. Alone in Havana, Ralph dodged the police who were arresting homosexuals. He finally escaped in the Mariel boatlift, as smaller craft capsized all around him. He was taken first to the Orange Bowl, then stuck behind barbed wire in Fort Chaffee, Arkansas, for a year. When he got to New York, he had to hustle to get by. He got HIV. Working in restaurants, eventually bartending, he hooked up with a succession of boyfriends, each one meaner than the last.

"Jesus Christ."

"What?"

Basil shook his head. "The shit you've been through."

"Yeah, well, it wasn't *my* idea."

"But you got *through* it."

"So what?"

"Why'd you never tell me all this before?"

Ralph shrugged.

The girly waiter took their orders, cruising Ralph shamelessly.

Red bandanna around his head, his biceps bulging through a flouncy shirt, Ralph looked like a pirate ready to grab the guy by his highlights and stick a big salty dick in his mouth.

"You want extra gravy with that?" the waiter lingered.

"Why not?"

The waiter took off to fetch Ralph's meat loaf.

"What I don't get is," Basil resumed, "you could have anyone you want. Why do you hook up with all these creeps?"

Ralph rubbed his forehead. "I guess it's a pattern. Joe's like, 'You think you're a piece of shit, so you look for guys who treat you like shit.'"

"Who's Joe? Your therapist?"

"Yeah."

"So, how's that goin'?"

"*Muy bien, gracias.* I'm here with you, ain't I?"

Basil stiffened. "What's that supposed to mean?"

"He wants me to make friends with guys who aren't like selling E at Escuelita."

"Oh. This is therapy."

Ralph frowned. *"Manganioni."*

"What?"

"Oh, come on." He put his hand on Basil's. "You *know* I like you."

Basil drew a breath.

"We're amigos."

"What's Escuelita?"

"A club—in Midtown." Ralph took his hand back. "You wouldn't like it."

"Why not?"

"It's like half drag queens. But the music's great."

Basil told him about the Ridiculous.

Ralph couldn't believe it. "You're such a fuckin' stiff."

"Oh, but not on stage, darling." Basil raised his chin. "I'm an *art-iste.*"

Ralph was not amused.

"I did straight parts too," Basil hastened to add.

"So why don't *you* have a boyfriend? What's wrong with *you?*"

"All the creeps are taken."

"You're a nice-lookin' guy."

"Y'know, the serious guys," Basil scrambled to say something, "the guys with jobs are all, 'Grow up, already, Baz. You're not gonna make it as an actor. Get a real job. Get a decent apartment.' The rest of the guys are even more fucked up than I am."

"Like me." Ralph smiled.

Basil wanted to hug him. "You're not fucked up. You've just had a hard life."

"So, what's the difference?"

"It's entirely different," Basil said. "You know, if I were you—I mean, if I'd gone through all the shit you've gone through, you know what would've pissed me off most?"

Folding his arms, Ralph sat back, grinning. "What?"

"My family leaving me behind."

Ralph eyes clouded over.

"Did they know you were gay?"

Ralph just stared at his drink. His grin slackened.

Basil felt like an asshole. "I don't mean to pry."

Ralph raised a limp wrist and tapped a finger to his stubbly chin. "Darling, what do *you* think?"

There was a line at the Visitors Desk. Hands on her hips, a woman was screaming at the unflappable Jamaican who handed out the stickers you need to visit a patient. Basil still had an ID from the days at the dawn of AIDS when he did volunteer work at Metropolitan.

He flashed his ID. A cop let him by. He took the elevator to the AIDS ward.

In the old days, the early eighties, they gave you a surgical mask: who knew how the disease was transmitted, back then? The patients Basil visited were black or Puerto Rican, drug addicts, mostly. There was a whole family there, three generations: Mrs. Hernandez, a diabetic; her daughter who had used one of her needles to shoot heroin and then returned it to the refrigerator; and a grandson, six weeks old. One guy with toxoplasmosis offered Basil his Nikes if he'd just get the CIA on the phone. Another guy was itching his skin off at such a rate, he looked like a log half-burned to cinders. After rounds, the volunteers met to share their feelings. The room they met in was adjacent to a room where electroshock therapy was given. As a Baptist minister offered counsel to the shaken volunteers, patients were wheeled in, sedated, strapped down, jolted, and wheeled out asleep.

"Can you tell me what room Raphael Perez is in?"

The nurse checked her chart. "*Raphael* Perez?"

"Raphael or Ralph."

She shook her head. "He's not on this ward."

"Are you sure?"

She picked up the phone and called Admitting.

Basil steeled himself: the worst things happen before you know it.

"He's in six-twelve."

"What floor is that? Intensive care?"

The nurse didn't want to say. Basil raced to the elevator.

There was no way he could forgive himself. It was obvious last night that something was terribly wrong with Ralph. He should've called him. The way he was racing around the bar and juggling shot glasses; it was probably toxo infecting the brain, overloading the circuits.

The sixth floor looked like a psych ward. Half-prison, half-kindergarten, every table was childproofed, every door was bolted. A guard buzzed Basil in.

"I'm here to see Raphael Perez. He's in six-twelve."

The guard checked his list and pointed. "Doctor Bijan's in there with him now."

Basil stopped in the doorway and made the sign of the cross.

What the fuck.

Sitting up in bed, Ralph appeared and disappeared, his torso glistening as he counted off sit-ups like a marine: "Forty-five, forty-six, forty-seven . . ."

"Come in." Dr. Bijan caught sight of Basil.

Ralph *looked* healthy.

A red book on her lap, Dr. Bijan, a sexy thirty-something, sat on the arm of a chair.

Ralph leaped out of bed in his underpants. "*Hola chico,* you're here. You won't believe what happened."

What was wrong with his neck?

"I thought I was going nuts." Ralph grabbed Basil's hand, put an arm around his waist, and started dancing.

Ralph's shoulders were hunched up so high, they touched his ears.

"I just had to keep moving." Shoulders rigid, he spun Basil around like a hunchback twirling a girl. "I couldn't sit still. I had to get off the bus. It wasn't moving fast enough. I ran from home all the way to the hospital. And my shoulders were stuck in this fucking position."

Baz looked to the doctor. She was smiling.

Ralph kept dancing. "I couldn't stand it. I'd hear this jet sound, Whoosh!, like a fuckin' seven-forty-seven was in my bedroom. These dogs, these pitbulls, with fuckin' blood on their teeth were jumping up on the bed. They were so fuckin' real. You have no idea. It's not like dreaming. It's like it's happening."

"It won't be long now." Dr. Bijan crossed her legs.

Her poise pissed Basil off. "*What* won't be long now?"

"The tranquilizer." Ralph let go of him.

"Oh."

"This silly bitch here wouldn't give me shit," Ralph said, shadow-boxing with the doctor, "till she figured out what was going on."

"This is one for the books." The doctor smiled. " I'll have to write it up for the medical journals.

"Can you wait? I'll be right back." Ralph headed to the bathroom.

"Sure."

Ralph slammed the door.

What the hell was going on?

Filling out Ralph's chart, the doctor explained.

A month ago, Ralph was prescribed a new AIDS drug, Viread. It made him sick to his stomach. So his internist gave him Reglan, a drug for nausea. Now, it happens that in a small number of patients Reglan has the paradoxical effect of speeding you up and making your upper body rigid. But Ralph didn't tell anyone this was happening. He just doubled and tripled up on BuSpar, the tranquilizer he'd been taking for years. By the time he got to Metropolitan, he was doing jumping jacks from the Reglan and hallucinating from BuSpar poisoning.

"So, he can't take his AIDS drugs?" Basil had a hard time keeping it all straight.

"No, no. He can take them. He just can't take the drug for nausea. We can give him another."

Thank God. "And he's okay now?"

"He should be." Dr. Bijan checked her watch. "I gave him enough Benadryl to put out a horse."

Ralph came out of the bathroom. His shoulders were a little lower. "I thought I was crazy." He raised his palm for a high five.

Basil managed.

"I think I can sleep now." Ralph climbed into bed.

"Don't lie down flat." Dr. Bijan grabbed a pillow and propped it behind his back. "The more BuSpar gets to your head, the more you'll hallucinate."

Basil pulled up the blanket.

"Tell Baz the good news," Ralph said, "about my viral load."

"It's dropping." The doctor picked up her chart. "We're gonna have our Raphael around a long time."

Ralph burst into tears and started wailing. His jaw dropped open. His limbs relaxed.

"Just let it out." Basil took his hand.

Ralph closed his eyes. His head rocked back.

"It's all over now."

Ralph let out a wail every time he exhaled.

The doctor headed off. "I'll be right down the hall."

"I'm sorry." Ralph kept apologizing.

"I told you: I'm Greek," Basil sat on the bed and put an arm around him. "You should've heard my mother when Reagan was shot."

Ralph reached for a tissue. "I was so fuckin' scared. I thought I was going to explode. It was my blood pressure."

"Next time something happens, you call me. Day or night."

Ralph wiped his eyes. "All right."

"We're amigos."

Ralph lay back. Basil grabbed a pillow from the other bed and stuffed it behind him.

"*Gracias,*" Ralph said. "I guess you got my call."

"Tonight?"

"I asked Joe to call. He said he left you a message."

"Oh, yeah."

"I just wanted to say good-bye."

Basil tried to look stern. "Oh, come on. You heard the doctor. Your viral load: it's dropping."

Ralph looked confused.

"You're gonna be around a long time."

Ralph laughed. "What the hell did Joe say?"

Basil didn't like being laughed at. "He *said* you wanted to say good-bye."

"To *you*. It's your last night at the Brownstone, isn't it? I wanted to be there."

Oh God.

"What the fuck is wrong with you?"

Basil couldn't help crying. "You remembered."

"Of course I remembered."

"I thought you were *dying*."

Ralph pulled him close. "Nobody's dying."

Basil wiped his eyes. "We're like two Greek widows."

Ralph was staring.

Basil reached for a tissue. "What?"

Ralph kissed him.

"You don't have to do that," Basil said.

"I know."

"You're hallucinating."

Ralph laughed, "No, I don't think so," and kissed him again.

They were eye to eye, holding hands, when Ralph's therapist, Joe, came into the room. "So, how's the patient?"

The front bar was jammed with guys wearing feathered masks and colored beads when Basil got back to the Brownstone.

Brian and Chad had tiaras. "Hey, Baz, where ya been?"

They sounded concerned about something. Basil was too happy to be bothered.

"Where the hell have you been?" Freddy rushed up. "I've been looking for you all night."

"I had to go to the hospital," Basil said. "One of our bartenders is sick."

"You gotta tell me what to do." Freddy pushed through the throng to the bar in the back. The doors were closed.

"What's wrong?"

"The fuckin' pipes burst."

"Oh shit." Basil felt guilty. He should've left his cell phone number.

"It's fuckin' *Poseidon Adventure* in there." Freddy pushed open the doors.

It took a second. Then—just like a movie—everyone yelled "Surprise."

Basil blinked.

There was a banner over the bar, THANKS FOR EVERYTHING, BAZ.

Don't fuckin' cry, he steeled himself; not *twice in one night.*

Three guys approached like the Magi: Krish had a cake; Black Bill had a red box from Bloomies; Chito held out a platter of his stuffed mushrooms.

Pressing his hands to his cheeks, Basil opened his mouth in an Edward Munch scream.

Everybody laughed.

"We didn't know how we were gonna get rid of you." Freddy handed Basil a glass of champagne. "Then like by ten, we started to worry: 'When the fuck is he coming back?' "

"God, I'm sorry. It was an emergency."

He knew so many people. Roberto and Frank. Victor and Cesar. Coming out of the bathroom, as usual, Mitch.

Freddy pulled over a handsome guy. "Baz, this is my friend, Ian, from *Eden Heights.*"

"Oh, nice to meet you," Basil said. Then, "Oh, I've met you before."

"I know."

Ian was supposed to have a wedding reception at the Brownstone. But it was canceled at the last minute.

"Call me tomorrow." Ian shook hands.

You want to make the gods laugh? Basil's father used to say: Tell them your plans.

"No, call me the day *after* tomorrow." Ian walked off with a tall black boyfriend. "Have a good time tonight."

Say, I ain't got nobody, and nobody cares for me

Emmett was imitating someone—Cab Calloway? Eubie Blake?— as he banged out his tune on the piano. His friend, Trey, who was some kind of producer, asked for a résumé. Basil said he'd send him one.

That's why I'm sad and lonely
Won't somebody come and take a chance with me?

It was an hour and God knows how many glasses of champagne before Basil could slip outside to use his cell phone. He wanted to see how Ralph was doing and say good night, if he was awake.

It had started raining. Yuri was lying at the foot of the steps like a mop. Imogen was reading a paperback. Basil thanked God he had five people to take to his desert island with him, but he especially thanked God for Ralph.

ABOUT THE AUTHOR

Kevin Scott is a screenwriter *(Key Exchange)*, playwright *(Hide Your Love Away)*, and critic whose arts reviews have appeared in numerous publications, including *The New York Times*, *The Washington Post*, and *Genre*. He teaches screenwriting at New York University, has taught film history at Princeton, and for many years was Literary Manager of the New Group Theater in New York City. *The Boys in the Brownstone* is his first book of fiction.

Order a copy of this book with this form or online at:
http://www.haworthpress.com/store/product.asp?sku=5408

THE BOYS IN THE BROWNSTONE

_____in softbound at $22.95 (ISBN-13: 978-1-56023-295-7; ISBN-10: 1-56023-295-1)

Or order online and use special offer code HEC25 in the shopping cart.

COST OF BOOKS_____

POSTAGE & HANDLING_____
(US: $4.00 for first book & $1.50
for each additional book)
(Outside US: $5.00 for first book
& $2.00 for each additional book)

SUBTOTAL_____

IN CANADA: ADD 7% GST_____

STATE TAX_____
(NJ, NY, OH, MN, CA, IL, IN, PA, & SD
residents, add appropriate local sales tax)

FINAL TOTAL_____
(If paying in Canadian funds,
convert using the current
exchange rate, UNESCO
coupons welcome)

☐ **BILL ME LATER:** (Bill-me option is good on
US/Canada/Mexico orders only; not good to
jobbers, wholesalers, or subscription agencies.)

☐ Check here if billing address is different from
shipping address and attach purchase order and
billing address information.

Signature_____

☐ **PAYMENT ENCLOSED: $**_____

☐ **PLEASE CHARGE TO MY CREDIT CARD.**

☐ Visa ☐ MasterCard ☐ AmEx ☐ Discover
☐ Diner's Club ☐ Eurocard ☐ JCB

Account # _____

Exp. Date_____

Signature_____

Prices in US dollars and subject to change without notice.

NAME_____

INSTITUTION_____

ADDRESS_____

CITY_____

STATE/ZIP_____

COUNTRY_____ COUNTY (NY residents only)_____

TEL_____ FAX_____

E-MAIL_____

May we use your e-mail address for confirmations and other types of information? ☐ Yes ☐ No
We appreciate receiving your e-mail address and fax number. Haworth would like to e-mail or fax special
discount offers to you, as a preferred customer. **We will never share, rent, or exchange your e-mail address
or fax number.** We regard such actions as an invasion of your privacy.

Order From Your Local Bookstore or Directly From
The Haworth Press, Inc.
10 Alice Street, Binghamton, New York 13904-1580 • USA
TELEPHONE: 1-800-HAWORTH (1-800-429-6784) / Outside US/Canada: (607) 722-5857
FAX: 1-800-895-0582 / Outside US/Canada: (607) 771-0012
E-mailto: orders@haworthpress.com

For orders outside US and Canada, you may wish to order through your local
sales representative, distributor, or bookseller.
For information, see http://haworthpress.com/distributors

(Discounts are available for individual orders in US and Canada only, not booksellers/distributors.)

PLEASE PHOTOCOPY THIS FORM FOR YOUR PERSONAL USE.
http://www.HaworthPress.com   BOF04